A REVIVED

MODERN

CLASSIC

ANNA ÉDES

ANNA ÉDES

BY DEZSŐ KOSZTOLÁNYI

Translated and with an Introduction

by George Szirtes

A NEW DIRECTIONS BOOK

Manufactured in the United States of America
New Directions Books are printed on acid-free paper.
First published by Quartet Books Limited, London, in 1991 and as
New Directions Paperbook 772 in 1993.
Published simultaneously in Canada by Penguin Books Canada Limited

Library of Congress Cataloging-in-Publication Data

Kosztolányi, Dezső, 1885-1936.
  [Édes Anna. English]
    Anna Édes / Dezső Kosztolányi ; translated and with an introd. by
  George Szirtes.
        p.   cm. — (A Revived modern classic)
    ISBN 0-8112-1255-6 (alk. paper)
    I. Title.   II. Series.
  PH3281.K85E3413   1993
  894'.51133 — dc20   93-1117
                                                              CIP

New Directions Books are published for James Laughlin
by New Directions Publishing Corporation,
80 Eighth Avenue, New York 10011

INTRODUCTION

The story of *Anna Édes* is one of innocence exploited. The very name of the heroine means 'sweet', and sweetness is part of her nature. A peasant girl up from the village, who receives employment as a domestic in Budapest, honest, hard-working and simple to the point of simple-mindedness, she is exploited by certain members of the newly recovered middle-classes of 1919 – a selfish and reactionary section of society which had suffered two severe shocks: defeat in the First World War, then a brace of short-lived socialist revolutions. A third great shock, the loss of two-thirds of the country's territory by decree of the Treaty of Trianon, was still to come.

Hungary had entered the war as part of the dual monarchy, her territory extending far into the countries that presently surround her. The various messily distributed nationalities naturally wanted independence, or at least greater autonomy, and as the war progressed they joined the Allies. The defeat of the dual monarchy increased the clamour for full independence. Then, as now, the crumbling of an empire led to a rise in nationalistic feeling. The first revolution in October 1918, known as the Autumn Roses Revolution, established the socialist government of Count Mihály Károlyi, who declared Hungary a republic. But the external pressure was too great. The Romanian army advanced on Hungary and in March Károlyi resigned to be replaced by Béla Kun, a Bolshevik who counted on Russian help. His soviet-style Republic of Councils (which included George Lukács as minor member of the government) instituted a Red Terror, then set about the nationalization of the land that Károlyi had only just begun to distribute to the peasants. By August the experiment was over. The unspeakable had happened and Romanian troops occupied Budapest.

Dezső Kosztolányi, who at the age of thirty-four was a witness to these events, had started to publish very early, when he was only sixteen. The son of a science teacher and occasional author, he was born in 1885 while his father was working in the city of Szabadka in southern Hungary. After school he studied German

v

in Budapest and Vienna. His reputation was made in 1907 by his first collection of poems, *Within Four Walls*. His second, *The Complaints of a Poor Little Child* (1910), confirmed his standing and enjoyed enormous popularity. Together with the friends he made at university, and who were to remain his literary companions for the rest of his life, he established a new literary journal called *Nyugat (Occident)*, which quickly became the foremost magazine of its kind in the country. Three generations of Hungarian poets were drawn to it by its high regard for craft and intelligence.

In a generation of elegant stylists, Kosztolányi was the most elegant. Handsome, witty and charming, he proclaimed himself an aesthete and established a career as journalist, commentator and first-rate short-story writer. Baudelaire and Rilke were among those writers he most admired. He was interested in psychoanalysis, made copious translations from various languages and moved with ease through coffee-house society. He also continued to publish a steady stream of poems of which some have established themselves as classics of twentieth-century Hungarian poetry. Though his touch was light – he loved bravura rhyme and was equally at home with free verse – it hinted at darker emotions. There was a nervous but disciplined melancholy at work in him which saved him from mere facility. Having been somewhat traumatized by the First World War and its consequences, he preferred to keep his distance from party political commitment and was sometimes mistrusted as a result. But he inspired enormous affection and loyalty among his friends.

Kosztolányi didn't begin to write novels until 1921 but soon displayed an impressive talent for the genre. His psychological insight was keen, his prose clear and classical. Indeed, there are many who prefer his fiction to his verse. His second novel, *Nero: the Bloody Poet*, which appeared in 1922 (recently republished in English as *The Darker Muses*), won an important literary prize and the enthusiastic approval of Thomas Mann, who wrote an introduction for it. The extended short story that followed this, *Skylark* (1924), is thought by some to be his single finest work. Others however award that honour to his fifth and last novel, *Anna Édes*, published in 1926.

The early elegance is certainly in evidence here, but the book is clearly driven by pity and anger. While it is full of comic, lyrical and psychologically acute vignettes it is considerably more than the sum of its attractive parts. The story begins with the flight of Béla Kun and the arrival of the unsophisticated Romanian army, and ends before the trauma of Trianon, at which time Kosztolányi's own place of birth disappeared into Yugoslavia. But the book's true interest is not in realpolitik: having established the historical moment Kosztolányi is concerned with the nature of his society rather than it specific fortunes. The ceremonial arrival in Budapest of Admiral Horthy, whose regency was to last until the latter days of the Second World War and who instituted a period of White Terror, is described almost in passing. But the spirit of the time, its cruelty and emptiness, permeate the household in which Anna's personal tragedy unfolds.

Her first appearance is delayed. Kosztolányi makes us see her through her employer, Mrs Vizy's eyes first. She notes that Anna doesn't look like a peasant:

Her nose was not merely 'normal' but of a decidedly interesting shape with wide nostrils: there was something piquant about it. She was slightly taller than average but fraily built, a shade underdeveloped, even a touch boyish. Her lips were pale and chapped. Her hands were as rough as you might expect in a servant, her nails short and square.

This is an owner's view of a prospective possession. Kosztolányi's sense of physical detail is extremely acute and is successfully transferred to his heroine who is terrified by the smell of camphor emanating from the Vizys' piano. This animal response to the unfamiliar smell sets the tone for the whole term of her employment and symbolizes the divide between her and the Vizys, who are substantial characters with complex inner lives but insensitive to the lives of others. They and their friends are part of a social fabric that is already partly fascist in nature. Mrs Vizy looks through people as if she didn't see them and is obsessed with finding the perfect maid. Her husband is climbing the career ladder of the civil service. But Kosztolányi's irony is not restricted to the obvious middle-class targets: it extends to the characters of the caretaker and his wife, as well as the other servants in the story. He is perfectly impartial and highly skilful in delicately shifting the narrative from one subject to another. These voices are then free to betray themselves without too much comment by the author.

The book rises to two climaxes: the eroticism of Anna's seduction by the cold-hearted popinjay Jancsi, a nephew of the Vizys, and the later murders committed by Anna. Anna herself is far from a cypher. Kosztolányi allows her the frail cocoon of innocence while managing to enter her subjectivity with complete conviction. A vulnerable and independent, if enigmatic, figure, Anna ensures that the book does not become merely an argument about social conditions but is raised to genuine tragedy.

Kosztolányi's narrative skill and clear, graphic prose have attracted a series of film makers. Three of his novels have been adapted for the cinema, *Anna Édes* being one of them. One can see why: it is a visual feast, the gallery of characters is appealing to actors, there is satire, romance, sex and murder, and in Dr Moviszter, the old ailing doctor, the reader discovers a protagonist who does try to see that some sort of justice is done. Kosztolányi himself was not at all religious and it is interesting that the doctor, who is, is obviously of an older passing world. Despite severe (and anticipated) criticism from the right, the book restored him to critical favour after a period when this had been slipping away from him.

Anna Édes first appeared in England in 1947. By that time Kosztolányi and his closest friends of the first *Nyugat* period were all long and prematurely dead: one by suicide, one through cerebral haemorrhage, one, like Kosztolányi himself, through cancer of the throat. Reputation has been a fickle goddess in twentieth-century Hungary. Although other, more radical writers of the thirties, such as Attila József and Gyula Illyés, rejected both his stance and his manner, by the time of his death in 1936 Kosztolányi's literary reputation appeared secure. After the Communist take-over in 1949, so called 'art-for-art's-sake' aestheticism met with official disapproval and despite the social conscience so clearly evident in his work he was thought to be unsound. The wheel has turned again since then: few people would now query the classic status that is usually accorded him.

His was an ill-fated generation but a remarkably lively and intelligent one. The last great *Nyugat* writer – of the third generation – was Sándor Weöres, who died recently, in 1989. With him the remarkable firework display of early and mid-century Hungarian literature came to a spectacular end. Kosztolányi's work formed a major part of that display. The reader familiar with the world of

Roth, Musil and von Doderer will recognize the place and find it enriched.

Having said that, I have left place names in the original Hungarian on the principle that we tend not to translate such terms from German, French or Italian. *Város* is town or district, *út* and *utca* are street and road respectively, *körút* is ring road, *tér* is square, *hegy* (often used as a suffix) is hill. The two districts which figure largely in the book are both in Buda, close to the river. The Vár or Fortress district was the old administrative centre, containing the royal palace. The Vérmező (literally Field of Blood) in the Krisztina district is an open space where the Jacobite rebels of 1795 were executed.

More complex are the old pre-war forms of address which have no direct equivalent in English, such as *nagyságos úr*, or *méltósagos úr* which denote subtle distinctions in civil society. They are generally used by lower ranks in deference to those above them, and are quite precise in their application. I have tried to imply these by tone and manner, and point them up when they are an integral part of the comedy or of some social strategy.

George Szirtes

Oremus pro fidelibus defunctis. Requiem aeternam dona eis Domine et lux perpetua luceat eis.

Circumdederunt me gemitus mortis: Dolores inferni circumdederunt me.

Absolve Domine Benedictus Dominus Deus Israel.

Et ne nos inducas in tentationem. Sed libera nos a malo. A porta inferi. Erue Domine animam eius.

Ne tradas bestiis animas confidentes tibi. Et animas pauperum tuorum ne obliviscaris in finem.

Domine Jesu Christe miserere ei. Christe parce ei.

Domine exaudi orationem meam. Et clamor meus ad te veniat.

Miserere mei Deus. Non intres in judicium cum famula tua Domine.

In paradisum deducant te Angeli: et cum Lasaro quondam paupere vitam habeas sempiternam.

Oremus. Anima eius et animae omnium fidelium defunctorum per misericordiam Dei requiescant in pace.

Rituale Romanum

The Flight of Béla Kun

Béla Kun was fleeing the country in an aeroplane.

In the afternoon – at about five o'clock – an aeroplane rose over the Soviet headquarters in the Hotel Hungaria, crossed the Danube and, passing the palace on top of the Várhegy, banked steeply towards the Vérmező Gardens.

The pilot of the aircraft was none other than the head of state himself.

He flew low, barely sixty feet above the ground. His face could be clearly seen.

He was pale and unshaven as usual. He grinned at those below and gave an occasional shabby and sardonic wave of farewell.

His pockets were stuffed with sweet pastry. He carried jewels, relics of the church and precious stones that had once belonged to well-disposed and generous aristocratic women. There were other valuables too.

Great gold chains hung from his arms.

As the aeroplane began to climb, and just as it was disappearing from sight, one such gold chain fell right in the middle of the Vérmező where it was found by an elderly and long-established resident of the Krisztina area, an excise clerk who worked in the Fortress, or Vár, district, in Szentháromság tér, the square dedicated to the Holy Trinity, one Károly József Patz by name.

Such at least were the rumours in the Krisztina area.

His Excellency,
the Comrade and Her Ladyship

The day the news spread about the necklace, on 31 July
1919, at six o'clock in the afternoon, Kornél Vizy called for
his maid.

'Katica!' he shouted.

A girl as plump as a pigeon stood in the kitchen. It seemed
she was about to go out. She was all dressed up in a pink
blouse, a white skirt with a black canvas belt, and a new
pair of patent leather shoes. She examined herself in a hand-
mirror, sprinkled a little white powder on her handkerchief
and dabbed it over her puffy face. She heard his shout but
stayed where she was.

The bell had been out of order since the previous political
administration so it was necessary to shout for the servants,
though if he was in the study he could knock on the thin
partition wall between it and the kitchen.

His voice was growing angry.

Noticing this, the girl crossed the long, narrow hall,
paused before the mirrored hatstand to adjust her hair, then,
her ample hips billowing, waddled into the dining room.

A man about forty years of age was sprawling on the divan
in such an advanced state of neglect he might have been
taken for a tramp. His shirt was creased, his winter trousers
worn at the knee, his shoes badly scuffed, and he was

without a tie. Only his aquiline nose and muttonchop whiskers suggested he might be a person of consequence.

He was clutching the latest issue of *Vörös Újság*, the Communists' official organ. He held it at a distance, almost at arm's length, since he was very long sighted. He was so absorbed in his reading he did not immediately notice the maid. The article before him proclaimed the imminent collapse of the state with the headline, *The Proletariat in Danger!*

Katica moved closer to the divan.

'You're here then, are you?' growled Vizy. 'How often do I have to shout for you?' He shrugged his shoulders glumly, as if to moderate his sternness.

The girl stared at the floor with bland indifference.

'All right,' said Vizy, more conciliatory now, but still morose, as if talking to himself. 'Shut all the windows.'

Katica set off.

'Wait! The shutters too. And pull down the blinds. You understand?' He hesitated. 'There was shouting outside.'

He threw down the paper. It rustled as it fell to the ground. The brown colour of the cheap straw-pulp looked as if it had been scorched in some universal conflagration. He rose from the divan and, hands in pockets, stalked over to the open dining-room window.

There below was the Bolshevik soldier who had cried out a few moments ago, but he looked so lonely and forlorn that hatred was wasted on him. A shrivelled, emaciated member of the proletariat, more embryo than human being, he was a figure upon whom the rifle with its fixed bayonet hung as if someone had slung it there as an afterthought.

The sunset streamed across the parched and flattened acres of the Vérmező as it had always done: it gilded the crowns of the Buda Hills and picked out the cross of a distant church.

At the top of the Granite Steps opposite, small groups of men huddled together, whispering in the now customary fashion, almost lip-reading each other's conversation. They

3

looked like sheep deserted by their shepherd and were the only sign of change.

Not a cloud in sight. A heavy drowsiness lay over everything, the kind that precedes summer showers, when the wind seems to hold its breath, when nature feels like an enormous room, when the trees look like toys and people stand about like wax dummies.

Everything was numb, no movement, not a sound. The only thing that gave an impression of movement was a poster bearing the legend *To arms! To arms!* on which a frenzied sailor was brandishing a flag with such superhuman vehemence that he seemed to have become part of it, his lantern jaw widening in a scream so vast it threatened to swallow the whole world.

Vizy had often passed this poster but had never really dared to examine it. In fact this was the first time he could look on it with equanimity, without a feeling of bedazzlement. A man can gaze at the setting sun without damaging his eyes.

Further off, on the Krisztina Boulevard a lorry laden with gaudily dressed children thundered into town as if it were a fire-engine on emergency call. It was returning from an excursion in the Zúgliget Woods, and the children were waving sticks at passers-by.

From the hill there rose the sound of thin childish voices in unison:

> *Rise, rise, oppressed of every nation,*
> *Rise, rise, ye starving masses, rise.*

Blissful in their ignorance, a dozen or so young clerks and apprentices were earnestly singing the words they had only recently been taught: those of the *Internationale*.

Katica, having shut the windows in all the other rooms, now closed those in the dining room. When all the windows were tight, Vizy sidled over to Katica and with a nervous, sickly smile whispered, 'They've lost.'

The news was of no interest to the maid, or if it was she

4

did not show it. But her master stood in front of her. His wife was not home yet and he longed to pour his heart out to someone.

'Katica,' he repeated. 'They've lost. The Reds have lost.'

The maid stared back at him, wondering what she had done to deserve her master's confidence.

'The scoundrels,' he added, his nostrils flaring, intoxicated with the sweet scent of revenge. No sooner had he said it than he heard a loud knocking at the door of the flat. He went quite pale. He stared at the air before him, as if searching for the word he had just uttered, so that he might wipe away all trace of it. He waved his hand vaguely, trying to clear some imperceptible fug of smoke.

'I'll answer it.' He strode with sudden decision into the hall, steeled for the worst. They might be looking for hostages, it might be a house search or state of emergency! He mentally prepared his defence: twenty years in public service, a social conscience, a general sympathy with Marxism though he deplored its excesses.

He was already a new man, no longer a martyr to Bolshevism but a victim of the old order which on innumerable occasions had ungratefully passed him over. He felt in his pocket for the trade-union card which only just that afternoon he had wanted to tear up. Fortunately it was there.

A little man stood before him in the corridor. He wore a scarlet-lapelled jacket like a postman, but his collar was uncomfortably undone.

'Good day, your excellency,' he bellowed, loud enough for the whole house to hear. 'May I have a word with your excellency?'

'Oh it's you, Comrade,' responded Vizy.

'Your humble servant, your excellency.'

'Do come in, Comrade Ficsor.'

The exchange was conducted with remarkable politeness in the historical circumstances. Both men were uncertain of their status, both anxious to give the other the advantage.

Kornél Vizy had been a ministerial councillor and it was the first time in four months that he had been addressed as your excellency. He felt some pleasure in hearing the title again, but was also a little disappointed that he had prepared himself needlessly. As for Ficsor, the caretaker of 238 Attila utca, he was crestfallen at still being addressed as comrade by the owner of the block.

The caretaker entered the flat and extended a hand to his excellency. Vizy took it. It was Vizy who had initiated the practice of shaking hands during the dictatorship of the proletariat, but ever since then it had been Ficsor who, out of courtesy proffered his hand first.

'They've gone!' enthused Ficsor, still at the top of his voice. 'The rascals are done for. They're packing up and leaving.'

'Really,' murmured Vizy, as if surprised at the news.

'Yes, your excellency. The national flag has already been raised over the Vár. My brother-in-law raised it with his own hands.'

'The important thing,' pronounced Vizy, avoiding the subject, 'is that there should be peace and security.'

'The dear old red-white-and-green,' gushed Ficsor in a fit of patriotic reverie, keeping a careful eye on Vizy's immobile face. 'Now there'll be some scores to settle, your excellency. Yes, now they'll have to dance to a new tune.'

Vizy noted the caretaker's air of desperation and maintained his own inscrutability. Ficsor was struggling for words.

'What I actually came about,' he stuttered, 'was the bell. The bell, your excellency. I thought, as I had a little time, I could fix it now.'

'The batteries are there.' Vizy pointed in the direction of the kitchen.

'I know, your excellency,' smiled Ficsor, who was deeply wounded by the idea that he, the caretaker, should not know where the landlord kept the batteries. 'If I may just borrow a stepladder?'

Katica, in her best dress, resentfully produced the dirty ladder. They had some trouble in positioning it correctly since the kitchen was tiny and unaccommodating, and was lit only by a tiny light-well so that even by day it was dark. Ficsor wanted to switch on the light but the bulb had long gone. He asked for a candle.

Holding the candle he climbed the steps to the batteries. From the top he explained the cause of the fault. He went into great detail, stressing the difficulty and necessity of repairing it, but in a highly respectful manner since he was only too aware that he was physically having to look down on the person he addressed as Your Excellency.

While Katica held the steps for him he fervently set about compensating for his deliberate neglect of recent times. He fumbled with the batteries, took each one down individually and placed it on the kitchen table. With his penknife he scraped at rusty wires. He put kitchen salt into the jars and topped them up with water.

At that point someone else knocked at the door. A tall, slim, hatless, distinguished-looking woman in a lilac frock entered the flat.

'Your servant, ma'am,' Ficsor bowed and scraped from the kitchen. Receiving no answer, he repeated, 'Your servant.'

The woman continued to ignore him and walked into the dining room. Vizy followed her and embraced her. He could no longer hide his great happiness. He was grinning all over his face.

'You've heard?'

'Everything. They say that by tonight we will be occupied. By the Romanian army.'

'Nonsense. The great powers would never allow it. It will be an allied army of occupation: Italians, French and English. Gábor Tatár told me so.'

The woman smoothed her beautiful ash-blonde hair and sank into the rocking chair. She gazed into space in her usual absent way, looking through everything, objects and people, as though they were not there, as if something beyond them engaged her attention.

'Where have you been? I've been worried about you.'

'I've been chasing about for something. This,' said Mrs Vizy, rocking gently, and she opened her white-gloved hand

7

to reveal a small parcel wrapped in newspaper. She threw it on to the table.

'What is it?'

'Butter,' she answered with a wry smile. 'It cost me three handkerchiefs.'

Ficsor was rattling about in the kitchen. He climbed the steps to replace the batteries. Mrs Vizy listened out for him, then turned away. 'What's that man doing here?'

'He is fixing the bell.'

'Now he bothers. We have been nagging him to mend it for months.'

'He himself offered to do it.'

'Why didn't you throw him out?'

'You're joking.'

'Certainly not. You have to kick his sort out. Bolsheviks.'

'Keep your voice down, he might hear you.'

'So what? You think he isn't a Bolshevik? Filthy swine. He's a Bolshevik all right. I'll show him . . .'

Vizy thought the time was not yet right for such things.

With unexpected ferocity the woman leapt to her feet and strode into the hall prepared to send the caretaker on his way.

But just at that moment the sound of the electric bell rang through the long neglected flat. It sang out in victory, in celebration, its harsh clatter bringing new hope and zest for life. Its fresh, gay, metallic trill refreshed the soul of the apartment, vibrated through its walls and woke it to new consciousness.

In the dining room Vizy marvelled at the sound. His wife looked for Katica, but discovered that the maid had once again sneaked off without permission.

'It's mended,' announced Ficsor with a bow, seizing Mrs Vizy's hand and administering a respectful kiss before she could remove it. He returned the ladder and, realizing that neither the kiss nor the mended bell were quite enough he took his courage in both hands and with a desperate confidence, as if imparting a great secret, practically whispered into the woman's ear.

'Your ladyship,' he began, his eyes downcast, 'I have a girl for you.'

'What?'

'A maid.'

Mrs Vizy could hardly believe her ears. She thought they were still ringing, that she must have misunderstood him. She looked at the caretaker with deep and undisguised interest. Her eyes sparkled. She would have felt no happier if someone had offered her a diamond.

'She's not a Pest girl, is she?'

'Not at all. She's a relative of mine, a peasant from the Balaton.'

The woman was positively excited. She had long dreamed of finding a maid privately, but a peasant girl! No one had come up with anything as good as this. She was certainly not going to negotiate the matter carelessly, and so, quite forgetting about her husband, she beckoned the caretaker into the kitchen, motioned him to sit down and, by flickering candlelight, she slowly went through all the relevant details with him.

When it was all finished she personally saw Ficsor out and returned to the kitchen. She picked up the handkerchief that Katica had left on the kitchen table and holding it between two fingers, she sniffed it and threw it to the floor in disgust. She pushed aside her hand mirror, closed the courtyard window and began to prepare a supper of tea and toasted bread.

3

A Sour Meal

Seeing that no one was at the outer door, Mrs Vizy went into the dining room.

'What are you doing?'

'Just trying it,' answered Vizy. 'It works.'

'I noticed.'

'You think he made a good job?'

'You can hear for yourself.'

'I hope you didn't say anything to him.'

'No. Leave off now!' she yelled at him as he tried the bell once more. 'What are you playing at? You're like a child.'

'I'm hungry. I'd like some supper.'

'But who are you ringing for?'

'For Katica.'

'Her highness has been gone for hours.'

'Where?'

'Where? Where she usually goes. Strolling.'

'Now?'

'Yes, now.'

'But nobody is allowed out on the streets today.'

'Fat lot she cares for that. Lajos is back.'

'Lajos Hack?'

'Him. He arrived on the barge.'

'And when will she get home?'

'I've no idea,' Mrs Vizy burst out. 'At midnight. For all I

know,' she continued to agitate herself, 'it might be dawn before she's back!'

'Has she taken the key?'

'I suppose so.'

'Very nice, I must say,' rumbled Vizy. 'Terribly nice of her. We have to sleep with open doors. She might bring anyone in.'

'Don't sound so surprised. You can't pretend it's the first time it has happened. You make me laugh!' She turned indignantly and slammed the door behind her, just as Katica used to.

In the kitchen she made a great fuss of clashing plates and rattling cutlery. At such times she needed an outlet for her emotions. When she tired of debating the endless and enormous cares of life with her lord and master round the table, her fury took the form of clattering, so that for a few seconds it might seem – at least to her – that it was all his fault.

She brought in the supper on a wooden tray. A cup of tea, a couple of slices of toast and the butter she had bought that afternoon.

Vizy, who had only had a bit of liver and some vegetable marrow for dinner, glanced down at the weak grass-green tea, the suspicious-looking slices of black and yellow maize-bread which looked unappetizing even after toasting, and enquired sourly if there was anything else.

'What else do you expect?'

'Won't you even lay the table?'

'We never used to in the evening.'

'Never mind,' sighed Vizy. 'It will do.'

He put his head in his hands as he often did when something went wrong with the housekeeping. He remained in this position for some time. He was dreaming of the white tablecloth, the rose-patterned porcelain of the plates and the wine in the cut glass which used to glimmer on the table whenever they dined here with his friends from the ministry.

'Are you not eating?' he nagged his wife.

Mrs Vizy rarely bothered with supper having suffered from nervous indigestion for some years. The recent excitements under the Bolshevik regime had only made her condition worse. She felt the acid in her stomach. She took out a cardboard box, extended her pale tongue and swallowed three dark-green pills with a shudder.

Her husband devoured the food all the more readily. Being healthy and male he greedily chewed and ground the dry slices of bitter-sweet maize bread on which he had expended every last smear of butter. Already it was gone. Still suffering pangs of hunger he added some saccharine to his tea and stirred it. At least it sweetened things a little.

Slurping his tea, he recounted the story of his meeting in Úri utca with Gábor Tatár who told him it was over, finished and done with. They had finished with Social Methods of Production, they could forget Revolutionary Self-consciousness, and there would be no more harrying of honest and industrious citizens.

Vizy had good reason for his boundless hatred of the Reds. He had starved under Bolshevism. When the commune took over he was demoted and put on half-pay. As it turned out they were so disorganised that he continued to be paid as before, but what could he buy for it? He had been ruined by the war, having from the outbreak sunk all his money – some two hundred and fifty thousand crowns in gold – in war-bonds and securities. He had had complete confidence in German arms. Only this three-storey house remained, and it produced no income. They lived in the four rooms on the first floor and the floor above was divided into two flats which were occupied by the local practitioner, Miklós Moviszter, and a young solicitor called Szilárd Druma. The house being situated in the immediate vicinity of Mozdony utca, it quickly caught the eye of the young Leninists. They took Druma hostage and kept him imprisoned for two months, and constantly harassed the clerically minded old doctor. On their first visit to Vizy they arrested his wife. She had been shaking out a tablecloth at the window and they charged her with secretly signalling to counter-revolutionary forces. They had dragged her off to parliament and only allowed her home at midnight, by which time she had been broken body and spirit. The next morning a young functionary called, who produced a cane from his leather leggings, and proceeded, while insolently strutting about, to requisition two of their rooms, the dining room in which they presently sat and the adjoining drawing room. It was lucky that the system had collapsed before any lodgers had been foisted on them.

But worse than anything was the fact that Vizy had been condemned to political oblivion. He was infinitely ambitious and with no prospect of advancement he was like a mill without grain, the wheels ground on within him uselessly. These were months of desperate frustration for him.

He used to be a reserved, somewhat sullen man who never discussed the office with his wife. Now he began to talk. On long walks in the Buda hills or sitting at home, waiting for the dreaded visit, he lectured her about his personal political creed and those young louts who were busy crippling the ministry.

Now it was proving difficult to resume the old domestic routine. When he had drunk his tea he stalked about and discussed the events of the counter-revolution, which had already assumed a comfortable historic distance in his mind.

'Do you remember?' he kept asking. 'Do you remember?'

He mentioned acquaintances who had been hanged, the colleague who had been executed before the parliament building for distributing handbills in churches, and the Ludovicans, those boys from the Military Academy, who had been denounced as 'counter-revolutionary brats'.

'And then there were the boats, the monitors. Do you remember when they stormed up the Danube under those great bouquets of smoke? I was just shaving. We thought it was the Communists who were doing the shooting. We hurried over to the Tatárs to watch it from the attic. People

13

were swarming like ants on the embankment. That's when they murdered poor Berend, the famous paediatrician.'

He hesitated before continuing.

'Then, of course, the Corpus Christi procession. That was quite a different sort of affair. Some commissar character in glasses wheeled up on his bicycle and swore at the Holy Altar. Spat at it too, according to some witnesses. They had him on the ground before he could move, carried him to the gate and beat him to death. Apparently it was a waiter who delivered the final blow.'

But the most exciting things, the thing that started it all, was the Krisztina rising. They had both followed its progress from close quarters.

'By the time you arrived those dark curly-headed terrorists had roared up on a lorry and started firing at the church. And the crowd ran screaming into the school where they were enlisting men for the Red Army. But you weren't there at the beginning. I was. It started with the crowd waving handkerchiefs. Krisztina tér was a mass of white. Trams stopped, people removed their hats and everyone sang the national anthem. I'll never forget the scene. They tore down the red flag and burned it. It was some blonde actress who lit the flame, just in front of the chemists. And when the volleys rang out we all rushed home. It was a windy day, rather grey for summer. A little girl was running in front of us with an ivory-covered Bible in her hands. The poor thing collapsed right in front of our house. The excitement was too much for her. She lay there on the pavement like a piece of wood. She couldn't tell us anything about herself. You brought her a glass of water. Do you remember?'

This too was a miracle, that they could speak about this now, so openly, so loudly. There was no response from Mrs Vizy. Her grey eyes were wide open, staring at some remote object of interest. After a long silence she spoke. 'Tomorrow she'll be sleepy again.'

'Who?'

'Katica. She'll be dead to the world till nine o'clock, as usual.'

14

'Oh, her.' Vizy was still lost in the crowd, where history was being made, where fate was mercilessly dealing out her cards. 'Why did you let her go out? You should be firmer with her.'

'I intend to be. I'll give her notice,' she leapt at the opportunity. 'You should have seen the black look she gave me when I suggested that she should occasionally stay in at night.' She suddenly leapt up and mimicked Katica's loud wail. ' "I won't come back at all if you like." The impertinence of it! Then she swans out, like this,' She proceeded to demonstrate, even imitating the maid's walk.

Her husband watched astounded while his wife acted out the whole furious charade, as though she were an actress performing to an invited audience. He felt he should say something. 'And what did you do?' he asked.

'Do? What I always do. I took it. I'd love to have kicked that great lump of . . .'

'You know what these people are like.'

'All they do is gobble,' she lamented. 'Enough for two. And fool around with the soldiers. But this one,' she bent to whisper in his ear, 'to top it all, this one is not in the best of conditions.'

'What's the matter with her?'

'Just that. Her condition,' she added significantly. Mrs Vizy fixed her husband with a look of horror.

'She doesn't show it.'

'I saw the signs on her underwear.'

'She is fat after all.'

'But that's why she's so swollen. It's in the legs, those puffed-out calves of hers. They're repulsive. And her brother comes here too, that hooligan, the engine driver. Our house is nothing but a public bar. One feels frightened in one's own home. She is a viper in our bosom, and we pay her for it. If only I never had to look at that ugly pasty face of hers again. It would be bliss.'

'You want another maid?' asked Vizy absently. 'Forget it. They're all the same.'

Mrs Vizy took a deep breath and was on the point of

protesting, but decided to suppress her indignation for the time being. She had never in her life met such a bestial creature. Katica was slothful, rude, immoral and common. Above all, common. She waddled about the flat as if she owned it, as if she had nothing to do with those who happened to live here. When they asked her in the morning what she intended to cook that day she simply pouted and said she didn't care. Would you believe it! She refused to queue up for things. It was left to her employer to stand about at the grocer's with filthy servants, left to her to roam the streets for a packet of lard, even to the point of collapse. Katica in the meantime was out amusing herself with her fancy man, with that repulsive tattooed sailor, Lajos Hack, who spent a fortune on her, heaven knows where the money came from.

Not that she hadn't tried speaking nicely to her: she'd lectured her, reasoned with her, commanded her. All in vain. It went in one ear and out the other. What did she care that her employer was weak, that she had lost a lot of weight through all this rushing about, that she had grown positively thin? It didn't matter to her that she was left to do all the errands, all the work right down to the polishing of the floor. She just stood back and let her do it, the slut.

Hands in her lap, Mrs Vizy went on brooding in her usual solitary long-suffering fashion. What were the others like? Were her previous servants any better?

Certainly not, judging by Katica's predecessor. Lujza Héring was worse than a magpie. She stole everything but particularly handkerchiefs. She was sacked on the spot and they spent two months without a maid. Working-class girls from Pest were notorious thieves. One of them had robbed her of a gold watch that she had inherited from her mother, another had pinched the feathers from her duvet. As for peasant girls such as Örzsi Varga, they worked all right but they kept sending things home, jams and herbs and such. And they ate! Lord how they ate! They'd have eaten them out of house and home. Even while they were doing the cleaning they'd be munching bread. To be fair there were a

16

couple of reasonable ones but either their mothers refused to allow them to live as servants, or they were lured away by some relative or other. The Germans were clean but untrustworthy. The Slovaks were hard working but had loose morals. There was Karolin who had two lovers at once, one a corporal in the infantry, the other a well-known writer whom they found lounging on their settee when they returned from a summer holiday.

Who knows what they are really like? Take Lidi for example, plain little Lidi, the nursemaid with the funny plait on top of her head. Who would have believed it? She was as ugly as sin, but one morning, there she was in the kitchen, lying on a blood-soaked mattress, unconscious from loss of blood, her face ashen, already gasping for breath. The ambulance came for her in the nick of time. She had tried to perform an illegal abortion on herself. She went with anybody. If they sent her down for some beer or wine she would quickly find herself a man, there beneath the gateway. She was the siren of the local stores and shops.

Those who did not go whoring were no less difficult. They broke the sink, burned holes in the clothes when ironing, caterwauled from morn till night, hung about the Horváth Gardens, read theatrical magazines and burned with unrequited passion for the juvenile lead in some operetta.

One was a gossip, another was choosy about her food, left her vegetables and wanted to eat the same pastries and fine meats as her employers, and always harped on about her previous situation where she had the best lean bacon for breakfast. And even the precious Margit was something of a whited sepulchre. She only touched things with her fingertips for fear of getting dirty, but she was dirty herself dear girl, she wallowed in it, the dust lay thick on the furniture, the glasses were sticky and she threw the cutlery – knives, forks and all – into the drawer, just as they were, greasy. Fortunately she did not stay long.

The only trouble was that others kept leaving. Often they had hardly arrived, and not one stayed for more than six months. Mrs Ökrös was only here for two hours, having returned her advance with one hundred per cent interest.

Mrs Vizy was not afraid to experiment: she tried everyone. She even had a girl from the orphanage, and attempted to bring her up. She had been the rudest of the lot. Three months of it was enough and after the scandal she created, she thanked God she was rid of her. Then there were Mari and Victor and Ilona (Ilona Tulipás, that was), and Emma Zakariás and Böske. Böske Rózsás? Was that her name? Which one was she? A whole regiment of women trooped by before her, blondes, brunettes, thin ones, fat ones, all those who had passed through the house in the twenty years of her marriage. They were becoming confused in her memory. One's head had settled on another's shoulders, a second had lost her body entirely and a third was merely a headless torso. She continued to cast about in this peculiar lumber-room for a while then threw the composite monstrosity back where it belonged. It was a fruitless search, she found little to comfort her, she couldn't recall a single one who had amounted to anything. All had deceived her, exploited their positions of trust, and every time she was left with the exhausting task of finding a new maid. It was like living under a curse. She had to admit her husband might have been right: it was six of one and half a dozen of the other.

Her mind finally settled on the last of them. Katica was the one she hated most of all, since it was always the present incumbent she hated most, whose presence it was which most increased the sum of her misery. Her husband meanwhile was still pacing about the room, holding forth about the next day's meeting of representatives which would have to take up some appropriate position *vis-á-vis* the new political situation.

Mrs Vizy sat crouched in the chair, far, far away as usual. Her face darkened.

Suddenly the frowns vanished. Her face seemed to brighten as if artificially lit from within by one of those torches used by doctors to inspect the throat. 'There's a girl who might be available.'

'Excellent,' muttered Vizy.

'Excellent,' she mimicked him. 'You weren't even listening.'

'Of course I was. Who recommended her?'

'Ficsor did.'

'When can she start?'

'She's employed at the moment.'

'Where?'

'Not far from here. In Árok utca.'

'Whose place?'

'Some people by the name of Bartos.'

'Who can they be?' pondered Vizy. 'Bartos . . . Bartos . . . let me think. No,' he exclaimed, perplexed, 'I don't know them.'

'How could you possibly know them,' retorted Mrs Vizy, who couldn't bear her husband's ditherings. 'How could you expect to know everybody. You say the oddest things.'

'And what does this fellow Bartek do?'

'To begin with his name is Bartos,' she corrected him. 'He is a revenue inspector. What on earth does a revenue inspector do anyway? I've no idea.'

'It's financial post. He deals with income. He has his own department. He performs inspections round the country.'

'Yes, that fits, he always seems to be away. He is a widower with two children.'

'What about the girl? Is she fit, capable and hard working?'

'How should I know? I know no more than you do. In Ficsor's opinion she is excellent.'

'In that case dismiss Katica.'

'What, and be left alone again. No thank you.'

'All right then, don't dismiss Katica.'

'All Ficsor could tell me,' her voice hardened, 'was that it is possible she might be available. Might!' she emphasized. 'We'd have to lure her away. That's not so easy nowadays. And for all I know I might be getting the worse of the bargain.'

Vizy hated arguments like this which turned in never-ending circles, but he could see no easy way out.

'Why don't you get someone else? A number of people have offered you servants.'

'For instance?'

'Mrs Moviszter.'

'Mrs Moviszter should shut up. I don't want her consolations. "Oh my poor dear, I'm so sorry for you with this constant stream of awful girls, but just you wait, I'll find you one." She has been leading me on like this for two years. All she thinks about is the theatre. First nights and poetry readings.'

'What about Mrs Druma?'

'As you know she is jealous. It pleases her to see me in difficulties. She comes down here to "marvel" at Katica. It's easy for her. Her Stefi might be crazy but she gets everything done. She even nurses the children. As for the Moviszters, Etel has been with them for twenty years, assists that sickly doctor and even helps out in the surgery. Her mistress is never home. She pays half what we pay to Katica. They don't provide any better food than we do. But the maid remains, God knows why. It's a matter of luck as everything is. All we need is a bit of luck. Some people are lucky I suppose, we're not. I don't know what we have done to deserve it. Well,' she sighed, slowly beginning to remove her tortoiseshell hairpins, 'one goes on taking the punishment and paying through the nose for it, losing out as always. Life isn't worth living.'

Vizy too grew sombre. He suggested that they should go to bed. It was getting on for ten o'clock. The light could be seen even through the shutters, and they should put it out in case the soldier on patrol noticed it. Once in July he had fired at the window.

'Why don't you come to bed,' urged her husband who had already started to undress in the bedroom. But the woman just stood at the door as if frozen there.

'Come on,' he pressed her. 'What's the matter with you? Are your nerves playing up?' He was astonished at her behaviour. 'You're like a child. You're always fretting about these servants. Nothing but servants all the time. It's really very petty! Tell me, is it worth it? All because of a servant? Aren't you ashamed of yourself?'

Mrs Vizy stepped into the bedroom and turned back the covers. It was then he noticed that she was crying.

'Angéla,' he pleaded with her, and sitting himself down on a chair he watched her smoothing the pillows while the great tears sparkled and rolled down her cheeks, as Asta Nielsen's did in the movies. 'Your nerves, like everyone else's, have been shattered by this dreadful period. But it's over now. A new age is about to begin, an entirely new and happy age. Life will change. We shall start our lives anew. Today, 31 July 1919, is no ordinary day. It is a historic day.'

Mrs Vizy pulled on a hairnet for the night.

They lay down together in the wide double bed, where for a long time now they had done nothing but sleep. Vizy turned off the bedside light. Darkness fell on them, shadows ran like waves along the floor, and the furniture lost definition and merged with the wall.

Vizy suddenly sat bolt upright. 'I can hear shells exploding,' he whispered.

'No,' answered Mrs Vizy, who had also sat up.

'They're shells all right, near the Vérmező.'

But now it was silent. Only the air still trembled. Cars were speeding along towards the Vár which at times of political change invariably served as a register of the city's, and indeed the whole nation's blood pressure. A few dogs were barking.

'Perhaps it was only a burst tyre,' suggested Mrs Vizy. 'Go to sleep.' In the past few months they had got so used to the sounds of bombardment that they could fall asleep as easily as troopers in the trench.

After a few minutes she spoke again. 'I think we'll try this girl after all.'

'Try her out then,' yawned Vizy. 'Do what you like. Try her out. Goodnight. Go to sleep.'

For a while they lay flat beside each other, naked under

the thin summer sheets. Then a curious light kindled behind their closed lids. They suddenly stood up, left each other, walked through walls, down long passages of years, each going his or her own way, crossing unknown landscapes, fully dressed now in the strangest theatrical costumes. They were in the grip of the most ordinary of miracles: they were dreaming.

4

Anxieties

Kornél Vizy slept cautiously. He rolled himself up into a ball, like a hedgehog, occupying as little space as possible. From beneath the shelter of his white pillows he gave out ambiguous statements and smiled on his foes, the Bolsheviks. He remained a politician, even in his sleep.

When he woke in the morning he ought to have felt as if his hopeless life had taken a dramatic turn for the better, but having chewed things over in his mind so long the night before, he had quite forgotten the previous day's events. Once he sat up though, reality filtered back and he recovered his previous good humour which had grown more certain, more novel and even more fascinating in the interval.

He stretched once and leapt out of bed. A glass of water glittered silver on his bedside table. He decided to do without breakfast and go for a walk. Those who had seen him but a few days ago turned to look at him. He was a dandy of a bygone age come to life again. He wore a suit of dove grey, a freshly laundered white shirt and an elegant tie. Acquaintances and strangers on every side greeted him as he passed. His spats squeaked and sparkled as they caught the light. It was as if a grenade had exploded at his feet, showering him with golden sparks.

His wife was still asleep, breathing lightly, her face waxen and pale. Her waking was markedly different. There was a terrible shock in store for her.

Although she had prophesied that Katica wouldn't be home till dawn, she herself had not seriously believed it. But when she rose at nine she found the table still laid, the teapot unemptied, the plate dirty. She hastened into the kitchen where the campbed lay folded and covered with a horsehair blanket. She tried room after room, quite disorientated. A bitter lump rose in her throat. Here was the living room. The piano had been pushed into a corner, mirrors lay on top of it, and everything was covered in sheets as if someone had died. Beneath the sheets she found basketfuls of clothes. The laundry box was in the dining room and a ramshackle old sideboard stood close by ready for use in case the rabble attempted to force their way in. It was because of them that everything was topsy-turvy. In the morning light this rag and bone shop brought back to her all the horrors of the siege.

The curtains and the paintings were gone. On the bare walls only the crucifix remained – this she had refused to take down despite her husband's entreaties – and on the display cabinet stood the photograph of Piroska, her only child, six years of age, surrounded by flowers and candles as she lay on her bier. Piroska was in her first year of school. She came home one April morning complaining of a headache, was put to bed, and by dusk she was dead. The scarlet fever epidemic had carried her off in six hours.

Her husband was out. He was striding about the world again, wrapped up in his affairs, his adventures. She knew that he cheated on her. Mrs Vizy was in the sanatorium for years after the death of her child and it was then that he had grown estranged from her, that he began, politely and delicately, to cheat on her. He had continued to cheat on her ever since.

Then there was this slut of a maid who couldn't get home in time. She was the embodiment of all her misery. Seizing the feather duster Mrs Vizy furiously began to dust everything in an attempt to forget her frustration. And in the meantime she was plotting a suitable homecoming for the maid.

24

Katica had spent the night with her sailor friend carousing at The Woman of Trieste. It was ten in the morning by the time she returned, sleepy, unkempt, her lipstick smudged, emanating a faint odour of wine.

However Mrs Vizy tried to control herself, her voice trembled with excitement as she informed the girl that she was giving her her notice and that she could leave by the fifteenth.

Some people respond to a firm box on the ear with silent insolence. The girl gave no answer but took the duster out of Mrs Vizy's hands and went on with the cleaning. She could at least try to hide her hurt feelings by working.

It was only now that the woman took fright at having dismissed a servant without any certain prospect of replacing her. The die was cast. Feeling her world crumbling around her she rushed down to find Ficsor.

Ficsor was just at that moment removing the red flag from its bracket on the elevation and was attempting to roll the cheap paper-cloth around the staff. Mrs Vizy grabbed his arm and ushered him upstairs.

Even though accompanied by the honourable lady of the house, the caretaker took care to knock at the door and vigorously clean his shoes on the scraper before entering. He who had but lately been used to dining at the special canteen rigged up at the National Assembly Hall and had made himself very much at home in the Vizy's flat now trod rather nervously there.

He was aware that he had much to answer for. He was among those who had in recent times been referred to as 'old Marxists'. Having been for twenty years a fully paid-up member of the Party, he regarded himself as one of the Red aristocracy and his pride in this was no less than that of a real aristocrat in his family tree. Naturally he had acted as the official representative of the household. He collected rents, executed the orders of the Communist government, cautioned the 'bourgeois' against plotting, beat his breast and drew attention to his shaky legs which had been ruined by years of climbing stairs. It was whispered that he had requisitioned two pairs of tan-coloured shoes and first-class rations for himself while allotting second-class rations only to the owner of the house who bore the lower classification of intellectual worker. His greatest crime though was that on the day Mrs Vizy was dragged off to parliament, he deliberately disappeared, returning only late at night, and that Vizy, who had wanted his support in the matter, had had to wait forlornly in his kitchen. The Vizys made no secret of the fact that they intended to break his neck at the first available opportunity.

He fingered his neck and felt his poor head which had lately grown to resemble a bruised apple, the kind so cheap and plentiful they spill from baskets at the market. But Mrs Vizy affectionately invited him to sit down and placed her hand on his arm.

'Look here, Ficsor, you might be able to help me out. Bring this girl here immediately. I've already dismissed the other. Your kindness will not be forgotten.'

The caretaker started for the door which promised his freedom. She delayed him.

'You say she has spent three years in service in Pest? How come I have never seen her at your place?'

'Bless you, ma'am, she's that kind of creature. She doesn't go anywhere. She is neither to be seen nor heard. She is very quiet.'

'I hope she is strong though. Could she manage these four rooms?'

'Her? She could manage eight. She's a village girl.'

'And she's reliable?'

'You will see that for yourself, ma'am. I'm not going to make speeches about her, all I will say is . . .' he hesitated.

'Is what?'

'That the honourable lady will be satisfied with her.'

The caretaker returned at noon, beaming. He had spoken with the girl, she was willing to enter service and would come tomorrow to discuss the arrangements.

But she didn't keep the appointment for the events of that day upset everything. Budapest was occupied – not by the

26

Allies as Gábor Tatár and Vizy had forecast – but by the Romanians, who had crossed the River Tisza and, against the wishes of the great powers, taken control of the city. They swaggered about the ragged and hungry streets in their brand new uniforms like guests of honour at a historical occasion. They raised their trumpets to the sky and blew upon them constantly and deafeningly; it seemed they were unable to proceed a step without this musical accompaniment which was plainly supposed to evoke memories of the Emperor Trajan's all-conquering Roman legions: the startled, dishonoured country rang with the sound.

This was something that neither Hungarians nor the Romanians themselves would ever have been able to imagine, not in their wildest dreams. They glanced at each other astonished at this miraculous turn of events. It was literally incredible. Hungarians at their windows watched Romanian vehicles cruising the streets below but they didn't believe it. Not even the Romanians could believe it straightaway. Head waiters scraped and bowed before them, lift-boys conducted them up and down in elegant conveyances, they came and entered as they pleased. It was all a little overpowering. A dream. All heaven lay before them, nothing barred their way. At first they didn't know what they should ask for and in their childish greed they grabbed at showy knick-knacks rather than things of real value.

They started by confiscating telephones from private flats. Two lorries piled high with them trundled down Krisztina körút trailing cut wires. Then they began to appear in stores, in factories, in hospitals. In one hospital they were received by an elderly director wearing an old-fashioned frock-coat, who, on the point of tears, delivered a stuttering official protest in broken French, referring to the ban imposed by the great powers of the Entente. The officer waved him away: doors opened and materials and equipment, including patients' apparel and bedding, were whisked away in the name of compensation or reparation.

To civil security however they took a different attitude and strictly punished any attempt at looting or disorderliness

27

They went from house to house rounding up terrorists and led them away. Pale and handcuffed, the terrorists hung their heads as they departed. They had begun to dance to a new tune, just as Ficsor had forecast.

The Vizys' house was humming like a hive during the nervous intensity of these historic days. First it was the elegant figure of the lawyer, Druma, dashing up the stairs and waving his briefcase to announce that conservatives had taken over the government and expelled the ruling social democrats. Then it was Mrs Druma who ran screaming through the house with her child in her arms because of some affray in the street outside. Then Etel declaimed that yet another Communist had been allowed to retain his post. Patients leaving Dr Moviszter's heart-and-lung surgery gathered by the Vizys' door vehemently discussing political events. The next day it was Stefi, the Drumas' counter-revolutionary maid who used to attend rallies after she had finished the washing, who returned home flushed and full of arguments, and loudly held forth from the gallery of the second floor, demanding the rope for every Red or pinko.

On the rare occasions Mrs Vizy ventured out she collared Ficsor at his place by the stairwell.

'Look here, what religion is this girl?'

'Catholic, your ladyship.'

Mrs Vizy approved. Catholic girls were nice, more modest, less headstrong and demanding than the Protestants. It's true they tended to be careless, were continually singing and were easily ruined. Once they started downhill they were unredeemable: they fell directly from heaven through to hell.

Once she accosted him in Krisztina tér. 'Where was she born?'

'In Kajár. She's the daughter of my sister-in-law. I told you she came from down Balaton way.'

This was good news. One summer, when her own daughter was still alive, they had stayed at Balatonfüred for their holidays. The occasion held pleasant memories for her, full of the noise of waves, of children's laughter and gypsy bands.

28

She also seemed to remember hearing someone praise 'the Balaton girls'.

At the market she bumped into Ficsor's wife.

'What in fact is her name?'

'Well!' marvelled the big woman. 'Does your ladyship mean to say she doesn't know? It's Anna.'

'Anna,' repeated Mrs Vizy and was immediately attracted to this soft, feminine name, since she hadn't yet had a maid called Anna, nor indeed any relation with whom the association might have been confusing. 'Anna.' She mouthed the name again and found it had a reassuring sound: it fell upon her soft and white, like manna.

Ficsor did all he could to entice his relative away. He wasted no time in his campaign and he and his wife hastened to take turns to call at Árok utca. He knew what was at stake. Every morning he saw Communists being dismissed from their jobs. A young man slunk by the gate, mopping at a thin ribbon of blood which issued from his temple. Such sights made him redouble his efforts. But he had little to show for them yet. So far he had succeeded only in talking to Mrs Cifka, Mrs Bartos's sister-in-law, who was part of the revenue-inspector's household. The inspector would only let the girl go if Ficsor found them a satisfactory replacement. He couldn't convince Anna either. She hummed and hawed and failed to understand the situation clearly; she had grown fond of the children and felt sorry for them. Once she promised to call round but failed to do so. Later she said she had 'thought better of it'.

Mrs Vizy continued to pester him. 'Why haven't you brought her along yet? I'd like to see her at least.'

'It's laundry day today.

'You mean she does the laundry as well?'

'Naturally. She washes and irons. She's a real gem.'

Next time there was another excuse. 'She is taking the children for a walk.'

'Little Bandi, you mean?' she asked, for by now she was intimately acquainted with the family's circumstances.

'Yes, the four-year-old.'

'Now look here, don't lead me on. Be honest now. I have to know for certain whether I can count on her.'

'Of course your ladyship can count her. I mean that most sincerely.'

The caretaker disappeared for a while. He worked overtime at the post office and spent only a few furtive minutes at home. Mrs Ficsor's story was that he was at the girl's house. The end of the month was approaching with alarming speed. Mrs Vizy was already considering keeping Katica on, who since being given her notice – probably because the ties between them had been loosened – seemed somehow less annoying. Katica had fixed up a job at the chemists and was due to start on the fifteenth. It very much looked as though now, just before winter and in the midst of this general confusion, she would remain without a maid, her husband would be gloomier than ever and they would once more be in the position of being unable to receive visitors or to go out; it would be like those two bitter months after the departure of Lujza Héring, the memory of which still evoked nightmares and oppressed her.

It seemed as though she would have to give up Anna. But she was determined not to surrender so meekly. Her late father had been a colonel of the hussars, and both her grandfathers were military men. She had inherited enough of the fighting spirit of her ancestors: though some were centuries distant now they lent her strength for the siege. She took on the whole town. She spent whole days walking to and fro. She called on long neglected acquaintances to enquire whether they knew of anyone available. They usually responded with a sympathetic smile. This was her Calvary: she was all too intimate with the stations of her cross.

For the first time in her life she turned to the police, but the police had other headaches. The wagons were in constant use, overspilling with rich human cargo. The unpainted benches in the yard were packed with suspects – Communists of minor or advanced age, children, old men, women in silks or rags, their eyes red from weeping, all

30

awaiting their fates. Mrs Vizy left her calling card with the officer appointed to deal with servants.

He knew what she wanted and admitted her without an appointment. He looked at her with a certain indifference, like a neurologist with an incurable patient. He comforted her as best he could then directed her to the domestic agency.

And so, without too much hope, she set her foot on the road again. If nothing else they could give her some information. Little tin tabs in red and blue and green advertised the availability of cooks, housemaids, wet nurses and every kind and grade of domestic servant: it was a veritable long vanished Canaan, as anachronistic as those empty restaurants whose windows proclaimed in gold lettering, *Fresh Dishes Available – Day and Night*, or those tobacconists that promised *Native and Foreign Brands* but sold only cigarette holders and flints for lighters.

There wasn't a maid to be had in the whole of Buda. She tried district after district and it was only on the Pest side, in Ferencváros, that she found one or two. The agent bowed respectfully before her: she knew him well, as she did all the others. He was a pale, foxy-looking scoundrel, with a silver watch-chain dangling from his waistcoat. He fawned on every customer and, in the interests of the business, referred to the servants as his 'ladies'. His voice sank to a whisper as he offered his merchandise.

The unemployed female workforce sat by the wall in basketwork chairs, like parsley vendors in pathetic fancy dress. They fell silent when she entered. They tried to look directly and unconcernedly before them, concentrating on the fact that the contract involved the agreement of both parties, but they could not take their eyes off this unknown woman on whom their immediate fates might depend, and they stared at her with a mixture of wonderment and contempt.

She only had to glance at them to know that this was shopsoiled material, the kind that's left behind after the sales, rejected by everyone. After all who would send their

31

daughters into service at a time like this when money has no value, when peasant farmers were swimming in home-produced lard and could afford to give their children piano lessons? Nevertheless she decided to question some of them. The first did not rise from her chair but sat crossleg-ged throughout. The second stood up but there was some-thing ironic in her servile expression: she herself asked for the return of her employment logbook while the rest nudged each other, grinning impertinently, and instinctively with-drew from Mrs Vizy.

Only one was keen to come, a grey, sixty-year-old cook with eyes like poison, who, according to the agent, had worked in the finest country inns, who would have offered to scrub the floorboards had she not been so weak and exhausted through having given all her energy to the slop-buckets of inns at Cegléd or Kecskemét.

What use had she for such people? She stared, dejected, at the mosaic tabletop where filthy paper flowers attempted to raise the tone of the establishment. The air was thick with the female odour of the servants.

By evening she had developed a headache – a migraine on one side of her temple; it was a long time since she had suffered from one. She wrapped her head in a towel and sat in the dark room, wondering why she allowed herself to get so upset. It wasn't the failure that bothered her so much, since she had prepared herself for that, it was a sense of guilt that she had been faithless to Anna, that she had somehow betrayed her by looking at others, and she resolved, come what may, to obtain only her services.

5

Ministry and Mystery

Mrs Vizy fought this heroic battle alone. She didn't even tell her husband that she had dismissed Katica. Secretly she sought out Druma, whose reputation as a counter-revolutionary ensured that his office was besieged by the relatives of harassed Communists who wanted to entrust their defence to him.

The young lawyer's normally flushed face was now aflame with the fever of history. He would gladly have packed Ficsor off to prison for a minimum of five years, but the matter of the servant, he felt, was perhaps a little hazy from a legal point of view. In any case he had a letter typed and forwarded to the Bartos household, advising them that according to the letter of the law they should be prepared to release the girl from her contract.

Vizy was rarely at home, and then only to bolt down his dinner and supper. He was morose, nervous and uncommunicative. His wife would not have dared to irritate him with such trifling matters. Whenever she asked him where he was going or where he had come from he would merely mutter the words: the Ministry, in a tone so low and secretive that it sounded as if he had said: the Mystery. And indeed the vast universe of politics and public affairs was, for him, a form of mysticism, and anything that fell outside its scope was necessarily so piffling that it wasn't worth thinking about.

The ancient yellow building that housed the ministry was a babble of confidential voices. Whenever Vizy entered its portals his senses responded to its murmurous atmosphere, and as he climbed the stairs an unctuous smile of self-esteem settled on him as if to say that while everything here pertained to public life, it was nevertheless his own domain, that he felt far more at home here than back at the flat. Once more the doorman greeted him. His well-groomed secretary met him in the hall with a list of his appointments for the day, readily sorted and annotated, which he quickly surveyed before deciding who should actually be admitted into his presence. To those already there Vizy apologized for keeping them waiting and bade them take a seat. He complained of the pressure of work, and joked that he was so busy that he couldn't even fit the angel of death into his schedule. He played upon the little key of his buzzer with the delicacy of a concert pianist. He adopted an official tone with provincial visitors, called in references for some, examined others' individual files, gravely shaking his head as he read the file's contents, criticizing it in a friendly though patronizing manner calculated to demonstrate his superiority. Then he would generously offer the visitor a cigar and if it was accepted he would produce his keys from his back pocket and unlock one of the drawers of his desk, not too quickly so as to prolong the moment of pleasure, and lay the gilded box before him and lift the lid to reveal the cigars with their ribbons, the official ribbons that marked the advance in his career. And while he was busily lighting the visitor's cigar he would make a mental note that there was now one cigar less, and quietly close the gilded lid and lock the box away again.

He liked this ritual and he liked the spirit of the place. At noon a bell rang to announce the arrival of the minister. The building was in a moment transformed to a temple. Even the grave official trees in the yard took on a more ceremonial air in their cast iron hoops. Have you seen His Excellency? Is he in a good mood this morning? I need to wheedle some money out of him for that damned chamber

34

of commerce. Good morning, your Esteemed Excellency. Good morning, your Excellency, your most obedient servant. He was surrounded by friends who had emerged from counter-revolutionary cells in Austria, from estates in the provinces, all scrubbed and scented, breathing a confection of eau de Cologne and Egyptian tobacco. They embraced each other, slapped each other on the back and celebrated his return since they had heard something to the effect that he had been violently carried off to parliament. They too complained of their various trials and tribulations and how they had been robbed of this or that by those blackguards. Nevertheless here they were, they were still alive, the old and the young for once on equally intimate terms with each other, low-grade salaries with high-grade ones, like one big happy family. They swam in a bath of charm and filial sentiment, all ready to be of service, in and out of office, granting everyone the respect due to their title, maintaining a military discipline and a certain self-discipline as well as knowing that all was up for grabs, and that in the due course of their careers any one of them could ascend the ladder of success to the topmost rung. This was Vizy's world, far more than the flat: it was his universe.

Vizy was an outstanding bureaucrat, hard working and conscientious. This was a fact recognized by both his inferiors and superiors. Nor did he lack a social conscience: if someone in trouble turned to him he would immediately write the necessary memo to the relevant organization. He was capable – in his own fashion – of disinterested charity, as, for example, in the case of the establishment of an orphanage or sanatorium. On the other hand he did not like being harassed on an individual basis. What were organizations for, after all? You couldn't even accuse him of minor abuses of his office: not a penny was left unaccounted for. But he believed religiously in doing favours for anyone who might be able to repay in kind, merchants and manufacturers who happened to be old friends of his, who, when he went to shop at their establishments, refused to allow him to pick up the bill. Of course he protested each time and

35

did not consider it ethical, but he would have been hurt if such expected 'unexpected gestures' had not been made. On his name day he was showered with gifts of various sorts from stores and factories. They sent meat, cakes and liqueur in quantities sufficient to supply the festive spread. Occasionally he might receive a ring or a silver watch which his puritan conscience would not allow him to wear; instead he locked it in the display cabinet and only brought it out when he felt low. These presents were by no means commensurate with the scale of favours granted, but they were welcome tokens which increased his self-esteem and lent a certain poetry to his life.

Now he took care to cultivate these friendships: at the Municipal Assembly Hall, at committee meetings, at party suppers, night and day he wove his web. He looked, in these uncertain days, to leave behind the past ten years of stagnation in his career and skip a rung.

One evening he was invited to supper by the secretary of state. At such times Vizy became a regular lounge lizard. He chatted light-heartedly, even to his wife, and on this occasion she used the opportunity to bring up the topic of the maid. On their way out she enticed him into the care-taker's flat.

His approach to the negotiations was considerably differ-ent from hers. Not being acquainted with all the fine details of the matter he could be as high-handed as when someone at the ministry passed him a hasty ill-prepared file. His wife regarded him with pride. There was, after all, something rather effective in this straightforward masculine style.

'Well, what about the servant?'

'She promised to come, your excellency.'

'If she promised then she must come and fulfil her obli-gations.'

'Well, she would come, but her employer won't allow her.'

'What do you mean? Hasn't the servant handed in her notice? And has he not accepted it? If so, he cannot legally obstruct her. The law is perfectly clear concerning the contract between servants and their employers. He has no alternative but, *de jure*, to comply.'

'Yes, sir,' bowed Ficsor, mesmerized by the Latin words.

'Very well then, let's have no more fooling about. If she doesn't keep her word I'll have the police bring her over. You can tell her that from me. Either she comes or it's the police.'

This did for both Ficsor and his wife. They stared at each other, dumbstruck. They were aware of the shades of the prison house creeping across their lives. They raised their hands in a gesture of protest against the charge of carelessness or perhaps to ward off the blows of fate.

Vizy had finished. He was ashamed that he had brought his prestige to bear on a trifle such as this. His eye roved around the basement flat. The damp had crept at least four feet up the wall, decorating it with black flowers as big as a man's hand. There was an insidious smell of mould in the air which mingled with the smell of onions roasting on the hearth. The windows were so low you could only see up to the knees of the passers-by. This was where he watched and waited for Ficsor for hours on end that time his wife was taken off to parliament; there he had sat on that small chair which they now hastened to dust and offer him, so that he might sit down for a moment and so delay the inevitable. But he refused the seat. It was dirty. He was afraid of soiling his dinner jacket.

In any case it seemed to him that the kitchen used to be a more attractive place. Then he was grateful for its silence, its biblical simplicity. There was a settee somewhere he had very much wanted to lie down on. Could it have been that battered and worn sofa leaking great wads of seaweed stuffing? A china mug lay in a corner beside a shopping basket improvised out of the mauve-coloured velvet which used to cover railway-seats in first-class compartments and which, following the revolution, could frequently be found in working-class households adapted to various uses, including hastily patched children's trousers. He was shocked by the poverty of the room. He held a handkerchief to his nose and shot a nervous glance at his wife urging her to hurry, but she was still wrapped up in her negotiations, aimless and circuitous as only a woman can be.

'So you'll speak to her, won't you Mr Ficsor, and you'll be sure to tell her that she should make up her mind? Perhaps you could promise her increased wages.'

'That won't be much use. She's not bothered about money.'

'Indeed?' Mrs Vizy's eyes lit up. 'What is she bothered about then? Does she keep lovers?'

'Her?' Ficsor quite forgot about courtesies and dug his fat wife in the ribs. 'Hear that? Anna keeping lovers!'

Mrs Ficsor revealed her yellow buck teeth and roared with laughter at the idea that Anna, of all people, should keep lovers.

Mrs Vizy grew curious.

'Does she have a large appetite?'

'She eats no more than a sparrow does.'

'What does she like doing then?'

'Working, your ladyship,' answered Ficsor. 'She likes work.'

'She's the sort of girl whose hands should be cast in gold,' added Mrs Ficsor, and smiled beatifically at the vision.

Mrs Vizy was at a loss to know which impressed her more: the caretaker's blunt assurance, or his wife's simple, almost poetic turn of phrase. Both were commonplaces, but sometimes these are all the more impressive since they leave the imagination free to roam at will.

Katica was still with them but only just. She did more or less as she pleased now and they didn't even ask her to tidy the flat. Mrs Vizy took a perverse joy in watching the dust and dirt gather. While Katica continued in her bovine way, yawning and waddling in the kitchen, she saw the other maid beside her, behind her, moving with the delicacy of a pixie and putting everything right. For work was what she liked, and only work. And much as we save our special gifts for those closest to our hearts, as a mark of distinction, so Mrs Vizy was already reserving certain particularly difficult jobs for her. She expected miracles from her. When she closed her eyes she saw her image with those hands that should be cast in gold, the maid with those golden hands which, being gold, sparkled in the half-light and led her on to ever new horizons.

Then something else happened. The Romanians moved into their immediate vicinity. Those at whom she had stared in astonishment in the first few weeks of the occupation now strolled before her house as if they had been born round the corner. She got so used to them she hardly noticed them. On Sundays, reeking of scent, the slim dark corseted officers promenaded up and down the Vár with their entourage of chorus girls, or took excursions into the hills, or picnicked on the grass with their latest sweethearts and took photographs to commemorate the occasion. They were serenaded by gypsy bands at the Philadelphia, who played them old Hungarian tunes such as they might once have heard and passionately sung as students back in the Transylvanian hills.

The common troops were encamped on the Vérmező. At night they prepared supper in a cauldron, lit their fires, and were attended by the local servant girls who had not seen real soldiers for some time, apart from a few wretched deserters or the flushed faces of the Red Army. Lajos, Katica's boyfriend, had a long record as a burglar and had been arrested, so the girl found herself a Romanian, a shepherd boy from the 'old kingdom' barely out of his teens. The tin-helmeted warrior had never seen such a beautiful woman. His arm wound around her waist, taking her hand in his, he walked her round and round the Vérmező, admiring her rouged lips and her tinted blonde hair. He communicated to her by signs that he would marry her if only she would return to Romania with him. Every day he would wait for her with a bouquet of flowers and would often enter the house itself, which outraged everyone. Etel refused to talk to Katica and considered her nothing less than a traitor; Steffi, on her behalf, declared Katica to be a Romanian spy.

Mrs Vizy wrung her hands. Such a scandal! Such shame

on the house! but she dared not interfere, since she feared the vengeance of the troops. Neither was there an answer forthcoming to Druma's letter.

The situation was becoming unbearable. She took her parasol in her hand and prepared for action. It was grey and dusty outside, a midsummer dusk more like autumn when the evenings begin to close in and the wind hums in the chimney. She stumbled along the uneven slopes of the Tabán quarter. The sentries on patrol gave the familiar streets the air of some strange colonial outpost.

She knew approximately where the house should be for the caretaker had often described it to her. She knew there was a practising midwife called Erzsébet Karvaly in the block, and that her sign, showing a baby being bathed in a tub, hung outside; that the gate to the house had iron palings, and that the glazed door of the Bartos residence opened on to the courtyard by a mural depicting St Florian which had a red night-light below it.

Árok utca was a row of dilapidated hovels in a state of subsidence, each indistinguishable from the other. She lost her way among them. She asked directions from a feeble-minded old woman sitting before a ruined shanty, but she had difficulty in making herself understood. Eventually she learned that she had missed the house and that she must go back the way she had come. She scampered down furtively as if she were a criminal. People eyed her suspiciously. She began to feel afraid. Eventually from a small grassy eminence she spotted the sign with the baby, made out Erzsébet Karvaly's name, and crept through the gate. The picture of St Florian and the flickering red light invited her on.

Her plan was to ask the maid out for a word or two and then to entice her away, there and then if possible, but in any case to see her for herself. She fumbled in her bag for some money so that she could tip someone to pass the message to the girl. But there wasn't a soul to be seen in the street. As for the dirty narrow yard with its patch of livid sky above, it was quite deserted.

She stood irresolutely, listening to the voices of women and children from within the house. A window slammed shut in the draught. She flattened herself against the wall and waited.

Suddenly the glazed door opened and a little barefooted boy ran out into the yard. This was Bandi. Her heart skipped a beat as a woman emerged.

The woman was roughly the same height as she was, but muscular and sturdy, her face a golden brown, her great head of hair tousled and her thick eyebrows black as coal. A faded mauve dress hung gracelessly on her. She chased after the boy who ducked and weaved around the yard till she finally caught hold of his hand, admonished him, then took him lovingly in her arms, smothered him with kisses and carried him into the flat.

After a minute or so she came out with a tin basin. She filled it with water from the pump and, as she started in again, looked round. Their eyes met for the first time.

Mrs Vizy beckoned her over with her parasol. Then with her spare hand. The woman seemed not to notice or understand and went in.

She did not come out again. It was getting dark. Soon a man entered the gate, obviously the master of the house. He stared at her, wondering what a respectable woman might be doing here. She thought it best to hasten away.

It hadn't quite turned out as she had imagined, but she didn't regret her adventure because at least she had now seen for herself what a strong, hardworking creature the girl was. What she liked most about her was her gentleness with the child. Her fantasies now had a basis of fact. At home she boasted to Ficsor that she had seen her.

'How did the honourable lady like her?'

'She's quite a handsome girl.'

'She has a wonderful nature. Your ladyship will be convinced of that.'

'Yes, but when?'

'Any day now. We've found someone to take her place

there. They told us today they are letting her go, you needn't worry anymore.'

Etel and Stefi were on the second floor beating eggs for a cake-mix.

'She's called Anna.'

'Really?'

Mrs Druma, who had a keen nose for gossip, wasted no time in spreading the news. This bland and conspicuously uncultivated woman had been an ordinary nurse during the war and had hooked her distinguished-looking husband while he lay wounded in a provincial hospital. She sneaked and prowled about the inner staircase like a little mouse. Even her voice had a squeaking mousy quality. Once she crept up on Mrs Vizy and assaulted her in her usual tactless, confidential manner. 'We know all about it. Yes, we do. What will you pay her?'

From her the details were conveyed to Mrs Moviszter. The doctor's attractive wife was wearing a flowery hat and, having received a complimentary ticket from a theatrical acquaintance, was on her way to a dress-rehearsal. As usual she was accompanied by the latest literary discovery. She spotted Mrs Vizy in the fashionable Kigyó tér, and, having stopped her, brought the conversation round to the subject.

'Surely not, darling! You mean she hasn't started yet? Everyone thought she began yesterday.'

Mrs Vizy shook her head. And meantime the days passed by. The generous form of Anna hung before her ever more mistily, ever more distant. She began to think the whole thing was a figment of her imagination, that perhaps the maid did not exist at all.

6

Anna

It was 14 August, hot and bright, a beautiful summer's day.
Vizy had popped down to the Municipal Assembly Hall for
coffee. His wife was contemplating what was left of her rice
pudding. A few stray grains of rice revealed themselves as
she pushed the plate aside. She counted them, there were
seven.

How did they get there? She didn't know. She was sure
she hadn't spilled them, since she had not moved her plate
once during the entire meal. She thought about the number.
Why precisely seven? It must portend something. After all
even the most insignificant things may be used by the world
beyond to convey an important message. Having quite
clearly witnessed the appearance of her daughter at frequent
seances and heard her voice, she did not doubt this.

She placed three pills on her tongue, swallowed them
with a glass of thin wine, and was pondering what good
news the seven grains of rice might portend when someone
softly knocked at the door, and before she could answer
Ficsor's head appeared.

'Should we wait, your ladyship?'

'Who's that with you?'

'Anna. May we come in?'

'Yes, do. No. Wait!'

The head disappeared and the door closed. Mrs Vizy clut-
ched the edge of the table. This sudden unexpected turn of

events left her dizzy. Her legs were bare but for slippers, and she was wearing the old lilac frock which she used to put on in the days of the commune when she hoped to be taken for a working woman.

She made for the wardrobe and changed into a white frock, champagne-coloured stockings and brown shoes. She selected these quickly like an actress before her entrance. She consulted the mirror. Her face was tired and careworn. She tried a smile but it looked forced. Then she experimented with a more serious expression but finally settled on a middle course. She lightly powdered her face, and slipped a gold bracelet on as an afterthought.

On tiptoe she hurried into the dining room. Her husband's housecoat lay on the divan with the sleeves turned inside out. She folded it, but some things still worried her. The tablecloth did not fully cover the table, the greasy plates still sat by the remaining rice pudding and flies had settled on the sugar bowl. She would have preferred to tidy up a bit but there was no time now. She was afraid that if she kept the girl waiting Katica would put her off.

All she could do was to straighten the tablecloth and replace the aluminium-tipped cork in the bottle. She resumed her place by the table and leaned on her elbow as if to suggest that she had been sitting there for some time thinking such thoughts as ladies of her station were wont to think. 'Come in,' she called in a low voice.

Ficsor entered. No one else. Not for three, four or even five seconds.

'Well?' she said. It looked as if they had cheated her again.

'She's here,' the caretaker assured her. 'Here she is.'

And then the girl came in. She came straight over to her, and curtseyed and kissed her hand so naturally and effortlessly, it seemed she had known her for years. Mrs Vizy did not withdraw her hand at once: she liked to have her hand kissed, enjoying the damp touch of lips. Ficsor told the girl to do something but Mrs Vizy did not – could not – hear it since the blood was pounding in her ears and her whole attention was directed to the girl who had retreated to the door and was holding her employment book in a clean handkerchief, her eyes fixed on the ground.

Mrs Vizy adjusted her lorgnette: her face was a mixture of shock, disappointment and wonder. 'Is this her?' she asked, indicating the girl.

'Yes, your ladyship,' Ficsor confirmed, incomprehendingly. 'This is Anna. Anna,' he repeated. 'Is she not what you wanted?' He inclined his head and squinted at the honourable lady.

'Yes,' answered Mrs Vizy, still doubtful, still a little hazy. 'So this is her . . .'

But it wasn't. At least it wasn't the person she saw that evening in Árok Street. The woman who ran after the boy had been taller, much taller, much more muscular; her face golden-brown, her hair and her eyebrows both black, black as coal. She remembered this quite clearly. It must be a simple misunderstanding. She must have taken her for someone else, perhaps for that relative of Bartos of whom Ficsor had spoken once or twice.

Although this was immediately plain to her, it was some minutes before she could dismiss from her mind that woman in mauve whom she had mentally appointed, accommodated, filled Katica's bed with and put to clean each room; that woman whom she already considered her own and who now had to surrender all those imaginary virtues with which she had been invested: now she had to strip this woman of her decorations and hand them on to the rightful claimant, a total stranger, this ungainly girl who stood before her obviously struck with stage-fright.

The disappointment and amazement slowly faded from her face and gave way to a pleasant sense of expectation. Once again she cast her eye over her. She didn't even look like a peasant. She wasn't as thick-set or ruddy-complexioned as Örzsi Varga had been, but rather lithe and somehow delicate, her face oval, her bone-structure fine and well proportioned. She wore a neat checked gingham frock under which her small childish breasts swelled out: there was something unselfconscious and toylike about them,

45

like two little rubber balls. The girl had some inexplicable quality which attracted and repulsed her at the same time; in any case she found her fascinating.

Mrs Vizy removed her lorgnette. Even when she was no longer looking at her but simply allowed her presence to enter her consciousness, she felt that this was the girl she had sought all these years in vain. She was aware of an inner voice that had guided her at all the turning points of her life, that encouraged and commanded her to forestall argument and act, to take this girl now and hang on to her. A powerful desire to seize and possess swept through her: she extended her hand as if to take hold of her and never let her go.

'You want her employment book, ma'am?' asked Ficsor.

'Yes,' Mrs Vizy answered, controlling herself, as she skilfully turned her misunderstood gesture into something more prosaic. 'Yes, let me see the book.'

She raised her brow.

'Your name is Édes?' she asked. 'Édes as in "sweet"?'

'That's her name all right, Anna Édes.'

Mrs Vizy read the information half to herself, under her breath.

Anna Édes was born in the village of Balatonfőkajár, in the district of Enying, in the county of Veszprém in Hungary.

Personal description

Year of birth: 1900 (nineteen hundred)
Religion: RC
Height: average
Face: round
Eyes: blue
Eyebrows: blonde
Nose: normal
Mouth: normal
Hair: blonde
Teeth: healthy

Beard: none
Inoculation: yes
Distinguishing features: none
Signature: Anna Édes

'Yes,' she said, and gave a secret smile, perhaps because of the name or because she couldn't picture Anna with a beard. She glanced at the book, then back at Anna, and checked through the curt details which hardly gave an accurate description of the girl. Her hair, for example, which was by no means thick and which was pulled back from her rounded brow and smoothed back over her head, was not blonde but somewhere between chestnut and blonde, almost auburn. Her nose was not merely 'normal' but of a decidedly interesting shape with wide nostrils: there was something piquant about it. She was slightly taller than average, but frailly built, a shade underdeveloped, even a touch boyish. Her lips were pale and chapped. Her hands were as rough as you might expect in a servant, her nails short and square.

'How old are you?' asked Mrs Vizy.

'Nineteen, ma'am,' Ficsor answered for her. 'Isn't that right, Anna?'

'Can't you speak for yourself, girl?' Mrs Vizy turned to Anna.

'She's bashful. Very bashful.'

Mrs Vizy had not yet seen Anna's eyes. 'Why doesn't she look at me?' she asked.

'She's frightened.'

'Of whom? Of me? There's really no need to be frightened of me.'

The girl briefly raised her long lashes but closed them quickly before Mrs Vizy could really see her eyes.

Mrs Vizy studied the spiky spidery letters of the signature the girl had taken such care over at the desk in the police station, and noted the comments of previous employers. There were only two of these to date: the first, in 1916 (the year of her arrival in Budapest), Wild the warehouse manager, then Bartos the revenue inspector. She had spent close on a year and a half with each.

'What was her post?'

'Children's nurse'

'You mean nursery maid,' she corrected him.

The references seemed quite satisfactory. She was considered 'a faithful employee', her moral conduct was 'unexceptionable' and it was duly noted that in both cases she was 'healthy at the time of leaving service'. Mrs Wild conscientiously warned other potential employers that her work was 'not always of the top quality' and that she had 'not yet developed all the necessary skills'.

'Not yet developed all the necessary skills,' quoted Mrs Vizy. 'Natural I suppose . . .'

'She'll quickly pick things up,' Ficsor assured her.

'Of course, it's not the main thing. The important thing is that she should work at them.'

'If it comes to that, she is most industrious.'

'Can she cook?'

'A little,' added Ficsor modestly on the girl's behalf.

'A little? I would have preferred if you had said not at all. I know the situation. They all say this when they apply for the job, but once they stand before the cooker it turns out they have no idea. Do you remember Margit Mennyei, Ficsor? She said she could cook. So did Lidi.'

Ficsor remembered them both and nodded sagely.

'Never mind, I'll train her. But can she keep things in order? Can she wash? Can she scrub the floor?'

'Certainly.' The caretaker waved his hand in guarantee.

'According to this then,' she quickly ran through the list, 'she can do everything that is required round the house: she'll do the shopping, bring in the coal, darn stockings in her spare time, mend clothes, etcetera, etcetera.'

'She's not the choosy kind, are you Anna?'

'That's as it should be. Once you're here you'll have to work. It's not a female companion I want but a maid. The place should be spick and span.'

Anna did not look at her all this time but stared at the

floor. The voice remained disembodied, official. Confusedly she shifted from foot to foot. From the moment she had entered the room she felt sick: indeed she felt so unwell she feared she might faint. There was a vaguely foul smell about the place she didn't recognize, something like the interior of a chemist's shop, a sharp cold smell which invaded her senses and disturbed her stomach. Mrs Vizy kept a piece of camphor in the piano to protect the felts. Anna didn't know where this medicinal odour emanated from, she only knew she couldn't bear it and that she wanted to rush out immediately. Had she paid any attention to this natural instinct she would already have been halfway down the stairs and running through the streets; nor would she have stopped till she was back in the fields of her native village. However her uncle stood beside her and she dared not move a muscle.

If she did raise her eyes at all it was no more than enough to allow her to see Mrs Vizy's shoes and stockings and, beside her on the wall, the ebony case of the pendulum clock whose even ticking divided the silence and lent the dining room an air of stiff aristocratic authority. She even managed to peek into the living room. The mirror there was a smear of colours reflected from paintings. A long low divan covered with a piece of scarlet Torontal carpet extended below it, blazing in the afternoon sunshine. She had seen nothing like it at the Bartoses' or the Wilds'. She stared at it dizzy and bewildered. Her eyes kept returning to it. The whole flat seemed to be an enchanted castle.

'The question is,' Mrs Vizy declared, 'would she like to work here? Well? Would you?'

The girl kept silent. Barely perceptibly she shrugged her shoulders. It was a vague, sad gesture.

Mrs Vizy's visage darkened. She knew too well the insubordination in that dumb movement, and in that instant she sensed the ruin of all her hopes and efforts. She decided that this was the time for firmness, that she must bring this business to a head.

'I beg your pardon?' she asked sarcastically. 'I am not used to being answered like this. If you don't want the job, girl, here are your references.' She made a point of dropping the employment book on the table so it made a noise. 'You may go.'

'Anna meant no harm,' Ficsor hastened to the rescue. 'You do want the job, don't you Anna?'

'Does she or doesn't she?'

They both waited for an answer. Silence.

'Yes.' Anna's answer was barely audible. Her voice trembled. She had simply meant she didn't mind. Wherever she went she had to work.

'That's different. Speak clearly and comprehensibly as is the habit in any decent house. If you behave well you will find this a good situation.'

'It'll be a good situation,' Ficsor hurried to reinforce the honourable lady. Their combined power would win the day.

'There are only the two of us, I and my husband. There are no children.' Mrs Vizy cast an unwitting glance at the photograph on the wall and went through the usual idiotic motion of smoothing back her golden hair as if her bun were inordinately heavy and the skull beneath it cracking under the strain. 'Furthermore I am more relaxed about certain things. You won't have to pay for bread – you can eat as much as you like. I understand that in your last job you breakfasted on brown soup. Here you will get coffee every morning. Hot coffee. On Sunday there is pastry, twice a week there's meat. If your work is satisfactory we may be able to run to a pair of shoes now and then. Or a dress.'

'Imagine, Anna. A dress!' The caretaker smiled encouragingly at her.

'And perhaps in due course,' and this was always the joker in Mrs Vizy's pack, 'I may have you taught to sew.'

'Do you hear that, Anna? Taught to sew. The honourable lady will get someone to teach you sewing. But you must work hard. You'll be mixing with the gentry. That's the sort of household it is. You won't find another like it,' he continued, and looked around for something that would make a deep impression on her, 'not in the whole Krisztina district.'

'When can she start?'

'Immediately,' replied Ficsor.

This took Mrs Vizy back a little. She had expected her to start the next day.

'I've sorted it all out with them,' he boasted. 'If once I promise something, your ladyship . . .'

'Where are her belongings?'

'Downstairs, with us.'

'Bring them up,' she instructed him.

She waited till the caretaker had gone and then she stepped over to the maid. She stood so close their faces were practically touching. Frightened, Anna raised her big tired eyes. Here eyes were blue without any sparkle, a milky blue verging on violet, like the waters of the Balaton at a humid summer dawn.

It was the first time they had met Mrs Vizy's. A tall pale icy woman was staring at her who for some reason reminded her of a strange bird with a mess of bright decorative feathers. She backed away towards the door.

Anxious to calm the girl after that earlier moment of sharpness, and also because she wanted to hear her voice – the only word the girl had spoken till now was *yes* – she asked her in a conciliatory manner what her father had been.

'A servant.'

'What kind of servant?'

'A hired-man. At the squire's.'

'A day labourer. Does he have anything? A house? Some land? Some pigs?'

'Nothing.'

'No doubt he gets wheat? Ah, you're better off than we are. And your mother?'

'Mama . . .' she began. The word caught in her throat.

'What's the matter?'

'She died. I have a stepmother,' she replied in a strangled voice.

'Brothers or sisters?'

'An older brother.'

'Is he a farm labourer too?'

'He has just returned home.'

'Demobbed?'

'No. The French held him prisoner.' She shrugged her shoulders.

'You're doing it again. You are not to answer like this. You must give a straight yes or no. Never mind, you'll learn.'

There would be time for instruction later. She returned to the matter in hand. In a softer, more confidential woman-to-woman tone she asked her: 'Do you have a lover?'

Anna shook her head. She didn't blush but a slight red shadow ran across her sweetly rounded forehead.

'Truth now. Don't deny it if you have one since I am bound to find out eventually. This is a respectable house. You may not bring anyone here, by day or by night. In any case I look after the keys. You have no acquaintances?'

'No.'

'You must know somebody.'

'I know the Ficsors . . .' she hesitated. 'And her ladyship, Mrs Wild.' She hesitated again. 'And Mrs Cifka, Mr Bartos's sister-in-law.'

'His sister-in-law? That tall powerful-looking woman who lives with them?'

'That's her.'

'And no one else?'

'No one.'

'It's better that way. Acquaintances only ruin you. Naturally if some relative should wish to visit you – your father or your brother for example – then you may ask permission to meet them. In any case you have every second Sunday off, from three to seven o'clock. But you must be home by seven.'

Ficsor appeared with a small package of belongings tied up in a chequered headscarf. Mrs Vizy, as the lady of the house, exercised her privilege of undoing it. Examining the contents was her habitual way of determining whether the new maid was a thief or not.

She found few enough things there. A few ragged cotton handkerchiefs without any monogram – therefore presumably not stolen – one blue calico dress, badly worn, a couple of headscarves, a pair of man's shoes discarded by the squire and possibly received as a present, one cheap hand-mirror with a trademark and a steel comb in whose teeth there remained a few tangled strands of hair. There remained a dented yellow tin trumpet with a scarlet tassell attached to it, a child's plaything. She picked it up and stared at it. She couldn't imagine what possible use a servant would have for it.

At this point Katica entered to clear the table, her head raised haughtily with a smile of superiority, like a princess who had suffered some slight. Mrs Vizy forbade her to touch it, but sent her out and followed immediately after.

Ficsor used her absence to interrogate his niece.

'Well?'

Anna didn't answer.

'It's a good place,' said the caretaker. 'First class. Rich people. The house belongs to them, the whole house. He is a councillor. They're gentry.'

That was all there was to the conversation. Their common bond of poverty had little charm since even ties of blood mean nothing without pleasant communal memories: people might lodge together, but if they worked from dawn till night they led their own impenetrable lives till great chasms opened between them.

Mrs Vizy wanted to smuggle Katica out of the house the way a hospital does its dead cholerics. The healthy must not be infected. She pushed her wages at her and told her to pack her belongings at once, and while she packed Mrs Vizy watched her like a hawk to check she did not steal anything.

While Katica's pack was no bigger than Anna's she stood more on her dignity. Before leaving she made a grand gesture of returning a jumper that she had received as a present.

She too feared infection – by anything that reminded her of the house where she had been so humiliated. Mrs Vizy took the jumper and slammed the door behind her. When she came back she addressed Anna in an entirely new tone, the one she was to use from now on.

'Come along, Anna. I will show you around the flat.'

They moved from room to room.

'This is the study. The books need wiping daily, but nothing on the desk must be moved. My husband is particular with his things. You understand? Here's another thing you must be careful with.'

A stuffed owl stared at the girl with its yellow glass eyes. Anna followed two paces behind Mrs Vizy and Ficsor, trailing her pack.

'The dining room you have seen already. This is the laundry basket. That cupboard will naturally be moved from there.'

The living room followed. 'This could do with a good clean too. We'll have to clear it first. We ought to pull the piano forward. There'll certainly be no shortage of work.'

The divan was covered with a red rug. Anna stood beside it, deathly pale from the overwhelming smell of camphor which clung to her. Ficsor and Mrs Vizy were already in the bedroom. She could faintly hear the latter's voice urging her on.

'Why doesn't she come through? What a strange girl,' Mrs Vizy said to Ficsor. 'We'll have a hard time with her at first.'

From the bedroom a door covered in wallpaper with pale climbing roses led into the dark dampness of the bathroom where water ran copiously from the broken taps.

'Turn off the light,' she ordered Anna. 'Come along, my girl. Look sharp. Whenever you leave a room turn the light off. Waste not, want not, life is expensive enough as it is. And shut the door behind you. It's not much effort. There's a draught.'

They reached the kitchen. It had already taken on an empty, uninhabited look, as if Katica had never lived there.

'This is your . . .' Mrs Vizy began, but left the sentence

in mid-air. 'It's not big, but it has done for everyone else so far. No, not there,' she cried when Anna was about to put her baggage down on the table. 'I don't want your fleas in my flat. Is your head clean? You'll take a bath tomorrow.'

She showed her the pantry. 'This remains locked. Every morning I shall give you flour, lard and sugar. I don't want anything to go missing,' she warned her.

Ficsor took his leave. He was at the door by the time the thought occurred to Mrs Vizy.

'Of course, her wages . . .'

'If you please, your ladyship!' protested the caretaker, with an air of indignation. 'You pay her as much as you think she deserves. After you have seen what she can do.'

'All right. We shall see.'

She invited Anna into the dining room. She ordered her to clear away the dinner and watched her closely as she did so. She instructed her how the plates should be carried, how to wash up, how to put the knives and forks away into the cutlery cabinet.

In the evening they prepared the table for supper. They arranged the plates and cutlery on the table. They put out a large white loaf since white loaves could now be bought.

Once they had made up the beds Mrs Vizy gave her a loaf of uncut cornflour bread.

'Here is your bread and your supper,' she said handing over a slice of cheese. 'And this is your pillowslip.' She pressed a red striped draw-sheet at her. 'Put this on. Eat your supper then you may go to bed.' She excused her.

'Good-night, ma'am.' The girl kissed her hand.

'There's no need for that,' said Mrs Vizy but the girl kissed it again.

New Broom Sweeps Clean

Anna gazed at the unfamiliar kitchen.

She had been told to have supper first then go to bed.

She cut a slice of bread. She couldn't bear even to bite into it. Both the bread and the cheese smelled of the flat.

She fumbled with the strange campbed and eventually succeeded in opening it, drew her pillow slip over her one pillow, rolled herself in the coverless eiderdown which until tonight had been Katica's and, having blown out the candle, lay down.

'*Lordandfather – fatherloving – mypooreyes – aregently-closing – yoursthoughlord – areeveropen . . .*'

This is what little Bandi prayed, and Pisti too, and even Gyuri the son of Mr Wild the warehouse owner. She had taught them all.

'*Watchoverme – ereIwaken – tomyparents – beprotector – shieldmyevery – benefactor . . .*'

Then Bandi, beside whose cot lay the sofa on which she slept, would have to have the poem of the birds and the penknife.

This penknife was special: when you opened its blade birds flew out of it, a host of brightly coloured birds. The child would go to sleep thinking of this penknife and when he woke in the morning he would remember dreaming of the birds and the knife and start laughing.

Anna repeated the rhyme now and though she herself

could not fully understand it it made her pleasantly drowsy. But she didn't fall asleep. Not even though she had stayed awake for a long time last night at the Bartoses.

What time could it be? Her bed was on the wrong side, by the wall opposite the window, high up. She had never slept above street level till now. She saw in front of her the towering inner wall of the tenement block. Squares of fiery light blazed up and went out. The lodgers entered one or other minor compartment of the house, a pantry or a water-closet; they turned lights on and off. Somewhere someone was playing a piano. A woman with a beautiful voice was singing along with it. She started again and again. The walls and windows hummed, the whole house rose and fell on waves of music. Sometimes she heard a buzzing beneath her bed. Later she discovered that the piano was in fact on the floor above, directly above her.

The voice and the piano both fell silent. Silence and darkness settled round her. Now even the squares of light on the opposite wall had stopped glowing. Having grown slightly numb she felt disorientated. She searched with her eyes for the old sofa but found only the wall everywhere about her, she stretched out her fingers but touched nothing, only the emptiness of night. She thought the kitchen had spun round and that she would shortly disappear down a chasm.

High up, at the very top of the wall outside, a single light still burned. It seemed they were both keeping vigil. At first she thought it was a star but it was only a common oil-lamp. It burned brighter than a star. Lamps are invariably brighter than stars.

A little after midnight she heard the key turn in the lock outside. Having already obtained a night pass from the Romanians, Vizy was arriving home. He was whispering to his wife. Soon someone opened the door of the kitchen. Barefooted and ghostly in a long white nightdress, Anna's mistress drifted over to her and looked down to see whether she was sleeping. She returned again a quarter of an hour later but by that time Anna did not see her for she had buried her head in the pillow and fallen asleep.

This was a matter of some importance to Mrs Vizy. Once again a stranger's breath was mingling with the familiar air of the flat, augmenting its common store. An alien heart was beating there: someone was sheltering under their roof, a stranger in whose person friend and foe, the extremes of closeness and distance, all met. Every house has a secret guest, and here she was. However unsympathetic Katica had been, she at least was known. This new person was still a mystery. Contrary to her habit Mrs Vizy locked the doors leading to the drawing room and bathroom.

'Are you afraid?' asked Vizy.

'No. But all the same. It is the first night.'

Goaded by her curiosity she woke practically with the dawn. What she saw stopped her in her tracks.

The maid had already aired and mopped the rooms. How could she have done it? It was impossible. She would have had to get up at four and work so quietly that no one heard her. Now she was crouching behind the writing desk in the study in that blue calico dress and the men's shoes Mrs Vizy had noted in her pack.

Mrs Vizy merely nodded. She knew it spoiled a servant to praise her straight away. She got her to grind some coffee and boil a pan of milk. She sent her down to the baker's, had her lay the table for breakfast and sent her to call his excellency from the bathroom.

He was shaving before the mirror, his face covered with lather. He looked rather like a snowman. Anna silently stole over to him and tried to tap his hand.

'Careful!' he cried, with great severity, 'I might cut you!' He held the flashing blade high above his head. 'You are the new girl? What's your name? Your family name? Your father's? He sounds Hungarian,' decided Vizy, as usual preferring to take a broad political approach to these matters. 'Farm labourers. Correct. Smallholders.'

Breakfast was elegant. Ignorant of their habits, the new girl had spread the clean yellow tablecloth used only for special occasions. The silver teaspoons chimed in the old idyllic way. When Anna took the milk pan out Mrs Vizy carefully followed her with her eyes. 'Looks a sound girl.'

Vizy frowned. He didn't approve of confidence so lightly bestowed: the disillusion that might follow would be all the more bitter. Hadn't it always begun like this? His wife thought herself a good judge of character and would draw far-reaching conclusions from the slightest evidence but she referred to every new servant, in the first twenty-four hours at least, as 'a sound girl' and trusted that this one 'was not like the others'. She garlanded them with more attributes than a poet decking out his verses. Then would follow the disappointments. By the second day there would be no more talk of sound girls. On the fourth day she would remark offhand that the girl was 'a little slow', or 'a touch indolent'. Next she would object to her manner. The climax would follow with dramatic speed. By the end of the week she would call him aside with a significant gesture, shape her lips into a silent hiss, and almost inaudibly tremble out the words, 'she steals . . . just imagine it, she steals'. Finally would come the damning verdict: 'and she's a whore, just like the rest'.

Why fool ourselves. Let's sleep on it. All new brooms sweep clean.

The new broom did indeed sweep clean. She would grab her basket and run down to the market in her unlaced shoes. One didn't have to wait for her, she didn't hang about, she returned immediately. The table was cleared, the table was laid. It was like the magic table in the fairy tale. There was order and silence.

She knew the shops and stalls of the district. She didn't lose her way in town. When they sent her further afield she managed to find her way back from Vámház körút, even from Boráros tér. She was not the country bumpkin they took her for. Her three years in Pest had modified her country habits. Her walk was quiet, she blew her nose silently, she spoke in a correct manner. It was only her accent that occasionally betrayed her, and the fact that sometimes, forgivably, she used too high a form of honorific for Mrs Vizy, addressing her as my gracious lady instead of as my good lady.

But she did have one peculiarity: she didn't eat.

The corn bread and the cheese she had left on the first day was served up again the following night. Still she didn't touch it. She simply stirred her coffee and pushed it aside. Nothing passed her lips. On the third day she ate an apple while at the Ficsors'. This at least was untainted by the smell.

Despite all her efforts she couldn't get used to the smell of the place. Her nose was as keen as a dog's and protested against it. The effect of 238 Attila utca was intense: she gave an involuntary shiver whenever she caught sight of it, even from a distance. Yet it was a very pleasant house. It was after all the house of Kornél Vizy. It had the dainty air of a *petit palais*. The outside wall was embellished with stucco roses, its balconies, delicate as swallows' nests, were lightly tacked on. The two at the top, belonging to the Drumas and the Moviszters, were of the open kind, but the Vizys' was glazed like a veranda with a shaded lamp dangling from the ceiling: they could eat there if they chose. The residence accommodated only these three professional households. Two boards fixed to the wall proclaimed: 'Dr Szilárd Druma, Solicitor, Specialist in Commercial Law and Litigation' and 'Dr Miklós Moviszter, General Practitioner. Appointments 11–12 a.m. 3–7 p.m.

One day, having been sent up to the Moviszters' to borrow some eggs, Anna discovered the source of that beautiful piano playing. The doctor's attractive wife was sitting at the piano in a low-cut nightdress, her pale jewelled fingers straying over the keys, singing at the top of her voice.

She got to know the servants too. Etel, her apron-strings hung with bunches of keys like some familial patron saint, ruled the roost from her large well-lit kitchen. It was the centre of her operations. Here she made all the decisions regarding what should be cooked or served for supper. Here she could play the tyrant, and even, occasionally, curse her employers, who lived in fear and trembling of her. She slept every afternoon from three to half-past four and between these hours the Moviszters were obliged to creep about like mice, the doctor himself answering the door to his patients. She would drink a bottle of brown ale both at dinner and supper and tended to move rather awkwardly these days owing to her weight which had much increased due to her incessant consumption of strudels. She would offer these to Anna.

The Drumas' maid was at first a little unwilling to lower herself to this level. Stefi's previous employer had been a count with a house in the precincts of the Vár. Having grown tired of high society she sought a bit of quiet and a power-base of her own, which she found at the lawyer's flat. She spoke with benevolent condescension of the Drumas, for they were young and their means did not yet allow them to furnish their apartment in a fully becoming manner. In fact she took it on herself to educate them into certain habits of refinement. She would ceremoniously announce the guests, and served the butter in delicately serrated pats. She continued to wear a white apron and a black dress. She referred to herself as 'the staff'. She read the Christian journals, associated with office girls and attached herself particularly to Druma's secretary with whom she would conspicuously link arms as they walked, hoping in this way to be taken for a secretary herself.

The two servants took Anna into their confidence. They quizzed her about the Vizys' diet, came down to use the Vizys' phone when their own was out of order and invited Anna to join them for a game of cards in the afternoon with beans and nuts as stakes. They had a rather low opinion of Mrs Vizy. They called her a miser, a half-wit who communicated with the souls of the dead. They kept asking Anna if she were satisfied with her situation. She said she was. What could she have said? After all she couldn't account even to herself for her ever increasing sense of disgust.

She simply couldn't get used to it. She quickly adapted to electricity. They showed her how to handle it. Anna made use of it, as they did. Not that she understood any-thing of electricity, but then neither did they. When she turned on the light she saw the room brighten but still checked to see the bulb was burning. It was the same with the telephone. For the first few days she talked in sepulchral tones into the wrong end until she discovered her mistake. Thereafter she relaxed into an easy acquaintance with it. She had seen greater marvels out on the plains. She simply accepted the fact that such things existed.

Other things disturbed her, and the longer she remained, the stranger they became. Quite insignificant things. Once for example, when she happened to hear that her master was called Kornél, she really felt she could stay no longer. The stove, which she imagined was green, turned out to be white. The drawing-room wall on the other hand was not white but green, the table not swelling and circular but hexagonal and low, one door opened inwards the other out-wards. These constant minor surprises shook her entire being. There was a Macquart bouquet from which tall pea-cock feathers obtruded that effected her with a peculiar trembling. She felt the 'eyes' were watching her and she always looked aside when she passed them.

Then, when she raised her eyes, there was her mistress, her hair uncombed and standing straight as if she were in a fury, waiting to vent her anger on her. Since the parquet creaked she heard everything. Mrs Vizy was anxious to protect her flat from draughts (which brought on tooth- and ear-ache) and from light (which irritated her). She was for-ever at Anna's heels, following her like a policeman. She would lecture her with well-meaning cantankerousness: 'Not that way, girl ... this way ... put it down on the table ... not for Heaven's sake on the edge where it's bound to fall off ...' As a result Anna placed everything in the centre of the table. Her mistress, however, would correct and adjust the objects just sufficiently to put herself in the right. Nothing was good enough for her. If Anna was quiet she demanded to know why, if on the other hand she talked of how it was at the Bartoses, she was quickly reminded that things were done differently here and that she shouldn't follow her own silly notions but listen to those wiser than her.

Chiefly though Anna missed the children, who had been delightful playmates and animated toys to her. After all she had been paid as their companion. She'd have liked to have someone to nurse here, someone to whom she could tell tales and recite verses. But what could she do with these solemn adults whose private shuttered lives were continually rubbing up against hers?

Hardly was the first week over when a great row exploded. She was just sweeping the bedroom and listening to Mrs Moviszter playing the piano upstairs when she noticed a little dolls' house on the wardrobe. Its wooden furniture was covered in white lacquer, there was a gilded mirror, a tiny handbasin with a tiny jug on the glass shelf beside it, and a bed with a red silk eiderdown, under which slumbered a doll with genuine hair. She stood on a chair to wipe the little gilded mirror. Suddenly she dropped it. It broke into a thousand little pieces.

Instantly, Mrs Vizy was there.

'What is broken! Oh!' she screamed. 'You idiot!'

Anna leapt down from the chair and started gathering the fragments, trying to piece them together. The woman knocked them out of her hand.

'Leave it. It's done,' she cried and burst into tears.

'I'll pay for it,' whispered Anna.

'Pay for it? Can one pay for something like this? It was a memento. My daughter's. Quick, the broom.'

While Anna swept she stood behind her and lectured her.

'You are a clumsy oaf. Katica never broke things. But I'll deduct it from your wages. I will. That will teach you a lesson.'

Mrs Vizy spent the rest of the day fretting about the significance of the broken mirror. But then what had the seven grains of rice meant? She couldn't reconcile the two. She remembered Mrs Wild's caution that the girl's work was 'not always of the top quality' and that she had 'not yet developed all the necessary skills'. She breaks things, thought Mrs Vizy. It looks as though this one breaks things.

That evening Anna ran down to the Ficsors to announce that she was leaving. She would give notice on the first of the month. The caretaker and his wife were anxious to know the reason why, but she could only shrug her shoulders and say she couldn't get used to it.

Ficsor, who had been sprawling on the sofa, took his pipe down from its hook and started berating her. He threatened her with her stepmother. He would send her home all right, her stepmother loved her so much she could hardly wait for her to return! Then he chased her back upstairs. Anna never again considered leaving. She preferred to stop thinking altogether.

Only at night, when she stared at the solitary lamp on the wall outside, did her heart begin to ache. She would never get used to this place.

8

The Phenomenon

In the end she did get used to it. There came the day of the great washing. Mountains of grey sheets and blankets, shirts and underwear rose before her, the dirty deathly sweat of the revolution still clinging to them. The steam made her pleasantly light-headed.

She boiled the water in the pan. Her sleeves rolled up, she knelt beside the tub, beetling away at the cloth. Her fingers played and puddled sensuously in the warm soapy scum. She lugged great baskets of washing about from place to place, shook the cloth, pleated it, wound it through the mangle. Her tablecloths were soft as lawn, her collars shone like glass.

Spring-cleaning took three days. In order to prepare they emptied out the drawers. Suddenly, as in a game of hide and seek, things appeared in unexpected places. They shook one casket and nine regionally minted gold coins rolled out with a sly inviting giggle. They had to accommodate themselves to the game and chase them down. But they found plenty of other things too. There were the two door handles at the bottom of a chest, the Swiss francs between the pages of a book (francs which had been put aside in case of a sudden need to flee the country), the locket wrapped in newspapers at the bottom of a tub of curds, and the single earring. In the master's desk they discovered a packet of

Russian tea, a kilo of lentils in a paper bag and two tins of Belgian sardines.

Mrs Vizy, whose nightmare it was that she would end up as a beggar and starve to death, saw that she was much richer than she had thought. There were still more surprises. From beneath a wardrobe Anna produced her long lost sky-blue skirt, and the salmon-pink silk blouse she thought she remembered giving to a Swabian woman in the course of a previous clear-out. They found cotton reels, buttons and various scraps of leather which Mrs Vizy had fanatically stored away. She wasn't unusual in this. The last two bitter years had taught her that human life was worthless: it was things, the stuff that you possessed, that really mattered. After all having read in the newspaper that the Austrian army's estimate of a man's value – heart and brains and all – was, at thirty-six gold crowns, far lower than the value of a fully equipped horse, why shouldn't she of all people draw the appropriate conclusions as to what was valuable and what wasn't? Matter was omnipotent: she gave it her rapt attention. She inwardly swore to be even thriftier hence-forth.

From beneath the elder tree in the courtyard she dug up the copper mortar she had secreted there before the various requisition orders arrived. This copper mortar, the pride of her kitchen, had narrowly avoided being turned into cannon fodder. Rescued from the storms and buffets of the troubled century, it emerged tarnished and muddy from its tempo-rary grave.

Upstairs, the flat had to be returned to its former con-dition. They pulled aside the cupboards which had been moved for protection against the dreadful people billeted on them. The mess grew the worse for it. The furniture began to roam. An armchair which appeared to have wandered out by itself stood marooned on the landing gazing longingly down the stairs. The wall clock lay on its back on the floor, its pendulum benumbed in its wooden case along with the blade of a whipping fork. Tables made excursions to the yard below where cane chairs and divans were already sunbathing together with the couch, now divested of its red coverlet.

From morn till night Anna strove in an aureole of dust. She spat black and sneezed grey. She thrashed the mattresses as if she had a furious grudge against them. She dashed upstairs into the flat and downstairs into the yard on a hundred occasions. Window-panes streamed with water, filthy water swirled in the pail, rags slopped and squelched. She polished the windows while perched on crude scaffolding. Then she was scouring the floorboards, applying a pale coat of beeswax, dancing on brushes strapped to her feet, polishing the parquet, sliding, gliding, stooping and kneeling as if at church, engaged in some interminable act of prayer. Glasspaper scraped along rusted locks. She brought hidden carpets down from the attic, unwound them from their naphthalined cocoons, and belted the dust out of them on the carpet-stand. Quickly she rearranged the furniture: a chair here, a table there, the piano a few feet forward. Then to finish with there was the chandelier to re-hang with infinite care in case anything got broken, a few new light-bulbs to screw in, and lastly the cream-coloured curtains to be attached to the smoky gold curtain rods and sewn to the curtain rings, then all was done.

By the evening they had finished. Within an hour the hall which had served as a temporary dumping ground was also shining.

Mrs Vizy took her husband's arm and led him ceremoniously through the flat. 'Look!'

'I say!'

'What do you think?'

'This is more like it!'

'Isn't it just?'

'It looks much more welcoming.'

It was certainly transformed beyond recognition. The pale sickly flat, which for long years had been covered with a patina of historical dust, had suddenly regained its health. Vizy trod the Persian rug in the study. Curiously he examined its pattern of cherry-coloured little birds perched on branches.

'Which rug is this?'

'You see, you don't recognize it. It's the one which used to be beside your bed. She cleaned it up with sour cabbage.'

It was like receiving a pile of new presents. The living room was a well-stocked bazaar: pots and vases glistened, city ware and country ware, preserved by God's grace from generation to generation. The cigar cutter twinkled on the chess table. All the clocks were discreetly ticking, their mechanisms supported by porcelain hares or hidden in the bellies of bronze horses. Ancestors returned from their long exile. Vizy's late father in a black cape and silver-fringed tie reassumed his place on the wall, as did his wife's relative, the Bishop Camillo Patikárius, with his lilac sash and his yellow smile spread across gracious clerical lips, and one of her great aunts, Terézia Patikárius, with the swans'-feather fan that she used to sport at balls.

Vizy adjusted one of the pictures. He rubbed his hands together. He stayed in that night.

Mrs Vizy raised her finger. 'This girl is clean. That's what I like about her, she is so clean and clever.'

It was undeniable that she felt more trapped by Anna than by any of her previous servants. For the time being she couldn't leave her side. But it was equally certain that Anna was not to be mentioned in the same breath as the others: she was a jewel and it was worthwhile spending time with her, educating her, polishing her to perfection. She had even begun to eat. She was slowly working her way through the various food substitutes left over from the war, the chicory coffee, the saccharine and the margarine: she was certainly no glutton ever hungering for fresh bread, she wasn't fussy. She woke at dawn at half-past four and didn't go back to bed till her business was done. She didn't talk back or pull faces. You were never aware of her, only of the results of her work. She was the original good fairy. What more could one want?

And every blessed day would herald a new miraculous

68

discovery of which Mrs Vizy would hasten to inform her husband. 'Come here for a minute. Just for a minute. I want to show you something.'

The copper mortar had regained its place of glory on a wooden hook in the kitchen. Meat axes, cake-moulds, whisking-bowls, frying-pans, casseroles and biscuit-cutters sparkled along the wall. Without bidding she had covered the stands with blue paper cut into fancy shapes.

Occasionally Mrs Vizy would carry some trophy into the study and place it wordlessly on his writing desk.

'Plum conserve. She made it herself. Look at that beautiful sweet liquid. It's like rubies. She is certainly keen. She has a natural feel for it.'

They were eating strudel.

'Well, what do you think? The pastry is wonderfully light. It melts in the mouth. She's a first-rate cook. This girl has made good.'

Vizy was softening but refused to cave in completely. This was curious since he always used to defend bad servants in order to calm his wife. Now he took on the role of an opposition party, keeping a benevolent but wary eye on the government. He allowed the praise to die in his ear. He niggled away with tiny objections. That the girl was a little graceless. That she was never in a good mood and might even be said to be a little sour. And that she hardly ever opened her mouth.

Mrs Vizy assured him he was mistaken. After all there were times when the girl actually smiled. What else should she do? What reason had she to be downright cheerful? A servant that is always working obviously takes some pleasure in what she does. She's just shy. Would we prefer her to be as cheeky as the rest? Heaven forbid!

Everything was resolved now but for one cloudy issue, the most important, the most delicate of all: theft. Did this paragon of virtue steal? It was a most difficult matter to check.

Theft is underhand and unexpected. It is like a haemorrhage in the night. Something disappears, some wholly insignificant thing. It may merely have gone astray, one thinks one may have misplaced it, or lost it perhaps; but that's not the truth, the truth is that it has gone, simply gone. What a dreadfully numbing conclusion to come to. One begins to worry about other things, even those one still has. Each silver spoon, each sugar cube, each handkerchief. How many did one have? Where are they all? Has one locked them away? Mrs Vizy locked everything away in any case. She wasn't going to give up easily though. She experimented quite scientifically.

One evening she left a Russian twenty-five crown piece on the table. The money was still there in the morning. Once, as if by accident, she let a blue hundred-crown note flutter to the ground. The next day it was back on her bedside table. She left a ring on the divan. Anna found it while she was clearing up and personally gave it back to her.

Then she tempted Anna by leaving the wardrobe open, having first carefully stacked and counted her handkerchiefs on the shelf. Not one went astray. The groceries were next: coffee and sugar, which servants particularly liked to pilfer. She didn't lock the pantry. She didn't even check for a whole week. When she did take her candle to do a proper stocktaking she saw that every grain of coffee, every cube of sugar was in its place.

So the girl did not steal. She said so to herself but did not quite believe it. Later she did not bother to say anything but wholeheartedly believed it, as did her husband. This one needed neither money, nor jewels, nor spices.

'You know what this girl subsists on?' she asked her husband, and answered in the words Ficsor had used earlier. 'Work, nothing but work. I've never seen anyone like her.'

'You're right,' Vizy concurred. 'Nobody has ever seen anyone like her.'

Both felt a great sense of release. Vizy lived his official life at the ministry, and when at home, whatever else he might do, he did not spend his time complaining. Mrs Vizy could go out again. In the mornings she would walk down to the medicinal spring in Buda, near the bridgehead of the Erzsébet Bridge, and drink a glass of warm sulphurous water which she found was good for her stomach. She went to the dentist and had her teeth put in order. She busied herself with charitable work at the Krisztina Institute, distributing clothes to the children of poor local salesmen.

She even had some time left over. She popped in to visit the Tatárs in Úri utra, where handsome high-spirited young men paid court to the two beautiful Tatár girls. She began to entertain a few old friends. She had no really close friends since she tended to meet only the wives of her husband's colleagues. Her relatives, the various Patikáriuses, lived in Eger. Even her husband had only one female relative in town, a divorced woman, the pathetic Etelka, who went from house to house selling fake Egyptian cigarettes, tried to cadge money from people, including the Vizys, and was quite depraved. They hadn't met for years. Vizy would cut her in the street.

Now it was brought home to her that she really had no one, and that the day was long. She had Piroska's grave restored and took a fresh bunch of chrysanthemums down to the cemetery every week. On Wednesdays she resumed her visits to the spiritualist circle, whose meetings were held in a villa on Rózsadomb hill, in Áldás utca.

It was a stiff ceremonious place with doors that pushed open and walls hung with silk rugs, where classicist paintings mingled with classicist sculptures. The host, a wealthy self-employed businessman, greeted his guests with a handshake of complicity. Everyone knew that his son had been paralysed sixteen years ago and that he inhabited a solemn room somewhere in the remote depths of the villa.

A general of the infantry was the spiritual leader of the circle. They summoned the spirits of soldiers who had died heroic deaths. Their fathers and mothers were anxious for news. Next to Mrs Vizy sat an ailing circuit judge and a Catholic priest in ordinary dress. The medium was a highly strung girl who threw her head back in a trance and spoke in German. Invisible strands of the spirit world converged here from every corner of the universe. Piroska's soul had travelled from Jupiter. Using the medium's hand she scrawled in a childish hand *Mamma Mamma* across several sheets of paper. On one occasion she materialized on the breast of the medium in a grey marshlight, her form compounded of milky fog.

When she made her way home on Wednesday evenings, Mrs Vizy no longer felt her heart pounding, she was no longer haunted by the old nightmare of finding a ransacked flat on her return, with forced doors and empty wardrobes ripped open. Everything at home was in order. She left her money out without counting it first. Those days were gone when she stalked the rooms with her hands behind her back as if handcuffed, worrying about the maid's next move.

Anna moved among them silently. And when she went out conversation tended to drift to her. They were now united in her praise, in their general sense of wellbeing. The praise tended decidedly to worship, it was prayerful, it was an uncritical piece of idolatry: they had got a remarkably useful bargain and felt distinctly proud that she was theirs and only theirs. Once in the privacy of their bedroom they would talk in whispers about the events of the day, all of which witnessed to her conscientiousness, her unselfishness, her infinite capacity for work. They encouraged and assisted each other in the magnification of her virtues, they trumped each other's descriptions of her, imitated her, sometimes even mocked her with a superior smile as if it were amusing that someone should be so simple and good hearted, so exemplary in her sturdiness, so uniquely undemanding; then they would laugh, self-consciously at first, then ever more loudly and outrageously. This was the beginning of an idyllic period for them when they lived in constant awareness of their good fortune. It was no delusion. The ridiculously impossible had come true: they had found the genuine article they had been dreaming about for years.

Occasionally they felt an ironic urge to embrace her and thank her for her good deeds, or to smuggle her down to the photographer one night under cover of darkness and have a photograph taken of all three of them together, as if they were a family; but they were dissuaded from this course of action, this mischievous and extraordinary joke of an idea which flashed across their minds for a mere fraction, a mere thousandth of one second then disappeared before they could properly think it through and laugh at it, by their bourgeois sobriety, and the knowledge that they were after all talking about a mere domestic servant.

9

A Debate about Sponge Fingers, Compassion and Equality

Things were getting better. True, there were still problems. There was runaway inflation. People eyed each other nervously in the oppressive atmosphere. They denounced their neighbours in anonymous letters. Those who once refused to recognize their friends as 'good Communists' now hastened to offer them this long-denied recognition and readily handed them over to the authorities.

It was as if a plague of locusts had devastated the place. Consumed and exhausted, the town lay on the rubbish heap. The expensive porcelain shelves in the window of the baroque *konditorei* displayed a single desolate scone. Trams which had been painted under Communist rule were still to be seen in their revolutionary scarlet with revolutionary slogans daubed across them, dashing suicidally through town like refugees from a mental asylum.

But there were also encouraging signs of improvement. Middle-class passengers on the tram were no longer afraid to stand up to the bullying conductress who addressed them rudely. They took pleasure in reminding her that this was no longer a Bolshevist state. Men once again began to give up their seats to ladies. It was a new and glorious flowering of the age of chivalry.

Once again Viatorisz stood at the door of his shop and greeted his customers. This was a sure sign of the times.

Viatorisz always knew precisely which way the wind was blowing. When the war first broke out he merely nodded, later it was the customers who greeted him. He accepted this as his due and once the Bolsheviks took over he didn't even notice it he was so busy. Now he offered to have the goods delivered to Mrs Vizy, all she had to do was to give him a ring on the telephone.

The Vizys' flat became a venue for informal parties. One afternoon it was the Tatárs who dropped in. Druma joined them together with his wife, and so did Mrs Moviszter. One by one the lights were going on in the worn chandeliers of middle-class life. At first the light revealed some wear and tear as well as shortages of one kind or another, nevertheless after so much suffering it felt good to be able to socialize again. It was like the good old days.

Tea was fairly cheerless. Mrs Tatár took head of place at the table, her laced bosom swelling before her. They tried to brighten the atmosphere with a few counter-revolutionary jokes but they were damp squibs. From his pocket Druma produced an orange that had been smuggled across the Italian border by a client of his. They hadn't seen one for a long time and passed it from hand to hand. They talked about food, the various ways of obtaining it and where one could get cheaper flour or potatoes. Councillor Tatár, who was renowned as a cook, waxed lyrical about a paprika fish stew he had prepared as a lad from catfish, sturgeon and carp on an open fire by the shores of the Tisza. He went into such details and told it all with such relish that it filled their mouths with saliva. Then he too lapsed into silence and fell to eating, chewing vigorously, stuffing the food into the aperture between his delicate pink mobile lips festooned with the shaggy fur rug of his grey moustache and beard.

The conversation ground to a halt.

'Oh, of course,' Mrs Druma dropped these words into the general silence, 'I had quite forgotten about Anna. Where is Anna? I haven't even seen her today.'

'She's out in the kitchen looking after tea.'

'Is that the new servant?' enquired Mrs Tatár. 'Is she a

good girl? Is she clever? The flat looks marvellous. And is she trustworthy? She doesn't steal, does she, my dear?'

Mrs Vizy did not deign to answer, she simply gave her a straight look.

'Don't you know Anna?' marvelled the other women in chorus.

'No, I don't. I have not had the good fortune to meet her. We have not been introduced,' joked Mrs Tatár, secure in her position as lady of the manor.

They laughed. Mrs Vizy glanced at her husband and rang the bell.

In came Anna in her blue calico dress, carrying a glass tray of walnut sponge fingers. She hadn't had the time to change. Her shoes slopped on her feet. She advanced in some confusion to the table and put down the tray. She felt she ought to kiss everyone's hand individually but there were so many of them she didn't know where to start. She was surrounded by smiling faces. Even Tatár had stopped eating and strained his thick neck towards her. Mrs Vizy admired the dumb show for a while, then beckoned her over and with a humorous but proud gesture introduced her. 'Yes, this is Anna. My Anna.'

When Anna closed the door behind her she heard laughter. It was as if a famous comic had taken a curtain call. The audience itself had little idea why it was laughing, but laughed all the same. The whole thing was wildly amusing: the awkwardness, the shuffling shoes, the manner of introduction. The atmosphere grew more lively. Cigars and cigarettes were lit. Vizy told some anecdote about Anna which was followed by loud guffaws.

It was into this den of jollity that Dr Moviszter, the old general practitioner, entered, having packed off his last patient at the end of surgery. He came to find his wife. He was immensely busy with his swollen list of patients. Once, in his youth, he had been assistant to a heart surgeon at a clinic in Berlin. On returning to Hungary he applied for a private tutorship at the university but they didn't want him. He had to live as best he could. His surgery was open ten hours a day and dealt mechanically with the usual mass of amorphous humanity that swirls round general hospitals and insurance agencies. He dragged his tired body about with the aid of a walking stick. When he smiled he exposed his loose teeth and inflamed gums. A few wisps of weedy hair trembled on the crown of his head. He was sicker than any of his patients. His diabetes was at a terminal stage. Colleagues and clinics had given him up for lost.

Vizy hastened to greet him, assuring him that he looked much better than usual. Moviszter thanked him ironically. He blinked uncertainly at the assembled company swimming in the smoke of cigars and cigarettes. He felt as if he had unwittingly stumbled on to the stage in the middle of an unfamiliar performance. He couldn't understand the reason for all this gaiety. They had to explain to him that they had been talking about Anna, the famous Anna. Vizy was prevailed on to repeat his amusing anecdote.

Moviszter did not touch the food. He retired with the men into the study. He refused a drink, but amiably clinked an empty glass with the rest when it came to a toast. Later they drifted back into the dining room to join the ladies, their cigars and cigarettes alight, their faces pleasantly rosy from the wine. Tatár leaned against the door-post listening to the conversation.

'Still on about the servants!' he exclaimed with horror, puffing out his narrow chest beneath the neatly fitted white silk waistcoat. 'That's women for you. They are incapable of talking about anything else.'

But the men, too, showed an interest in the subject and kept an ear open for what was being said. Vizy brought the wine back into the dining room. Moviszter sat himself down in the rocking chair and, closing his eyelids, gently rocked to and fro.

The subject was still Anna.

'You know,' Mrs Druma was saying, 'she is pretty, too. She has quite a sweet little face. Nice figure as well. Slender. She's really attractive.'

'Yes,' added Mrs Tatár in a philosophic mood. 'These

peasant girls quickly blossom once they get to Budapest. The same goes for mine, my Bözsi. I brought her from the village last year. She was thin as a rake and ragged as a scarecrow. Well, I quickly fattened her up and fitted her out with a wardrobe. I bought her a white piqué dress . . .' She coughed at this point like someone beginning a speech. 'Last Sunday my girls had a party. Bözsi opened the door for the guests. Ervin arrived, Ervin Gallovszky, who has recently returned from a Russian prisoner-of-war camp. What do you think happened? This boy,' and she herself smiled at the recollection, 'this boy kissed my hand in the hall then stood before Bözsi and formally introduced himself to her, and put out his hand for her to shake it.'

'The servant?' marvelled Mrs Vizy.

'The servant. If I had not signalled to him he would have shaken hands with her!' Her asthmatic chest heaved with laughter and turned to coughing. 'He thought,' she added in a strangled voice, 'that she was my Ilonka or Margitka, or perhaps one of their friends.'

'And what did your maid do?'

'It was as if someone had set fire to her face. She hid her hands behind her back and – would you believe it! – burst into tears. She was in tears the whole afternoon. She refused to serve to save her life. The girls teased Ervin dreadfully.'

Tatár nudged his wife. 'Don't forget the cat.'

'Oh yes, the cat!' Mrs Tatár exclaimed. 'When she first came to us we had a two-month-old kitten which belonged to Ilonka. It was called Cirmos. One morning I could hear Bözsi enticing her with some milk, calling, 'This way, Master Cirmos, here's your breakfast, sir.' She addressed the cat as if it had been her superior. It was ages before she dared be familiar with it. You see! That's what they're like. Unfortunately it doesn't last for long, they lose their innocence far too quickly. Nowadays she always wants to be visiting her village for one reason or another, a funeral, a harvest or a wedding. I have a whole tribe of relatives to put up with.'

'My maid,' contributed Mrs Druma, 'takes a great interest in politics and the cinema. She is devoutly religious.'

'And mine,' added Mrs Moviszter, 'is a tyrant. Etel is used to command. She promises not to dismiss us – providing we do what she says.'

'Mine,' observed Mrs Vizy, and all attention turned to her since she had listened to the others' woes with a certain malicious glee, 'mine is interested neither in the cinema nor in the theatre. She doesn't even sing. There is no one courting her. I have never met her family. She is an orphan. She never goes out. So far she has not even taken a Sunday afternoon off.'

'That Anna is certainly a remarkable creature.' The murmurs of appreciation were so unanimous that she feared she had overstepped the mark, and now, having found herself the centre of attention, she felt bound in all modesty to distance herself a little.

'Mind you, you shouldn't envy us too much. She was far from perfect at the start. I've had my struggles with her. And she still has her faults.'

'What?' cried Vizy, wounded, raising his head from the cloud of wine. 'Do please tell me, what fault has she?'

Mrs Vizy searched vainly for a fault. What fault can you find where there is none. She couldn't answer.

There was a general hubbub of approval which was suddenly cut short as the object of their speculation entered.

Anna began to clear the table. They watched her even more attentively than before, taking note of her every movement. She darted between the table and the sideboard with uncanny lightness. It was as if a silent robot were moving among them. She's like a machine, they thought, a machine.

When she had put the tray of sponge fingers on the sideboard, Mrs Vizy called her over with the air of one who had just been struck by a delicious thought. 'Bring it here, Anna.'

The guests rose up and formed a circle round Mrs Vizy. They seemed to freeze in their positions as in a tableau with the maid as the focus of their attention. Moviszter's chair stopped rocking and he leaned forward a degree or two.

Mrs Vizy selected two sponge fingers and presented them to Anna. 'These are for you.'

The guests began to smile. Tender feelings flooded through them as if they were present at some almsgiving for the deserving poor. But hardly was the girl offered the fingers before she pushed them away.

'Thank you.'

'What's the matter? Don't you like them?'

'No. Thank you very much. I don't like them.'

A painful silence followed. It was broken by the decisive tones of Mrs Vizy. 'In that case, girl, just put the tray back. I wouldn't force you. Not for the world. You may go.'

The guests continued standing in a circle, still wearing benign expressions but slightly overcome by the confusion. Their astonishment left a horrible sense of numbness hovering about the company.

'Did she mean to reject you?' wondered Mrs Tatár.

'Of course not,' Mrs Vizy explained, 'that's just the way she is. She won't eat any delicacy. She even leaves the apricot jam. What do you think she has for supper? You'd never guess. Nothing. She has coffee in the morning, and a spoonful of stew for lunch. She doesn't want any more. As regards sponge fingers, it appears she doesn't like them.'

'It may be that she likes them too much,' said Moviszter, who was still leaning forward in the rocking chair.

'What did you say, doctor?'

'I said she may like sponge fingers very much indeed.'

'But she herself said she didn't.'

'That's precisely why.'

'I'm sorry, I don't understand.'

'Servants are often afraid to like what they like, so they convince themselves that nice things are not nice. That's their defence. Perhaps it prevents them from too much suffering. Why should they desire things that can never be theirs? They're right too. They couldn't live any other way.'

'Then what should we do with her?'

'Why don't you try giving her sponge fingers every day.'

'Sponge fingers every day?'

'Yes. Lots of sponge fingers, so many she couldn't possibly eat them. Then you would see how much she liked them. That she liked sponge fingers better than anything else in the world.'

'But why? She isn't ill. A diet of sponge fingers is only good for invalids.'

'Fine thing it would be too,' grumbled Mrs Tatár. 'Sponge fingers wasted on their coarse palates. Sponge fingers!'

'This is just another of your peculiar ideas, my dear Miklós,' Druma admonished the doctor who had once again closed his eyes and was rocking to and fro.

Mrs Moviszter lit a cigarette, went through into the sitting room and began to play a foxtrot on the piano. The ladies followed her. Vizy filled the glasses. The gentlemen sat down in their places and washed away the bitter flavour with more wine.

Having wiped his dripping moustache with his handkerchief, Tatár returned to the issue of the sponge fingers which continued to bother him. He addressed Moviszter. 'But you know, my dear doctor, these people are after all different from us. Their stomachs are different and so are their souls. They're servants and that's what they'll remain. They themselves demand that we treat them as such. The other day, for example, I rang up a friend of mine. A strange voice answered the telephone. 'Are you an employee?' I asked. 'No,' answered the voice, in a markedly impertinent manner, 'I am a servant.' You should have heard it. I was so surprised I couldn't even tell why. I continued holding the receiver in my hand while this voice crackled on, growing angrier, more challenging and arrogant. They actually enjoy referring to themselves in these terms simply in order to upset and insult us.'

He sipped at the amber yellow wine and continued.

'People have often tried to treat them with affection. I had a friend once, poor fellow he's dead now, Karcsi Zelándy, God rest his soul. He was a sound chap, a little eccentric perhaps. His head was always full of theories. He was a vegetarian, he wore moccasins, he even went to visit Tolstoy at Yasnaya-Polyana. When he returned he was determined to tackle the servant question root and branch. He took one on and informed her that they were absolutely equal: there was to be no master, no servant, they would take turns at serving each other. At the first opportunity he sat her down at the family table along with his wife and children. He recounted the occasion to me later. Well, it was a pretty sad affair. The unfortunate girl felt awful receiving such inordinate attention. She languished there in her stained skirt with its kitchen smell, hiding her hands under the table or touching her face, and said nothing at all throughout the whole meal. She was of course tired, having been cooking and baking since the crack of dawn. Suffice it to say, the meal being finished she changed her clothes and announced that she would not stay a minute longer in a place like this. And there and then she went.'

Debating with himself as much as with the doctor he none the less addressed his pointed remarks to the latter. 'Now, my question is, why did she go?' and he pressed his forefinger against his fleshy nose so hard that he quite squashed it. 'I ask because however they questioned her she wouldn't say. Well I'll tell you. She went because she had more brains than her master. She went because she realized that the situation was unnatural and insincere. The sincere course of action would have been for my friend to unconditionally offer her his house, his land and his livestock down to the last calf, down to the last nail. These simple people on the lowest rung of society live in absolutes. They have much more imagination than we suspect. They are not content with half-measures. They want either to be masters – and absolute masters at that – or absolute servants. The rest is all comedy. It was the same with the Romans. They also tried to perform the comedy. But,' and here he hesitated, 'only once a year. I can't remember the name of the festival but the patricians dressed up as slaves and invited the slaves to take over their tables and served

82

them with mead and roast capons. They said it was in remembrance of the golden age when everyone was equal. But when was this golden age? It's nothing but a myth. They themselves couldn't remember it. Besides, even our hands are different,' and he held up his soft pudgy hand which indeed resembled nobody else's. 'There's no such thing as human equality. There are only individual differences between people, doctor. Dammit!' he wound himself up artificially like an orator in a passion, 'masters and servants have ever been and ever will be. That's all there is to it. It's a fact we cannot change. So let them remain the servants.'

He looked around. His speech met with general approval. The company whose rights he had defended closed about him gratefully. He had made his point, but turned to the doctor and drew the natural conclusion. 'There's no alternative.'

'But there is,' replied Moviszter from the rocking chair, fiddling absent-mindedly with the medallion of the Virgin Mary that dangled from his watch-chain.

'I am curious to hear it. What alternative can you offer?' enquired Tatár, raising his large wise head.

'Compassion.'

'Compassion?' repeated Tatár, happy that the argument could take a fresh direction.

'There is a place where everyone is both master and servant at once, where everyone is equal, every day of the year.'

'What place is this?'

'The Kingdom of Christ.'

'But that's in heaven.'

'It is in the soul.'

'Very well, but just you try to realize it here. With the Bolsheviks and their comrades.'

'One doesn't have to realize it,' responded Moviszter, with annoyance since his illness made him crotchety. 'It is unnecessary. That was the problem with the Communists too: they tried to realize an ideal. One shouldn't try to realize ideals. Not one. Once you do they're finished. Let them remain where they are, in heaven among the clouds. That's how they remain effective, that's how they survive.'

'Excuse me, doctor, would you have your servant sitting at table with you?'

'No.'

'Why?'

'Perhaps,' he pondered, 'because she doesn't expect it. It would be precisely the comedy you describe. At least, now, here on earth.'

'Then we're both in the same boat.'

'Not exactly, councillor. Because in my soul my servant is always at table with me.'

'That's all right I suppose,' said Tatá, wrinkling his arched brow. 'Why not? But let me tell you something. Your servant would never sit you at her table, not in a million years. Let them scrape together a little nestegg and they become regular tyrants. I've seen them. The first thing they do is to hire a servant of their own, and they are quite merciless, quite heartless with them. God save me from criminals-turned-policemen. There is nothing worse than being the servant of a servant. You'll find little compassion in them.'

'That has nothing to do with the case.'

'I beg your pardon,' Tatár started, anxious to lead the conversation on to a new track, 'I expect you regard yourself as a humanitarian.'

'Me? I'm nothing of the sort.'

'Pardon?'

'I don't like humanity, because I have never seen it, because I don't know it. The concept of humanity is perfectly hollow. And take note, councillor: every confidence-trickster is a humanitarian. Those who are greedy, those who would not spare a crust for their own brothers, those who are the worst of scoundrels, they all have a humanitarian ideal. They hang people and murder them, still they are humanitarians. They desecrate their homes, they kick their wives out, they neglect their parents and their children, and what are they? Humanitarians. There's no more comfortable position. It obliges you to nothing. No individual has yet come to me announcing, I am humanity. Humanity requires no food, no clothes, it maintains a decent distance somewhere in the background with a halo round its brow. There is Peter and there is Paul. They are only people. Humanity does not exist.'

'What about patriotism?'

'Same thing,' said Moviszter and hesitated, seeking the best way of putting it. 'As you know it is a very beautiful, very general concept. Much too general. Think of the sins committed in its name.'

'Then who or what do you like?'

'The clergy,' Druma teased him. 'Miklós likes the priests. Or perhaps the Bolsheviks. I'm not too sure myself now. I do believe,' he frowned, 'that you are a Communist beneath the skin. No, don't deny it, my dear Miklós!' And he embraced him with such vehemence that the old doctor's frail shoulder-blades nearly cracked under the pressure.

'No, God bless you. Have a drink, you old Bolshevik!'

Druma proceeded with a vivid description of what the Communists had done to a genteel sixty-year-old woman who had been imprisoned with him. Every night at precisely midnight they led her out into the yard to execute her. They made her kneel down, pointed their guns at her, and spent minutes taking aim at her forehead. Vizy riposted by pointing out that his dining room and sitting room had *de facto* been requisitioned from him.

'That is of course what they want,' Tatár smouldered, 'a role change of world historical significance. They want you down in the cellar and the caretaker up here in your flat. It's a merry-go-round. As one bucket goes down so the other comes up. Myself, I do not doubt for a second that you could produce an outstanding breed of gentlemen from the raw material of caretakers. But this would take about three hundred years. They would first have to be fed to bursting point till they are disgustingly fat, then have the time to grow bored of it all. Their sons would have to learn riding and swordsmanship as our sons do, their spines would have to grow a little straighter, their feet and hands a little more slender. In the meantime we would slowly get used to baked beans and the room in the basement. Slowly we would grow as scraggy as they are. But this too would take some time. And what would be the point of it? No point at all.'

The conversation drifted on to politics. Vizy had been quiet till now, since he did not like to commit himself to any view and believed theoretical argument to be sterile. Now he took the floor. He talked about office matters, committees and programmes of reorganization.

If only the whole world could have seen him in this mood! 'It's our turn now!' he proclaimed, and rested his hand on Gábor Tatár's shoulder in a sweeping gesture of solidarity, as if he were seeking comrades-at-arms for the great battles ahead. As was his habit at such moments his eyes darted to one side and his face assumed a sly expression of readiness and rapaciousness transfused by the basest overwhelming greed, but within a moment he had reassumed control of his features and modulated the expression into one of enthusiasm for the common good.

If one had asked him what the aim of politics was or what was the goal he had been seeking under various governments since his early youth, he would have summed it up neatly in one sentence: 'The eradication of corruption.' He shrank from recasting the latinate diction into common Hungarian terms, because that would have made it too obvious and it would have lost the patrician gravity he associated with Cato. He preferred to leave it as it was in its cloaked, passionate generality, and refused to countenance the possibility that politics might be merely the eternal agitation of those who are hungry and unable to escape from mediocrity, that every political system assumes power only to place its allies in favourable positions so that it might weaken and crush its opponents. Corruption to him was invariably associated with the activity of other people, people who sped by in official cars on their way to rendez-vous with their girlfriends, and he was all the more inclined to condemn this because he remembered one delightful

86

night when he too swept past the trees in the park with an actress friend in an official car borrowed for the occasion from a friend, and recalled the feelings of pleasure that mingled in his breast when, at the end of the ride, the peaked chauffeur duly saluted him with an enthusiasm he wouldn't have summoned even if he had been generously tipped.

Moviszter was growing bored. He continued rocking for a while in his chair then shuffled into the sitting room where the women were huddled round the chess table. They were still discussing the subject which had sparked the debate between their menfolk.

Mrs Vizy was engaged on a long monologue of lamentation. 'Certainly she works hard enough. But what does she want?' she asked with some annoyance. 'She gets food, she gets lodgings. She even gets clothes. She can bank her earnings. What else could she desire in these difficult times? What problems has she? She doesn't have to maintain this large flat, she doesn't have to bother her head with what to cook, or how to find the money, she can live without a thought, without a care in the world. I often think that nowadays it is only servants who can live really well.'

The women sighed as though they had all chosen the wrong career, and now regretted that harsh circumstances utterly prevented them from becoming servants.

The doctor beckoned his wife over. He complained that he was tired. He was always in bed before ten because by seven he had to be on a crowded tram on his way to the hospital. Mrs Moviszter stubbed out her cigarette. The Tatárs too began to make moves to leave. They wanted to get home before their front gate was locked. Mrs Druma stood in the hall with her ear pressed against the kitchen door.

'What is she doing?'

'Working, no doubt,' said Mrs Vizy. 'Let her.'

But Mrs Druma had already opened the door. A figure stood by the waste basket in the dark kitchen with a man's black shoe in her hand. She was polishing it.

'Good-night, Anna. Goodbye. God bless you,' the voices hummed at her. Anna mumbled something.

'What did she say?'

'She was begging your pardon,' translated Mrs Vizy. 'She can't open the door for you because her hands are pasty.'

'Pasty?' enquired Mrs Druma.

'Paste is what the servants call shoe polish.'

'Pasty!' repeated Mrs Druma. 'Fancy that. Pasty!' and the thought of hands being 'pasty' kept her amused all the way up the stairs to their flat.

10

Legend

The Vizys were still chewing over the events of their little party.

'Did you hear him? I should feed my servant sponge fingers. Sponge fingers!'

'Crazy, quite crazy.'

'Because that's what she likes best. I've never heard anything like it.'

'And that wasn't the end of it. There was his usual twisted logic. You know what I mean. Tatár soon settled his hash.'

'I don't intend to let her become a primadonna. That's all we need.'

'It looks as if he has finally lost his marbles. He's a sick man. He'll be lucky if he survives two months. They don't even bother to measure his sugar level any more. Did you notice how the flies kept landing on him? He was constantly waving them away. Poor fellow. He'll soon be pushing up the daisies. What will become of his wife?'

'But you were at fault too. What was the point of praising her to the skies in front of everybody? They might try to entice her away.'

The doctor infuriated her. She kept Anna on an even tighter rein. She had never employed a caretaker's assistant but now Anna was pressed into this service too. Once a week she had her scour the stairwell, clean the attic, and when there was nothing else to do she ensured that the

Ficsors kept her busy. It became Anna's job to put out the rubbish. When the dustcart's bell fell silent in front of the house she could be seen in the sunshine struggling with the waste bins of three households, tipping their grimy contents into the cart. She was also given a basketful of stockings to mend so that she should not get bored in her spare time.

Mrs Vizy tended to be neutral in expressing her satisfaction. She told the Ficsors that the girl would do. This was quite difficult for her since she was almost beaming with delight. But she controlled herself in the interests of education. She put on a hard face, but it was only a mask.

The month ended on 15 September. She paid Anna her wages. Not as much as she had paid Katica, who had been overpaid, but she let it be known that she would be prepared in time to give her a raise. And she didn't deduct the full cost of the mirror. Only half of it.

Anna needed no money so she asked Mrs Vizy to bank it for her or to buy her something. Mrs Vizy bought her a headscarf on the market in Roham utca.

On the fifth Sunday she deliberately sent Anna out to have a walk round town. Anna wore the gingham frock in which she had arrived. The desolate Sunday light trembled on the granite of the pavement. An interminable day of empty idleness yawned before her. She dawdled at gates, then ambling vaguely down Logodi utca arrived at a square with a church and a large hospital, a square ringing with noise louder than the cawing of rooks at the end of autumn. It was a place where servants tended to promenade: Swabian girls cackled and muttered and linked arms, chattering in their incomprehensible lingo, just as they would have done back in the village, going about in gaggles as always. They formed chains around the traffic islands where the gas-lamps stood, obstructed passers-by and held up the traffic. The trams had to ring their bells extra loud so that they could proceed. Anna was the only lone figure among them.

On her way home, by the Vérmező, a Romanian soldier pinched her breast. She took shelter in a doorway and waited for the soldier to disappear. Near the Southern Terminal she bought some sticks of barley-sugar at a sweet stall as a present for little Bandi in Árok utca.

Servants, when they visit their previous employers, always say, 'I've come to visit, if you don't mind.' The employers don't mind. It breaks up the daily routine, and once, after a little uncertainty, they have recognized the ex-servant, who is probably a little thinner or a little fatter, or at any rate older than she was, they too begin to reminisce about the old days and the time that has passed since. They receive a guest whom they treat as a guest. They offer her this and that. The guest for her part stands rather more self-consciously, burdened with graver memories, in a room whose every object she knows more intimately than the owners. Her arms, accustomed to heavy work in this very place, hang inactive and useless by her side; she cannot behave with the familiarity she once did when, willy-nilly, she was an extra member of the family; and it further depresses her to reflect that in her absence family life has continued as before, and that however kindly they receive her now, she has not been irreplacable. Everyone feels this now and then, but she feels it more completely, more disturbingly, and when the friendly visit comes to an end, without realizing it she grows sad and departs with a painfully stupid expression her face. Only ghosts, the revenant dead, feel quite like this.

It was Bandi who had once given her his toy trumpet as a memento. Now she gave him the barley-sugar. Bandi stared at her in wonder. Confused memories whirled around his little head. The barley-sugar had the required effect. He sat in her lap. She was the one he had once loved most of all, and whom, at the age of one and a half, he had called Mamma not Anna. But when she began to tell him about the magic knife and the host of birds that flew out of it, he no longer listened. He had forgotten the magic knife. Anna said goodbye and arrived back at 238 Atilla utca well before six.

All things considered it was better at home.

Mrs Vizy spent the morning in the kitchen. It wasn't

necessary to keep an eye on the maid any more, but there is nothing more interesting than a kitchen, which is after all the laboratory of life. Here she could discover what happened at the market, what was cooking at the Moviszters or the Drumas, or simply watch Anna pottering about in her usual amusing fashion. The food which is about to undergo its miraculous transformation before it finds its way on to the dinner table, is still strewn about the kitchen in its raw state. The water that will go to make the soup is throbbing in the big iron pan; the carrots, the leeks, the kohlrabi, the celery, the black pepper are all boiling in the pearly saline liquid along with broken eggshells that serve to reduce the froth or scum floating on the top. The smaller pans are bubbling and dripping too. The maid quickly snatches the saffron and the ginger from the shelf, cuts the onion into thin slices, her eyes and nose dripping, grinds the nuts and crumbles the bread roll, chops the parsley, splits the eggs dividing the yolk from the albumen, scrapes the turnip, guts the rabbit, dips the meat in the flour and throws it into the pan where the hot fat sizzles and hisses.

There was only one thing Anna wouldn't do: she couldn't bear to kill live chickens. She would rather run upstairs and call Etelke down to perform this most common of exotic murders. The old servant would graciously gather up the carefully chosen sacrifices, take them out to the standpipe in the yard, and with one dextrous movement wring their necks, and chop their heads off with a large kitchen knife, the blood spurting up to her elbow, sometimes even flecking her face. Anna turned away. Even Mrs Vizy found it hard to stomach. She knew it was necessary but would still ask Etelke how she could do it. Etelke would roar with laughter and say that whatever had to be had to be.

Mrs Vizy gave Anna to understand that she wasn't happy for her to spend too much time with these other servants. Etel wasn't a suitable companion, she was an old hag, loud and impertinent, and as for Stefi she snubbed her in any case and wouldn't be seen in the street with her. What would she want with such people? They laughed at her behind her back. Once or twice she actually denied Anna was at home, would not let them into the flat. Anna saw that her mistress was right. She made no great effort to seek the others out. Why should she go vainly chasing after them?

Instead she patched and mended things in the kitchen. A chicken scampered cheeping around her feet. She had personally bought it from the roost in order to keep it as a pet. She knew each chick by its feathers and its voice. Like most village girls she thought of a chicken much as she thought of other birds. She gave it little saucers to drink from, fed it with crumbs and talked to it. At night the chicken would jump on to her bed and sleep at her feet.

When they were together Mrs Vizy talked of Piroska and Anna of her stepmother, that gaunt young peasant woman who one winter night had chased her from home. Ficsor wrote to Anna's father, István Édes, to tell him of her new job but he never replied. He was fed up with her. She, for her part, slowly made herself at home in her environment. She no longer mentioned her previous employers, the Bartoses, nor did she hear any more about her predecessor, Katica. Those times were gone. She felt increasingly proud that her masters were richer than the Drumas or the Moviszters. She was happy when they gave her a new rolling pin. She referred to the sieve as 'our sieve', to the corkscrew as 'our corkscrew', and all these things were finer than the ones upstairs. She admired Mrs Vizy's clothes too, especially that black silk dress she wore to the seance on Wednesday afternoons. Mrs Vizy would joke with her, 'Look, I put this on just for you.'

After all Mrs Vizy found her maid quite a pleasant companion. Maids fulfil much the same function for their mistresses as whores do for their husbands. When they're not needed they can be sent away.

One particular evening, after the great political upheavals were over and all the heated debates had flared and settled, Vizy was waiting for supper in his study. They knew he was working so were careful to keep quiet. The beautifully tidy study was shrouded in silence: the inkwell, the sealing wax, the scissors and the stuffed owl lined up in their ranks on the desk. Vizy was writing to Ferenc Patikárius, his brother-in-law, who had charge of their vineyard in Eger. The letter was hard to compose. The easier it was to dictate memos to his secretary at the ministry, the more difficult personal letters became. He stopped, reread the contents, dusted the ink, and read through once more before finally licking the envelope, lighting the candle and marking the seal with his signet ring. He gave a great yawn. His heart, lungs and liver were in good working order, his stomach soundly digested whatever he deposited in it, and yet it seemed to him he was suffering. He fell prey to that *ennui* peculiar to bureaucrats who are left to themselves. He looked into the kitchen and tried to hasten proceedings. His wife was chatting to Anna who still carried the freshness of village life about her. Vizy too would have liked to sit down here and chat but his wife ushered him out. She told him that Anna should not disturbed, that she was a servant and not a tourist attraction.

Yet however she tried even she could not keep Anna's light hidden under a bushel. The girl was a daily caller at Viatorisz's shop. The grocer would greet the extraordinary servant with a generous wink. As his place was a local hub of gossip for all the women that shopped there, everyone got to hear about her. They mentioned her name at the baker's and the butcher's and at the laundry; even the undertaker knew about her. Even the enormously fat policeman, who would always respectfully salute the Vizys when they passed him on his beat along Attila utca was aware of her existence.

Her fame took wing. At first it was just in the immediate neighbourhood of Attila utca, Krisztina tér and certain points along the Krisztina and Attila körúts, but soon Pauler utca, Mikó utca, Logodi utca and Tábor utca were also ringing with her name. Once there, within a week it had spread into the Vár: into Úri utca where the Tatárs lived, the Bástya sétány, Ferdinand tér and the Vienna Gate tér.

Her reputation had lodged itself in the minds of men and women everywhere and was still growing.

They spoke of an exemplary servant. Many had not yet seen her and knew her only by her Christian name. She had not even taken a definite form in their imaginations. Those who knew about her felt like members of a society of the superstitious who had heard of a miraculous cure, some potent religious icon; they could not understand the supernatural powers at play but took them for granted.

Eventually the news spread full circle and came back to the Vizys. One day a friend called Vizy at the office asking whether Anna had a sister or an aunt since they needed a reliable servant.

Mrs Vizy was preparing packages for the poor at the Mária pharmacy. As usual the assistant chemist was chatting with her as she weighed out the prescriptions, and all of a sudden she too mentioned Anna. She talked about 'your Anna' with a knowing smile.

When Anna appeared at the market with her straw basket on her arm, the vegetable traders whispered to each other: 'Vizy. You know, the councillor. Him in the ministry.' When Vizy appeared, however, the whisper would go: 'Here he is, the man I told you about. That's him. Anna's master.'

In the evenings the gentlemen of Krisztina would walk out with their wives. One woman suddenly stopped dead. She stopped listening to what her husband was saying and was staring at a particular point as if she had seen an apparition.

'Look!' she whispered. 'That's her . . .'

'Who?'

'Anna. Who works for the Vizys. Anna, the Vizys' maid.'

The man peered about in the gaslight gloom but saw nobody since the vision was of the most fleeting kind. The ghost in the blue calico dress had flitted by the wall carrying a fresh loaf from the baker, had disappeared behind the gates of a coffee-coloured house and was already rustling up the stairs. She was irredeemably lost to their sight. They waited for a short while as others had done before them, then moved on silently, wrapped in their own mysterious thoughts.

11

Master Jancsi

One September morning the messenger boy at the ministry brought Mrs Vizy a telegram her husband had already opened. Its brief message was: *Arriving tonight Jancsi.*

In his letters to Vizy, Ferenc Patikárius made frequent mention of his twenty-one-year-old son, Jancsi, who was still hanging around Eger. Up to the age of fourteen Jancsi had been a student at the military cadet school at Sankt-Pölten. When his elder brother Sándor was killed in the Carpathian campaign, his father removed Jancsi from the school and enrolled him at the local *gimnázium*. He wanted his remaining son to be educated into a profession. The boy's next four years rushed by like a dream, its terms interrupted by enforced holidays owning to coal shortages all of which induced lax discipline. He watched his teachers and elders trooping off to war, becoming dead heroes from one day to the next. Like everyone else he quickly aged with the war. In his last year he was called up, given his training and attended his lessons in military uniform while waiting to be summoned to the front. But the summons never came. The revolution broke out in the meanwhile and he had just time to pass his military exams.

Then, with the iron discipline of the Lower Austrian cadet school behind him and the freedom of a generally imponderable future before him, he entered a period of drifting. He became something of a socialite. He danced his time away at parties, courted the local girls and developed a reputation as an impromptu wit. He dreamed of being a film star. He did not fancy any other career. For two years he stalled. He had no appetite for further study.

Eventually his father despaired of his torpor and appealed to his brother-in-law to make a man of this rascal whose life had been broken by the war. Vizy's advice was that on no account should he enter local or state service like some genteel pauper: instead he should perform his Christian middle-class duty and heed the spirit of the age by seeking some practical, financial position. This would be the best course for him. Ferenc Patikárius agreed.

Vizy rang a banking acquaintance who promised to employ the lad as a salaried trainee. It only remained to find a flat for him. At this time flats were extremely scarce in Pest. Mrs Vizy was jealous of her rooms and it was only with some difficulty that she was persuaded to accommodate her nephew until something turned up. She felt a certain obligation to her brother.

In the evening she set the table for three. Jancsi failed to arrive. This wasn't altogether a surprise: he was the most unreliable fellow in the world.

Three days after the cable, when they had almost forgotten their prospective lodger, at about eleven in the morning, the door burst open. Jancsi blew in like a hurricane.

'Aunti Angéla!'

'Jancsi, Jancsi!'

'I kissa da hand.'

'Hello, hello. What time do you call this? What a fellow! When did you arrive?'

'This very moment. I got the express. It was three hours late.'

'You are an idiot, you know.'

They were both talking at once, screaming and hugging each other. It was a theatrical welcome, somewhat over-theatrical in fact. Mrs Vizy disengaged herself and straightened her hair which he had thoroughly rumpled in his harum-scarum way. She gently pushed him away.

'Wait, let me look at you.'

She examined her nephew. Jancsi looked like a vice-admiral, in white from top to toe. He wore white flannel trousers, a white jacket and white sports shoes. The dark times appeared not to have touched him.

'How you've grown!' marvelled Mrs Vizy. She was trying to discern the prematurely aged cadet who was allowed home for a few days at Christmas and languished at the end of the family table with a sad little cermonial rapier at his side. To meet him like this after some years was rather disconcerting.

Like everyone else she liked to fix her distant acquaintances in a particular place at some precise point in time: time stopped for them as if they were dead, and she gently deceived herself by imagining that just as time had frozen them into a photograph so she too had been stopped in her tracks on the road to annihilation. Once they succeed in meeting, though, most people realize the deceit and smile in confusion as if seeing something pleasant rather than something terminal and terrible.

So Mrs Vizy talked nonsense. She looked into the far distance and smiled as she remembered.

'Come along, I'll show you your room. You can stay here as long as you need to. This divan will be your bed.'

'First rate,' said Jancsi and threw himself across it. Then he rolled off and stood on his hands, proceeding miraculously to walk round the room in this manner. His white face reddened as the blood rushed to it and his jacket flopped over revealing his fine zephyr shirt and the handkerchief in his top pocket, folded into a dove shape.

'You idiot!' Mrs Vizy admonished him. 'Don't you dare turn my house upside down. You're as crazy as ever.'

'So I am, Aunt Angéla,' he proclaimed, bounding to his heels and giving her an exaggerated bow.

He started to whistle.

Mrs Vizy watched the whirling dervish. Her memories of his old escapades whirled with him and echoed to ancient laughter. A notorious wag will always appear more amusing to his relatives than to a complete stranger. Despite Jancsi's mobility there was something deliberate about him which implied a sense of distance. His perfect, almost neurotically elegant clothes conveyed the same message. He was strong and muscular but his chest was narrow. His small hands were dry. He never sweated however hot it was. His short spiky copper-coloured hair was firmly plastered over his neat and surprisingly delicate skull, from which his flat ears hung loosely as if cut out of paper and merely pasted on. His thin lips were stubborn and cruel. His face was lifeless, wooden and irregular, a series of whimsically contrived planes set tumbling over each other within a roughly pentangular frame. A cubist sculptor might have carved it.

Abruptly he stopped whistling. His baggage was being brought up, two suitcases of the finest English pigskin. He grew serious and devoted his rapt attention to the opening of their locks. It was all here. Eleven suits, tails, smoking jacket, winter overcoat lined with opossum fur, beautiful shirts, silken underwear, patterned socks, lacquered shoes and low-cut shoes for leisure wear with long protruding leather tongues, a manicure bag, various perfumes, and glycerin soap in white ebonite jars since he couldn't bear anything but glycerin soap on his skin. Right at the bottom there were two books, one a set of famous literary parodies by the humorist Karinthy and the other a brief textbook entitled *How to Master English in an Hour*.

Aunt Angéla wanted to help him unpack but Jancsi wouldn't allow anyone else near his clothes. He lacked nothing. He had even brought clothes brushes with him. He went through his jackets, brushing them down, flicking the odd speck of dust away with his fingers. He smoothed his trousers and fixed them in their presses, then hung everything away in the wardrobe his aunt had put at his disposal.

He took his toiletries into the bathroom then started on his ablutions. He washed thoroughly and long. He soaped himself, showered, and despite already having shaved that morning, applied the keen American razor to his smooth face. He puffed some deodorant under his arms, changed his underwear, put on a dark-blue suit and a rust coloured necktie and emerged as if newborn into the dining room where Uncle Kornél was waiting for him.

'*Hello,*' he greeted his uncle in English. '*Hello. How do you do?*'

'Welcome, you ass. And how are you?' Uncle Kornél embraced him roughly and, as family custom dictated, gave him a buss either side of his face.

'*Thank you very well.*'

'What do you think!' exclaimed Mrs Vizy. 'He speaks perfect English. He wants to go to America and be a film actor.'

'He'll have to make a living here first.'

'Your Uncle Kornél has found you a post in the bank.'

'*Yes, yes,*' Jancsi nodded.

'Now you listen here, you young jackass! Tomorrow morning we will go down together to meet the manager. You must introduce yourself.' He explained the nature of the job but Jancsi was unable to pay much attention. There was a dark-brown wart on the left side of Uncle Kornél's face: it was the feature he remembered most clearly. Now as his uncle talked it jogged up and down and Jancsi felt the urge he often felt in childhood, to grab hold of it between his fingers, lift it and pull at it until it snapped off and Uncle Kornél let out a scream.

Aunt Angéla gave some instruction to the maid about setting the table. In her white dress, her blond hair gleaming, his aunt illuminated the room like a tall candle shedding unearthly light.

Jancsi eyed the couple. To him they were merely actors who had chanced upon their masks somewhere and wore them now because they felt like it. He was unable to see that lives other than his might be as strictly necessary as his own. He was still possessed by the merciless nihilism of youth. It confused him and he tried to cover it up. He coughed and remarked that his family looked forward to seeing them in Eger, that they really should pay a visit. All the while he was fiddling with the cutlery.

They sat down to eat. He took his place opposite Kornél and fixed his eyes on the tablecloth, darting an occasional glance up at his uncle as he drank his soup. Not for long.

'What is this?' he suddenly cried out and held his spoon high in terror.

Mrs Vizy opened her eyes wide as at something miraculous. It was a bad omen. The spoon that Jancsi had been dipping into the soup had wasted away and there was only the handle left.

'Is this your doing, you scamp?' she asked her grinning nephew.

'Funny, eh?'

'Silly prank. Where did you get it?'

'In Vienna. Last month on a visit. It was in a bazaar. Look,' and he took a similar spoon from his pocket.

Uncle Kornél wasn't angry.

'Look here, young man,' Mrs Vizy reproved him, 'when will you grow up and come to your senses?'

Jancsi showed them the complete set of practical jokes an Austrian company produced for the general conviviality of mankind. He had a cigarette case from which if you tried to remove a cigarette the whole contents sprang out. There was a cigarette which exploded with stinking rockets when you lit it, a matchbox filled entirely with duds, a brandy glass which appeared to be full of yellow liqueur that could not be drunk because the top was glazed, a small pistol that mewed, and a printed tramticket which entitled the bearer to lie down on any tramline of his choice.

Aunt Angéla lamented the incorrigibility of the boy. He had been no different when he was small. Once in Eger he pulled the chair from under the choirmaster. Another time when they were painting the fence he covered their white dog in green oil paint and the poor creature remained green to the day it died.

Uncle Kornél tried to drink from the brandy glass, fired the mewing pistol then warned him that this was enough, no more jokes now, tomorrow the serious work would begin.

The next day they drove together to the bank. They sought the manager but were directed to the office of a departmental head and it was only after some delay that they found the correct waiting room which in any case was full of customers. Vizy sent a message to the manager who sent one back begging their pardon but he had to attend to a minister from Bulgaria and he would be with them soon. A secretary wearing glasses ushered them through into a small plain room where they used to hide personal visitors.

In a few minutes the manager, a short powerful thick-set Jew, appeared through a side door. His suit was creased and he was smoking a cigar through a holder.

He took Vizy and Jancsi by the arm and steered them into a vacant consulting room. He was so busy, he confessed, he barely had time to breathe between appointments. When Vizy had carefully presented his request and reminded him of his kind promise, which in the meantime he had forgotten, the manager took a pad from his pocket and asked Jancsi for a pencil – fancy him not having a pencil of his own! – and immediately wrote out something, chatting and smoking all the while. The ash dropped from his cigar on to his waistcoat. He ignored it. When they had finished he shook hands with them and made straight for another side door where a committee was waiting for him.

A smart gentleman now stepped into the room. He had already been informed of the arrangements and happily shook Vizy's and Jancsi's hands on which he could evidently feel the still warm and magical imprint of the manager. He escorted them into the lift and to the ground floor, then down some iron stairs into the armoured vault. Here Jancsi was given a desk, introduced to his colleagues and put to work.

It was a world of marvels. Every day Jancsi grew to admire it more. The enormous building in the middle of the square rose so majestically, so festively towards the heavens it might have been a cathedral. Even the haughty procession of fast cars waited patiently by the pavement before it, and the pedestrians who passed by its doors peered respectfully and curiously into the hall, lowered their voices and all but doffed their hats. Those who believed in nothing else, did at least believe in this; it reassured them to feel that there was something to life after all.

Even the porter in his braided cap stood in the doorway with a certain air of self-importance; his office included the street but it also extended into the sanctum itself, surrounded as he was by dubious hordes of visitors who ignorantly insisted on seeking unauthorized entrance. He was the one who made the first decision as to whether a person might or might not set foot inside, and he performed this duty in a quiet tactful manner, dealing with hysterical paupers in much the same way as Jesus had with the money-changers and publicans in the temple. This temple was equally short with unbelievers.

Jancsi liked to loiter in the entrance and in the gilded corridors of green marble where sunbeams filtered through stained glass. In the distance he could see the branched staircase dividing, and glimpse panelled halls and reception rooms with luxurious armchairs and divans. An air of abundance and supreme wellbeing emanated from them. The paternosters trundled round, the great cashier-hall clattered with thirty typewriters, and a hundred clerks in glass booths were stooping over desks.

Where he worked, down in the vault, the lamps were always burning in honour of the local god. This section which dealt with stocks and shares was guarded with particular care. The rooms were divided by steel doors half a metre thick and alarm bells rang at the slightest touch. At dusk the security guards appeared with their electric torches. Here the clients carried trunks loaded down with currency or gold or jewels, and filed into cubicles like confessional booths where they examined not their consciences but the contents of their bags which they personally proceeded to place in safes of steel. The air was loud with the ringing of strange bells, at the sound of which officious little ushers appeared from one door or another.

Above him in a wing of the first floor reigned the omnipresent figure of the man he had met but once, the manager, who was always here and never here, who appeared only for a moment and even in his car was likely to be negotiating with big American corporations. He stole up in the lift unseen, entered his office unobserved and was surrounded by a ringing choir of phones, humming tubes of internal post, squadrons of telegrams and a bevy of bright and busy secretaries, company managers and directors who served as votaries, attendant priests and old fat bishops respectively. Thus attended he would retreat to the deepest sanctuary and perform his holy offices at the altar where he might survey – for minutes at a time – the one deity in which the twentieth-century still believed, the god of gold.

How fascinating all this was, and how secure. Jancsi felt he was at the still point of an unstable world, a minor clerk of a new religion. Suddenly and for the first time he could imagine himself as an independent adult.

Later he discovered that Józsi Elekes was also employed here and worked on the second floor in the currency department. They bumped into each other in the corridor and fell into a delighted embrace, chortling like country cousins. They arranged there and then to meet for a drink together at a café concert. They couldn't bear to part till late at night. Jancsi escorted his friend to Vienna Gate tér where the Elekeses had their flat. Elekes in his turn escorted him to Attila utca, and so they continued until they ran out of conversation on the one topic that fully absorbed them, the seduction of women.

Elekes had been two years above him at the Eger *gimnázium*, and had already been with the bank for a year. He regarded himself as a native Budapester. He had a wide circle of friends. He spent mornings on the office telephone arranging their daily entertainment.

Jancsi's first task was to find a new sweetheart in the city. He couldn't bear not to have one. He felt he hadn't properly moved in until there was a girl to whom he could pay court, some one and only he could think of each night before he went to sleep, one who would be the chief concern of his life. There were two candidates for this post, Elekes's sister and Ilonka Tatár. Eventually he settled on the latter.

As many as ten or fifteen young men would flock to the Tatárs' of an afternoon. It was partly because Elekes was stalking Margitka that Jancsi favoured her sister. Ilonka was a gay and charming girl, rather pretty if a little on the plump side. In due course she would end up as fat as her parents.

Jancsi's romance consisted of casting his first glance at her when he entered the room, of lingering over their formal handshake and of leaning on the piano and asking her to play some old Hungarian tune. He sent her flowers too: often, before office hours, he could be seen in the Krisztina florist's, flitting from bouquet to bouquet, sniffing at the white violets and ordering them to be delivered at the Tatárs with his personal card.

Mrs Vizy found their guest less inconvenient than she had feared. The bank had lent him some gravity. By nine he was out of the house, returning for lunch at half past two. After this he would roll a cigarette at the table, or tend his nails and make conversation with his aunt.

'Poor Ilonka,' she teased him.

'Why, Aunt Angéla?'

'Take my word for it, dear. It's because you men are incapable of real love. You are attracted to one or other pretty face then you forget her. *Andere Städtchen, andere Mädchen.* You needn't pretend. Don't lead the girl on.'

Jancsi blushed and protested feebly; he was flattered that she took him for a rake. He made disparaging comments about women. Mrs Vizy chided him, while taking pride in her manly nephew. In his face she read secret debaucheries.

By four he was already prepared for the evening. He rinsed his mouth with scented water and waited for Elekes, who arrived dressed to the nines, wearing a monocle. They left for the *beau monde.*

At home he bothered with nothing but his clothes. He

106

saw nothing, he heard nothing. He would look for something he actually had in his hand. He had been with them three weeks and was still calling the servant Kati, mixing her up with the maid back in Eger. He would have been pushed to recognize her in the street.

Anna, for her part, had her hands full with him. She would wake him each morning at eight, and leave a gold-rimmed cup full of cocoa, a croissant and a glass of water on the chair beside the couch. The young gentleman found waking rather hard. It took half an hour of coaxing before the thought of the bank roused him; then, panic-stricken, he would throw on his clothes, upset the glass of water or the chamberpot, snort over the washbasin, leave the taps running, flood the bathroom and trail wet footprints across the newly polished floor. He really required a maid of his own.

When he had stopped whistling – he was a real songbird, continually whistling – Anna would go into the bathroom which would still be heady with his scent. She swayed dizzily in the misty perfumed air. She tidied away his nail files and scissors. Once she pressed one of his sprays. Cold scent shot out of it so terrifyingly fast that she immediately replaced it on the shelf.

Jancsi never communicated with her but by way of command. As he was leaving with Elekes he stopped at the kitchen door to ask her to tell the good lady of the house that he would be home for supper at such and such a time.

Late one afternoon Anna was alone, doing her ironing in the hall. She was steaming a pair of trousers with a damp cloth. The board was placed across two chairs. Jancsi dashed in at the door. Seeing that she was in the way, the girl started to move the board, but the young gentlemen motioned her to let things remain where they were, took a few steps back to the door and leapt clean over the ironing. He stopped at the dining-room door to see the effect he had made. Anna was ironing with an indifferent expression on her face, her legs gently spread. Her calico dress clung to her limbs. Her feet were bare.

At the beginning of October, Ferenc Patikárius invited the Vizys down for the grape harvest. They decided on a four-day round trip. Vizy asked the ministry for a few days off. At first the arrangement was that Jancsi would accompany them, but he preferred to continue at the bank, since he wanted to stay in Pest and visit the Tatárs or go to the cinema. Mrs Vizy instructed Anna on what to cook for the young gentleman. They left on a Wednesday from the Southern Terminal.

Jancsi escorted them to the station, since the Vizys, who remained provincials at heart despite their twenty-five years in the capital, laid much store by these formalities. They had a first-class half-cabin. Vizy overwhelmed his wife with courtesies. He offered her the window-side seat, ran out for a magazine and was generally solicitous for her comfort. Aunt Angéla nodded.

As the train jolted into movement she leaned out and once more admonished her nephew on the platform to take good care of everything, especially the house. Uncle Kornél waved with his handkerchief.

Jancsi whipped off his straw hat and shouted after them. 'Hurrah!' he cried. 'Hurrah!'

12

A Wild Night

The train was still drawing away, he could still see Aunt Angéla's face and Uncle Kornél's handkerchief, when all of a sudden he decided – and the decision took even him by surprise – not to return to the bank as he had intended, but to go home and there and then sweep Anna off her feet.

The thought was so deliciously exciting, his throat went dry. He clung to an iron pillar and looked up at the station clock which was showing precisely twelve. He took a deep lungful of the foul smoke-sour air.

Outside, before the station, he had the sensation of arriving in a strange town where a million new experiences were waiting for him. He took no notice of Baross tér, its colours bursting with brilliant light and its sombre eponymous statue, he saw only Anna in her chequered dress, ironing at the board balanced between two chairs in the narrow hall, her feet bare, her thighs gently spread, and he felt a keen desire to be there now, to embrace her from behind, and, as was the custom with servant girls, unceremoniously to upend her like a sack of flour.

He started to run. The warm October noon scorched his clothes. He leapt aboard a passing tram but leapt off again at the next stop. He whistled up a cab and promised a large tip if the man drove fast.

How slowly the fellow drove. Each turn of the wheel seemed an eternity. In the meantime the image that so unexpectedly presented itself to him continued to haunt him, teasing him, moving, ever more lithe and lively, like a film. Anna put the iron down, smiled uncertainly and sat in his lap.

But neither she nor the ironing board were in the hall. Where was she? In his confusion Jancsi looked into the kitchen.

'Is it dinner time yet?'

'Already?' asked Anna, at the stove. 'I thought . . .'

'What did you think?'

'I thought it would be at half-past two as usual.'

'Oh. No.'

'I can have it ready in a few minutes.'

'I say . . .'

'Yes?'

'What is there?'

'Clear soup.'

'And?'

'Roast veal.'

'And?'

'Poppyseed pudding.'

'Poppyseed pudding,' Jancsi repeated, frowning. 'Poppyseed pudding.'

'Is it not to your taste, sir?'

'Oh yes. Very much. I'm very fond of poppyseed pudding. Very fond.'

He was babbling without any idea of what he was saying. His brain however was hard at work, comparing this girl in this wholly new situation, quite different atmosphere and different dress, to the one who was ironing in the hall the other day, and he was trying to bring the two images together to realize the object of his desire. Anna was no longer barefooted. She was wearing her shoes and this disturbed him even more.

In the dining room she laid the table for him alone, giving him Uncle Kornél's place. He looked around and once again felt the heat surging through him as it did at the station.

For several minutes he was incapable of movement. He was alone, quite alone with her.

On tip-toe he hurried through into the bedroom. He looked for the key in the flush door, transferred it from the outside lock to the inner one, locked it several times, then opened it again. From here and the dining room one could lock off the entire flat. The hall door was covered in milky glass. No one in the corridor could see through that, not even in the brightest light.

He was deep in thought. He touched a pillow and shivered. He contemplated the tall mirror and established that it was big enough to show the reflection of two naked people kissing and embracing. He stroked the bedcover. Everything in the room, each object, each piece of furniture became an element in his design and glowed with its electricity. The deserted flat no longer looked like a family hearth: it was a den of vice, a willing accomplice that silently played along with all his plans.

He lifted the writing case, poked around in it, explored the cupboards, tugged at locked drawers, sat down in all the chairs and spread himself across the divans, even Aunt Angéla's divan. He had never rested on it before. He buttressed himself with cushions and propped his shod feet on the white silk cover. So what if he messed it up! No, on the contrary, he gloried in the knowledge that all this was someone else's and that he could do whatever he wished with it; some inner excitement led him on, a youthful instinct for vandalism, tempting him to kick things, break the locks and open everything, to foul, wreck, cleave and smash the lot.

He planned his assault for dinner. Anna served up the soup but didn't glance at him. He deduced from this that she must already suspect something. Over meat he noticed what appeared to be a little smile flickering at her lips: if he addressed her now she would laugh out loud and ruin everything. He decided to hold the plan till the sweet course. Nevertheless when it came to it he said, 'Thank you,' and left it at that.

111

After dinner he lay down on the couch in a mood of helpless fury and despair, covered his face with his hands and cursed his own stupidity. He was incapable of speaking with women, particularly when he most wanted to. His remarks at such times were so obscure they didn't understand him, or so offensively crude that he blushed from ear to ear at his clumsiness. Usually he could do nothing but joke with them. This was all right in its fashion as far as Ilonka Tatár and her crowd went but was absolutely useless with Anna.

In any case there were many things about Anna that put him off. Her hair was straggly like most peasant girls', drawn into a narrow knot, since servants, unlike their superiors, quickly lose their rich thick head of hair. He noticed a light down on her upper lip which in the heat of the kitchen had gathered a few beads of sweat. There was a small spot by her nose. Her figure was far too thin. Only her eyes were beautiful, and her teeth.

Jancsi tried to console himself and take away his desire by dwelling on her faults. She was as bony as a boy, she had a moustache, she sweated, a bright summer spot glowed by her nose and she had that stump of a bun on her head. But the longer he pondered the more clearly he saw it was in vain. Far from abating, his fever actually grew. The little imperfections which had at first rendered her strange and almost unattractive now made her all the more tangible, all the more suited to the purpose for which he had selected her. He groaned as he lay and turned over.

For Anna this was the first day she could work without supervision. She bustled about happily as if she were head of her own staff. As soon as she had done the washing up, she took his excellency's jackets and trousers from the wardrobe to dry-clean them with a spot of benzine. As she struggled through the door with the great heap of clothes she spotted the young master on the couch. He was lying stiffly with a glass tube sticking out of his mouth. She had no idea what it was.

'Are you ill, sir?' she asked him.

'Not at all,' cried Jancsi, taking the thermometer from his mouth and shaking it without looking at it. 'I thought I might have a temperature, so I decided to measure it. I seem to have caught . . .' and for no reason at all he emphasized the last word, 'a chill.'

But his mind was elsewhere. 'Now's my chance,' he thought. 'One joke, any common joke, some rib-tickling, side-splitting vulgar joke and she'll reel with laughter and fall flat on her back. That's the way with maids. On your back, Susie! . . . Leap on her, raise her skirt. What can happen? At the worst she'll slap my hand. So what. She's no virgin anyway. You've just got to look at her. Her tits are small and loose. The upright sort. Elekes said as much. But she might be a hot little tart. A sweet piece of fluff. A kind of peasant whore.'

He encouraged himself with words like these and others cruder still: it was like licking honey from a milk-jug, the sweetness of the words irritated his throat. They made him cough.

Anna was speaking.

'I could call down Dr Moviszter, sir. He's usually at home at this time. He hasn't even opened the surgery yet.'

'No need at all,' laughed Jancsi in a heavily forced manner, and propped himself up on his elbow to survey her.

He was thinking. 'Ah! she is looking into my eyes. I was wrong at dinner. She suspects nothing. But why should she suspect anything? Her sort don't understand innuendo, they're too simple. I ought to say something. Nothing crude, something with a touch of subtlety. Every moment is a moment wasted. If I fiddle around for too long then it will all come to nothing. I've already lost today. There are only three days left: Thursday, Friday, Saturday. Sunday's too late. Do something.'

He opened his mouth, convinced something would come out. His mind was blank. He merely repeated her name.

'Anna.'

'Yes, sir?'

'Look here Anna, I shall stay at home the rest of the day.

I won't go out. But if I ring, come to me at once. Wait a minute, Anna,' he added though she hadn't moved. 'Yes. That's all I wanted to say.'

She went away. Jancsi sprang up and dashed to the dining room door but froze there. It would be ridiculous to run after her in the kitchen when she had only just left him. No point in ringing either just yet. He turned his thoughts elsewhere and lay back on the couch which was still warm from his own damned heat. What was the matter? He couldn't understand it. He had never felt anything like this, only once perhaps, on that one occasion.

Yes, it was then, on his return from Vienna after his exams, travelling alone in that dimly lit carriage on the evening train. He pressed his eyelids in the effort to remember.

It happened shortly before they crossed the Hungarian border that he noticed a low-browed woman with a large hat-box in her lap. It wouldn't fit on the luggage rack. She looked exhausted and neglected, vaguely sickly. She wore a thick grey dress of broadcloth. Her heels were worn down. He had no idea who she might be, how old, whether married or single, whether German or Hungarian speaking, but as soon as he saw her he could not take his eyes off her. Above the train the sky was dull and leaden. Rain was slowly trickling down the panes and the air was as close as in a steam bath. As the conductors shouted out the names of the stations their voices died in the soft cotton-wool mist. Before he could speak to her the woman got off at Bruck on the border. She struggled with her hat-box and dragged her feet through the mud beside the rails under the pounding rain. She hadn't brought an umbrella with her. She kept walking until she faded into the grey. For a long time Jancsi stared after her through the window. He would have given his life to follow her, to take her hand and kiss her drooping mouth, then take supper with her in the room of some frontier hotel, where there was only a single table, one cupboard and one bed. He had forgotten all this the next day.

114

Obviously Elekes was lying when he said it was easiest with servant girls. Perhaps they were the most difficult of all. Furiously he changed clothes and went out.

He started off for the Tatárs but turned back on the Zerge Steps and crossed the Alagút tunnel beneath the river into Pest. He sat in a cinema and watched a seven-reel romantic film from Italy. Then he bought a ticket for the Pathefon and listened to Wagner's *Flying Dutchman*. It was growing dark outside. The half-light emboldened him. He imagined taking the girl quite simply by force, with one wild cry. He scampered up the stairs.

The kitchen, however, was empty. Like a murderer who bursts into a room with a dagger drawn to find his long intended victim absent, he flopped on to the kneading stool and laid his head on the table. At least it felt good to be here, in this ugly kitchen with the lingering smell of benzine.

Anna was startled to find him there.

'Where were you?' Jancsi enquired.

'At the butcher's, getting a chop for supper.' And she took a package wrapped in newspaper from her basket.

Jancsi waved it away. 'I don't want it. I won't have any supper tonight. Some black coffee will be enough.'

So he had a black coffee. He stood before the window and watched the night. At ten Ficsor locked the gates, Mrs Moviszter stopped playing the piano and the house grew quiet. The maid's room was dark. He too undressed and turned the light off.

For a while he stood in his nightshirt in the dark. It was impossible to tell what he would do.

He took a step. The boards creaked so loudly that every-one in the house must have heard it and suspected what was going on. He stepped back. Once more he hesitated, then slowly, yard by yard, he felt his way forward as cautiously as if he were a piece in the endgame of a chess final. The floorboards snapped like machine guns. Gritting his teeth he decided to run, no longer caring what anyone thought of his night excursion. Door-handles shrieked, doors wailed.

He had arrived in the blackness of the kitchen. He held his arms before him and felt his way to the wall. He had no idea where the bed was. He tried to locate it.

'Are you asleep?' he asked quietly and uncertainly.

'No,' answered Anna immediately, her voice wide-awake.

'I ... I thought,' stuttered Jancsi, 'I thought ... you know ... you might be asleep already.'

He found the bed. With a daring that terrified even him he sat down on one side of it. There was a tiny noise, some light sweeping of cloth against cloth, a hesitant movement.

The girl sat up. Only then did she know she was not mistaken, that, incredibly, somewhere in the dark a voice was really asking if she were asleep.

'You don't mind?' asked Jancsi in a choked voice.

Anna just sat in her bed, simple and honest, as if she were ill and were waiting for the doctor to examine her. She didn't quite understand the situation. She had heard stories of masters visiting their servants at night, even that the maid might be her master's lover and that occasionally a child might be born. There was such a girl in Kajár who was dishonoured by a lawyer from Pest. She had heard the girls gossiping of this and much more. Despite the fact that all such seductions happened in this way, she was filled with a stupid sense of wonder.

'Are you afraid?' asked Jancsi, still perched on the side of the bed. 'If you're afraid I'll go back.'

Anna was a little scared, but felt flattered by the young gentleman's interest in her and her fear of him going away was stronger than the thing she first feared.

'No.'

Jancsi lay down on the edge of the iron bed. The girl drew back to the other edge. There was space enough between them for another.

But they were already under a common quilt, that coverless maroon woollen quilt which Jancsi had regarded – even though it was Aunt Angéla's – as so dirty and unattractive as to be fit only for a pox-ridden invalid. Now he drew the quilt up to his nose.

The forbidden heat was quite astounding. He felt as if he were passing into an immediate fever and would burn away in its flames. He moved his legs through the darkness with lustful stealth, into the unknown depths of the servant's bed, expecting each moment to come upon something filthy or bloody, some terrifying object of horror, a bedbug perhaps or a toad. His trembling fingers stroked the ragged cotton sheet.

At his feet something stirred: a black form. Frightened he cried out. 'What is that!'

'The chicken. Off with you,' Anna clapped and chased the chicken off. It scuttled from the bed into a corner of the kitchen where it fell asleep standing up.

Jancsi drew closer, not hurrying, slipping first one finger then another towards her. He was hardly able to bear the excitement. There was no need for caution. He laid his left arm across the girl's breast.

Anna let him. A pleasant warmth began to rise within her. It was love. She knew she was being embraced. Back in the village the boys had often caught her up and touched her breasts for a joke. But then she started to laugh, loudly and with good humour. 'If only they could see me!'

'Who?' started Jancsi in a panic, snatching his arm from Anna's breast and straining to hear a noise on the stairs. Somebody was slamming a door. 'Not my aunt and uncle?'

'Not their excellencies.'

'Then who?'

'The young ladies,' laughed Anna from her heart, teasing and coquettish. 'The noble young ladies.'

'Them!' snorted Jancsi, flattered by the thought. 'What do I care for them.' His superciliousness condemned a vast congregation of doting paramours to death with the merest gesture. 'I don't want them. Not them, nor the noble young ladies. Because I've had such lovers before – your honours and your worships,' he said translating them into terms a servant might understand. 'It's not them I want. It's you. You are beautiful.'

'Why didn't you please to say so this morning, sir?'

'You noticed then. Was it when I came back from the station? Or at dinner? Was it already at breakfast?'

'If you'd told me in the morning at least I would have been beautiful all day.'

'No,' pleaded Jancsi, deeply affected by her rough wit. 'Don't say that, don't. You are beautiful,' he croaked with desire. 'I swear you are.'

'That's a sin, young master,' she lectured him.

'Why is it a sin?'

'To swear so lightly, on a bean . . .'

Jancsi resolved to put a stop to this. Such broad peasant banter seemed to mock his pale desire; he longed for silence, a hothouse silence which would nurse them towards consummation. Again he extended his arms over her breasts. Anna evaded him with a single movement.

'Listen, my love,' he pleaded, and gabbled in an effort to prevent her common, mocking laughter. 'Don't laugh, don't say anything. Not a word. Just listen, my dear. I won't hurt you. I swear. You are so beautiful. I love you. Only you. I love thee.' Having addressed her formally so far, he whispered the last pronoun. It signified intimacy and seemed to link their identities so closely it inflamed his desire; even as he spoke the roof of his mouth broke out in a feverish rash. 'Thee, thee. Say it. Thee. You say it too. Say it to me. Thee . . . thee . . .'

The girl wouldn't say it. She was reflecting on the immense distance this one little word could bridge. Jancsi's eyes grew accustomed to the darkness; he could make out the shapes of things: he could see Anna. Her two white breasts glimmered and lit the night around her. He plied her with questions about her lovers, if she had had any and if so who they had been. For a while Anna gave short ambiguous answers then ceased to answer altogether. Had she taken belated offence at his earlier demand that she be silent? Jancsi interpreted her silence to mean that she had been more or less anybody's and that he was merely the last in line. All the better, he thought and made moves to take her by force, now with flattery, now with violence.

118

Anna easily beat back his awkward advances. When he tried to grab her round the waist she gave him such a shove the bed almost collapsed. 'No,' she said harshly.

'But why?'

'Because you mustn't, that's all.'

'Listen . . .'

'Would you please leave me alone. Go to your proper young ladies. And stay there.'

Would you believe it? She didn't even call him sir or young master. She appeared to have assumed mastery of her bed. Jancsi pressed his head into the pillow case, biting at its edges, his face streaked with tears and spittle. She could hear his bitter sobbing. He lay on his stomach.

Then an arm suddenly closed round his neck and she embraced him with such intensity it almost hurt. He couldn't breathe. Slowly he sank into its ecstasy and allowed himself to be immersed in this enervating, liquid warmth where he could drown as sweetly as in a bath of sugared milk.

She was terribly strong, this peasant girl, and even thinner than he had imagined. As he encircled her she seemed utterly without flesh, simply muscle, sinew and bone: he felt her frail skeleton, her pelvis, the crucible, that secret well of creation. Several times they rose and fell in the pattern of death and resurrection.

Then they talked for a while.

A little after midnight a carriage stopped before the house. Someone rang and the caretaker opened the gate. They whispered to each other, wondering who this late visitor might be. Whoever it was passed their door and made his way up to the second floor where he knocked. They heard Dr Moviszter's voice. A few minutes later two people came down, the doctor sat in the carriage and they drove off. It was an emergency call.

Around dawn Jancsi noticed the light on the wall opposite and asked Anna who lived there. Then he returned to his own bed, along the route he had followed the night before.

The sun was not yet up. His heart was pounding with

happiness as he threw himself on to the couch. It was done at last. It was monstrously delicious. He was convinced his conquest was unique, that never in the history of the world had anyone committed a sin like his. But that was why he enjoyed it so and was unashamed of it.

Ilonka Tatár must still be asleep. Her father is bearded. At the end of each party he always comes and chats benevolently to the young men and has a piece of left-over cake. Her mother keeps a careful eye on proceedings, gauging their progress with a glance of approval or disapproval.

Jancsi laughed out loud. At last he understood why he had been so scared of girls, and why he was so happy when these formal rituals of courtship were over and he could dash home, whistling all the way. But this girl's relations were complete strangers to him. She was as unattached as a bird on the tree.

As he crossed the hinterland between waking and sleeping he was still marvelling at something. That this was all there was to it, that this most important of human affairs which adults take such care to hide from the children, was itself so childish, so comical, so like a game.

He began to nod and as if to echo his thoughts, an ugly smile of triumph spread across his face.

13

Love

Jancsi was sitting in the armoured vault. The bank was gloomy. It was a typical morning in the office. The department head passed him a file with a column of figures as tall as a skyscraper. His task was to add it up. His pencil clambered up it, storey by storey, then he lost count and had to start again a few floors lower down. In the end he grew bored with it, pushed it aside and stared at the window.

He thought of Anna's mouth. He hadn't even kissed her lips yet. When their flushed faces touched during the night Jancsi had turned away in disgust at the thought of a servant's mouth. Now it seemed even more exciting than possessing her body: the abasement of kissing those pale cracked lips, to press them apart with his and to prevent them from closing till the two of them were united in one breath, till they were crushed and squeezed together like exotic fruit.

He took his hat and sneaked away.

He found her in the dark bathroom.

'Stay,' he panted and kissed her. The kiss was strangely cool. It failed to satisfy him. Again and again he raided her mouth, pushing past the gates of her teeth to find her tongue which had a peculiar piquancy for him. Its wetness was intoxicating.

'More,' he cried. 'More, more.' He was a child gorging on

strawberry cream. As soon as he finished he wanted to start again.

Anna, who hadn't seen him since they were together, blushed in her shame and leaned back against the tub, fainting with happiness. He could do what he wanted with her. She had prepared his cocoa in the gilt-edged cup at eight as usual and left it on the chair: he had drunk it and left. She would have thought it perfectly natural if he had failed to recognize her again after their midnight encounter. This new situation surprised her more than the original night visit.

'Why don't you kiss me back? Why don't you speak? You don't love me. O thou . . . and I . . . thou,' he stuttered the ultimate interchangeables of love once again. When his satisfied lips fell from hers and he stopped to take breath she slipped out of the room.

'Wait!'

Jancsi caught her in the hall and kissed her again. From there they moved to the kitchen. In every place the kiss tasted different.

'Go to the window,' he commanded her. 'Here. In the corner. Next to the wardrobe. Into the light. I want to look at you. You look at me too.' He watched her with a wild intensity.

The eyes are the furthest outposts of the brain: stationed on the projecting ramparts of the skull they are themselves an observing, independent organ of intelligence. Somewhere in the fever of recognition, when existence itself irrupted into the cosmos, they knocked two holes through their walls of bone, and peered out through narrow slits to discover the purpose of creation.

But these two pairs of eyes were fixed entirely upon each other, exploring, searching and striving together for enlightenment and blessing.

'Now,' said Jancsi, 'you are not to touch me, nor I you. This is what you must do.'

He placed his arms behind his back. Their lips became the only point of contact between them.

Anna obeyed him as readily as if he were asking for a brush or a shoehorn.

The next day he didn't go into the bank. He telephoned to say he had a throat infection. He put on his fine woollen shirt and his white flannel trousers with the smart leather belt and lounged about the flat without his jacket. They had the whole day to themselves. Occasionally someone would ring with a bill that Anna would pay, or with a letter, but otherwise they were undisturbed.

Anna came in with the brush and pan. She wore a fancy headscarf and looked very pretty. She looked like an actress at the operetta, a soubrette, the archetypal sexy maid.

Jancsi asked for her hand. Only her hand.

'Give it to me,' he said.

'Why?'

'Just give it.'

'It's dirty,' she protested and started to wipe it on her apron.

He seized it all the same. He held it as gently as he would a butterfly, he stroked the palm which had touched many disgusting things in the line of duty, he enclosed it in his own delicate pampered hand and squeezed it tight. There was something in the roughness of those blistered fingers that was indescribably sweet. He took each of them separately and began confusedly to kiss them, not knowing what to do with the object of his desire. Suddenly he closed his lips about her hand.

'What are you doing?' the girl exclaimed, outraged. 'Isn't sir ashamed of himself? He should leave me alone!' She snatched her fingers from his mouth and, blushing deeply, ran to the refuge of her kitchen, where she fell to sulking. This was too much for Anna. She didn't understand.

At night when he came to her barefooted and the floorboards creaked beneath him she was glad and was not afraid of showing it. She had already made space for him in the bed. It was only in the daytime she couldn't bear this hocuspocus. She didn't understand that her young master was descending the ladder of desire and that since he had succeeded

123

in completely possessing her he was trying different approaches, each one a rung lower in his descent from heaven to earth. There was much she didn't understand.

After the kisses and the squeezings of the hand came the moment when he began to address her as a social equal. He asked her to address him in the same terms and drop the 'young master' tag. He quietly repeated her name, the most lovely of feminine names, a flirtatious name full of conditional promise. He could be with her for hours saying nothing else. Before he kissed her he would first ask humbly for her permission.

He was seized by ridiculous whims. She constantly had to be changing her clothes for him. First he would send her out to put on her gingham frock but she was to return on bare feet. Then he had her change into calico and wear her laced shoes. Nothing would absolutely satisfy him. Once he actually asked her to wear nothing but Mrs Vizy's evening wrap about her naked body. This she firmly refused to do.

Later he started to talk so much it made her head spin. He knelt before her. He lay down on the floor. He told her that at midnight, when everyone was asleep, they would creep into the garden and make love until dawn among the ash trees and lilac bushes. And that in the evening they would hire a carriage and drive out of the city to some country tavern where they would have supper and that they would make the barman believe that she was his bride, and after that he would even take her to America, buy her high-heeled shoes and long silk stockings and a sparkling tulle skirt such as actresses wear, and that they would roar along the highways of New York in a large sedan, her head on his shoulder. Anna just shrugged her shoulders and laughed at him.

On Friday the young master had her lay the table for two. When she brought in the first course he demanded that she should eat with him, or at least share his dish, sitting down, face to face with him. Anna would not have sat down, not for the world.

It took him long enough to persuade her to come to his couch just the once in the daytime. She did so on the last day, on Saturday afternoon.

Jancsi closed all the shutters and lit the chandeliers as if it were night. First he took her to the bathroom and sprayed her all over with scent. The girl stood solemnly in the cloud of perfume, only shrieking once when the spray tickled her breast and ran down her belly. Then they went into the sitting room and consecrated every inch of it with kisses and embraces. Their pilgrimage concluded on the couch.

Round about seven Jancsi lit a cigarette. He longed for something new.

'Anna,' he yawned, 'bring me the telephone.'

The girl brought the handset over with its fifty-foot extension trailing behind like an enormous dead snake.

'Thank you,' said Jancsi, already raising the receiver. 'You may go.'

He rang Józsi Elekes.

'Is that you? . . . Nice of you, I must say . . . you never even enquire after my health . . . I haven't been in for three days while you . . . No, old man, no . . . something bigger than that . . . I'll tell you all about it . . . No, not over the phone . . . All right, come round straightaway . . . Fine . . . I'll expect you . . . Hello, hello . . . What? . . . I don't understand . . . And you with mine. Ratface yourself.'

He slammed the receiver down, smiled at his friend's bold suggestion and felt pleased with his own response. He tidied himself up, sat down at the piano and played the one piece the knew, a popular one-step. He hummed the English words.

> You made me love you
> I didn't want to do it,
> You made me want you
> And all the time you knew it . . .

Elekes was knocking at the door but he was still bawling and hammering at the piano:

You made me happy
Sometimes you made glad,
But there were times, dear,
You made me feel so bad.

'So?' enquired his friend. 'You weren't ill?'

'No,' Jancsi replied.

'In view of that I must say you look pretty awful.'

'Really?'

Jancsi stood before the mirror. His eyes were bloodshot, his face pale. He was glad. 'Perhaps I do. I do in fact have a headache.'

'What, with an empty head like yours?' Elekes never lost an opportunity to show his wit. 'What can possibly ache in that?'

'Leave off, Elekes. This is a serious matter.'

'Are you in love?'

By way of answer Jancsi tinkled a few high notes on the piano. They made an ugly piercing noise.

'Single or married?' Elekes probed. 'Where did you pick her up?'

'In the *konditorei*. The Gerbeaud.'

'A tart?'

'An actress.'

'Ah. Which theatre?'

'Here and there. She's a dancer.'

'I see. And when did you cook her goose?'

'Wednesday night. I got talking to her in the little bar. You wouldn't believe it, old man! What a wildcat! What a demon! She came with me there and then. In her car. She has a car. We're lovers.'

'And where do you meet?'

'Here.'

'Hm,' thought Elekes and smiled jealously. 'You miserable so and so. So you bring her here?'

'Every day, since the old folk left. Every night. And during the day. She has just gone, this minute. She was still here when I rang you. Right here.' He pointed to the couch.

126

Elekes took a deep sniff. He could smell the delicate perfume and see the lit rooms. Perhaps it wasn't so unlikely after all.

'Buxom?'

'Slender.'

'Blonde?'

'Chestnut brown.'

'What's her name?'

'Promise not to tell?' They shook hands on it while Jancsi pondered some gigantic whopping lie, but he couldn't think of anything. 'Marianne,' he sighed. *'Liebe* Marianne.'

'Well, well,' acknowledged Elekes. 'She must be quite a dish. But you'd better be careful,' he warned Jancsi, 'don't yield yourself up entirely. She sounds like the hysterical sort.'

'I know, but what hysteria! Her eyes roll when I kiss her. She is delirious. And you know what, Elekes? Just listen to this . . . are you listening? . . .

Jancsi's mouth hung open: he stood dumb. As he was talking Anna stepped into the room and announced that tea was ready. He glanced at her and then at Elekes who had turned his back and was also looking at the girl. He expected Elekes to burst out laughing and point at her, recognizing her at once in his precise description of the actress. All would be revealed.

Nothing of the sort. Elekes stubbed his cigarette out on the ashtray and followed Anna to the table. Jancsi's spirits sank. A dull, shapeless misery descended on him, such as he felt when he was alone.

He could never cope with sadness, not for a minute, and protested vigorously against the idea of trying to understand it, or of surrendering himself to it and enjoying it. He would turn to the most artificial diversions. He was like a morphine addict: only a new shot would relieve him. He quickly poured himself a strong cherry liqueur, clinked glasses with his friend and drank it down, whistling. After tea he took his favourite book and read its irreverent parodies of high-minded poets.

Then they tried a practical joke on the telephone but it was not a complete success. They rang a mutual friend who happened to be out and they had to be content with talking to his widowed mother. They instructed her to tell her son to report the next morning at eight o'clock at the political security unit, if he knew what was good for him.

Elekes looked at his watch and, despite Jancsi's entreaties, took his leave. He too had a rendezvous. With another actress no doubt.

Jancsi remained and continued drinking alone. With a clumsy movement he knocked the bottle over. The liqueur spilled over the white Persian rug.

Anna cleaned the rug, swept up the cigarette ash and generally tidied up, since the two rascals had made a thorough mess of the place.

The young master sat very straight. The drink had not gone to his head. He was dry drunk, so to speak, stiff and solemn. All the same he had to say something to her. He rose from the table, and approached Anna steadily without swaying. 'Look,' he said. He attempted to amuse her by sticking a pair of red glasses on his nose and squinting at her through a piece of parchment paper.

She didn't laugh.

'How horrible!' she gasped. 'How ugly you look!'

Jancsi took the revolver from his pocket and pointed it at her, took aim and fired. The gun mewed.

'Did I scare you?' he chortled and followed the girl who backed away from him holding her two arms out in front of her. 'Don't be afraid. It's only a joke. Come here. I want to show you something else.'

He took a dark banknote from his wallet.

'Have you ever seen one of these? It's American. A dollar bill. Do you know what it is worth? A fortune. This note is French. And this one's Dutch. It's proper currency.'

When he had stuffed the notes back into his wallet he stretched. He felt as though his head had been pumped out and his spine were made of glass.

'Make the bed,' he said. 'I'm having an early night. Their

128

excellencies arrive in the morning. Don't tell them I didn't go into the office. And not a word about Mr Elekes. I'll take care of that.'

Over the last four days Anna had done all the jobs she had been asked to do. She had darned many stockings and patched many skirts. She had tied them up in two separate bundles. She had also scrubbed the main stairs. She was ready for her ladyship's return.

This night she waited in vain for the young master. He didn't visit her. But tonight of all nights she was scared to be alone. She kept seeing the white face with the red spectacles. It mockingly pointed a revolver at her.

At two o'clock the kitchen window rattled. She got up and closed it. Outside a cool wind had sprung up. The trees were whispering.

Later she heard the rain start.

14

Something Very Bitter

Come the evening, it was still raining. It was a persistent steady rain, a constant blubbering that slopped in the yard. The gutters spewed up filthy water.

When she looked out Anna saw that the whole sky was one mass of grey. There was not the merest patch of blue. How good it would be, she thought, to take a long-handled mop and clear it away as if it were a spider's web in the corner of the room.

She hurried down the stairs and waited for her masters under a rickety umbrella. Let them not know anything, let them not tell anything from her appearance, for she would surely die of shame. She draw her headscarf down over her eyes.

The Vizys, who had returned on the overnight train, were driven down the street in a coach which dropped them before the house. Anna saw her ladyship first. She was already leaning out and shouting. She wanted to know if the house was all right. Anna nodded that it was. And was all well with the young master? Yes, quite well, she answered, after a little hesitation, then waited as if she had something more to say.

Mr Vizy was the first to leap off the carriage. He was wearing his travelling cap and a leather flask was slung round his neck. Anna took the bags and made her way upstairs. Heaven knows, she was quite glad they had returned and that they could get back to their normal routine. Mrs Vizy was glad too. The maid she had left behind was still here, had baked a sweetloaf as a surprise and had kept the flat in sparkling order. This was no more than she expected of her now. On the other hand, meeting so many new people under unfamiliar circumstances had yielded new experiences, and she could view her own household a little more clearly and objectively. She was not long in recounting how the maids in Eger rose every day at four and helped on the land for practically no wages at all.

They unpacked, and drank some tea. They had been chilled through on the journey. Jancsi was still asleep. He lay on his couch, white as a corpse, his eyelids half closed, his mouth hanging open.

The rain poured down all Sunday and for the next three days. Suddenly – and rather too early – autumn was here. The little house in Attila utca grew even smaller, closer and darker. The air had cooled considerably. Cold mornings were in order. Mrs Druma, whose husband's earnings continued to increase, bought herself a new pair of galoshes and a new overcoat. Druma himself came and went on the stairs in a transparent English mac. Mrs Moviszter drove with a coach and two to her artistic gatherings or to rehearsals. At home she recited verses in the sitting room, wearing a plunging négligé and dramatically waving her arms.

Stefi and Etal no longer idled on the gallery. They warmed themselves by the stove and wrote letters in the evening. Only briefly would they peek out to wave a hot iron, describing fiery circles in the darkness. The Ficsors lived like moles in their basement hovel. The woman would cook a thin egg soup for breakfast. Ficsor would appear like a ghost in the foggy corridors in his dripping postman's cloak, cursing that someone had left the attic door open again. A pipe burned in his mouth. He coughed. The yellow shoes he had so famously requisitioned for himself were already worn out. It was the end of a short summer. The poor slowly divested themselves of clothes, the rich put more on.

131

Jancsi worked at the bank. Liberated from his self-imposed close confinement of four days he took a deep breath of genuine relief as he stepped out into the street. He no longer felt comfortable at home. His memories filled him with shame and he would talk to himself aloud in his nervousness. The girl was unbearable. Since Elekes's visit that evening the whole affair seemed incomprehensible. Now that his uncle and aunt were back and the old order had reasserted itself he was unable to look at her and was in physical pain each time she entered. For the time being he took refuge with his relatives. He fled from her.

He spent much of his time in the street ogling passing women. He furtively followed each one with his eyes and mentally undressed her. He yawned his time away at the Tatárs' party and took his leave in English. He picked up a waitress at a *pâtisserie*. He didn't find her attractive but he still brought her to a quiet and modest hotel in Buda where they were glad to accommodate guests for an hour or two. After the waitress came a model, followed by one who called herself an actress. He'd meet her in a cab. He hardly ever went home for supper. Instead he and Elekes set themselves up at the Club des Parisiens, where a regular table was reserved for them.

The decor of this newly opened bar was rather showy for the times, with rows of mirrors, dripping chandeliers and gilded stucco columns. There was also the constant screaming of a jazz band. The great advantage of a jazz band is that it makes not only thought but sensation of any kind quite impossible. And this was precisely what the elegant clientele of this club wanted. It was the haunt of foreign middlemen, successful arms dealers, officers of the Triple Entente and of better-class prostitutes, those merry little war-widows, once brides of heroes, who had fallen on hard times and sought here the gratitude owed to them by posterity. They were happy to hear the black band wailing like wild animals, happy to hear its sick martial retching which drowned out their own nausea and despair. The music maddened them a little, then they danced to it.

The dance floor itself was something special. It was covered in a sheet of glass lit from below by pink electric bulbs wreathed in flowery patterns so that the whole floor looked like an enchanted ice-rink. Jancsi spent every night here and stayed till closing time. The girls knew him, cadged cigarettes off him and rather liked him. He danced the one-step with a certain formal elegance. He could often be seen swirling through the smoke, clutching a woman, his pale face bent to the floor fascinated by the brilliant lacquered shoes gliding across the glass.

It was dawn before he arrived home. The key slowly turned in the lock. He pulled his shoes off in the hall and crept to his couch on stockinged feet so as not to wake the Vizys. Anna always heard him. She couldn't get to sleep until she heard the young master's footsteps in the sitting room. She waited for him each night. And through the day too, constantly. She waited for him, for something to happen. Perhaps only for him to say some kind words to her, to smile at her, or, if nothing else, for him to ask her for something. Jancsi said nothing. He was glum and in a hurry. Obviously, he must be angry with her.

Yet she was paying more attention to herself now for his sake. She combed her hair several times a day, would frequently glance at the mirror and wore her best outfit, her one gingham frock, even for work.

By November the nights had grown even longer. The hooting of trains at the Southern Terminal was clearly audible. A stray engine would now and then moan in the dark, as touchingly and sorrowfully as a child.

On Sunday Mrs Vizy went to church. Mr Vizy too left early. The young master woke late. He was arranging his trousers before the wardrobe. Anna opened the windows so that she could start the cleaning. As she passed the wardrobe she gathered her courage and spoke to him.

'Excuse me, master . . .'

'What is it?'

'Please forgive me . . .'

She burst into tears. She cried silently but in such distress

133

her entire body shook. Jancsi stared at her. For a while he was completely lost for words. Is it possible he could have loved her, that he had been in love with this? She wiped her tears with her knuckles, she snuffled and her nose was as red as a drunken peasant's. She had tied a long scarf around her waist. It brought a damp autumnal smell into the house much as a stray dog might have done. The draught was whistling through the open window as Anna's tears rained down and kept on falling. She was muttering too, though he could only make out one word: '... shame ... shame ...'

'That's impossible,' said Jancsi. 'Quite impossible. Out of the question.'

'But it's true ...'

'Stop crying. Do please stop crying,' he begged her and stopped his ears to shut out her weeping as he once had her laughter.

'If only you'd stop crying ...'

'Oh, master ...'

'Be quiet. This is no way to talk. Will you stop it! Well. So. The first thing is: it is by no means certain. Not at all. One must wait.'

He shuddered with disgust that he had to discuss matters like this with her in such horrible intimacy.

'Whatever the case one must wait,' he repeated and shrugged his shoulders. He only half believed it. She might be trying to blackmail him. Nevertheless he took care to ask her each morning from then on. Anna just shook her head.

In the *Club des Parisiens* Jancsi buttonholed Elekes on the subject of a certain actress. 'Look, old man,' he began, leaning back in his armchair, 'I'm in trouble, my friend, in deep trouble.'

'Is that all?' replied Elekes and leant forward to whisper in his ear.

'Are you sure?'

'Certain. We've used the method time and again.'

That night Jancsi stood by Anna's bed.

'A footbath. In plenty of hot water, as hot as you can bear it.'

The girl made the water so hot she could have plucked and boiled a chicken in it. She dangled her feet in the bowl and hissed with pain.

'Well?' asked Jancsi after a couple of days.

Again, she just shook her head.

'Incredible,' he mumbled. 'Truly incredible,' and he snapped his fingers.

He was in a real pickle, up to his neck. Just his luck! What a repulsive business, and what a scandal there would be next spring.

Elekes suggested a gynaecologist, someone who was particularly sympathetic to the arts, especially actresses. Jancsi thought it convenient to arrange an appointment for his actress. His pal introduced him to a sympathetic chemist who made his living currently by smuggling silk in from Vienna and smuggling Hungarian arms out to Czechoslovakia. He gave Jancsi something.

Jancsi waited for an opportune moment when his aunt had popped out into the corridor. 'Here it is,' he whispered to her urgently.

'What is it?'

'Medicine.' He slipped four small packages of powder into her hand. 'Hide it away,' he insisted when she started examining the little paper sachets. 'Then take them.'

'Should I swallow these?'

'You don't understand. It's *in* the packets. You open them, dissolve the powder in water and drink it.'

'Now?'

'Before you go to sleep. By morning it will have done the trick. But let nobody see it. Because it's illegal. If they found out they could put you in prison for it.'

'But then perhaps I shouldn't take it, master?'

'Nonsense. Of course you should. But say nothing to anyone. Be careful.'

Anna did as she was instructed. When the flat grew dark

135

she opened the packets. They contained a white powder like fine flour. She sniffed at it. It had no smell.

She emptied the contents of all four packets into a glass of water. But she was too scared to drink it in the kitchen. She went into the toilet. Then she shut her eyes and drained the glass in one gulp.

Dear Jesus, how bitter it was, O Mother of God, blessed Mother of God, how bitter. She had never tasted anything so bitter in her life. And it only reached its peak of bitterness once she had gone into her room and lain down on the bed. Its stinking bitterness seared the roof of her mouth and burned her throat. Only poison could be so bitter. She clapped her hand to her mouth and fingered her tongue hoping to touch the bitterness, amazed that anything could be so bitter. Each individual hair on her head was suffused with it.

She slept till one or maybe later. She opened her eyes wide and stared at the window. The bright orange light on the wall opposite was leaping about with such energy she was lost in wonder. Were they ringing bells somewhere? She heard the boom of distant bells which grew silent then, with a deep grumbling, approached ever nearer. She rose to see why they should be ringing bells at this hour.

Then someone came in, a vast figure, she had never seen someone so huge. How could they come in when the door was shut. The figure stood by her bed like a horse.

We-e-ell, what's up with you-u-u? You can stay where you are. Father, dear father. Just look. His head was a piece of ham. He'll never harm her. He'll just sit in the chair, like the broom. He's mad. He'll go away.

I ought to sweep up anyway. The place is crawling with filth. I'll pull that drawer open, and – would you believe it? – it's full of millet.

Oh your ladyship, how you startled me. I thought you were going to fall off the wall.

What is she doing here? Go to hell, idiot. I'll burn the omelette, the water will boil away in the pan. Let go of me.

'What's the matter?' asked Mrs Vizy, bending over her. 'Are you ill?'

Anna was so fast asleep she could hardly hear her breathe.

'Anna,' she shook her. 'Anna. Can you hear me?'

The girl turned over.

'She is ill,' thought Mrs Vizy. She touched her brow. It was quite cold. Her hands and her feet were like ice.

'Is she going to die on us?' she wondered. She ran up for the doctor. Moviszter was out on a call and would only be back in time for surgery.

In the meantime she offered the girl tea with rum and exhorted her to drink it, it would warm her up. Anna shifted and pointed at something. She asked her to turn on the light.

'Why?' wondered Mrs Vizy. 'It's morning. Half-past eight,' she said, frightened.

Anna waved her arms round in terror then squeezed her hands to her eyes. She couldn't see a thing. The whole world had gone black: she was blind.

Once again she fell asleep and did not wake until the masters came home and started on their meal.

Mrs Vizy was just complaining that this was all she wanted, a sick girl on her hands, when Anna appeared in the dining room with the tray.

'Are you feeling better?' Mrs Vizy enquired.

Anna could see everything now but she couldn't hear. She could only see their mouths moving.

'She must have caught a chill,' said Vizy.

'Of course,' Jancsi agreed. 'It's a chill.'

'All the same, I'll call the doctor down,' Mrs Vizy fretted.

'Just as you think,' said Vizy, 'but you know what these peasant girls are.'

'Yes,' added Jancsi. 'And in any case she is better.'

By evening she was feeling so much better that she herself asked them not to bother the doctor.

For days her vision was impaired and her ears rang. Once she couldn't see the ice box, once she dropped a silver spoon and didn't hear it fall. She also felt a great pressure on

137

her heart, just as she did that night: she felt so small and everything around her so large.

'Perhaps you have upset your stomach,' Mrs Vizy quizzed her. 'Try to remember. What did you eat? You must have eaten too much of something you like.'

One day when no one was about Jancsi skipped over to her and asked if she was all right.

'Yes.'

'You see. I told you.'

'It was just that it was so bitter,' Anna replied with a faint sickly smile. 'So terribly bitter.'

'Bitter?' repeated the young master. 'All medicines are bitter. The important thing is to get them over and done with. Well, goodbye.'

But he had had enough of this affair, and of the Vizys too who were always nagging him about his late nights. He took the issue of his accommodation into his own hands. He showed the minister's calling card at the housing bureau and asked to move into the room in Márvány utca that he had been promised a fortnight ago. Within forty-eight hours the room was his.

It was on the third floor, not particularly big, but it did look out on to the street and – most importantly – had its own entrance. That very day he packed up his belongings, kissed Aunt Angéla and Uncle Kornél, and didn't even return for the evening.

Jancsi sat in his new room in his beaver-fur coat. He was chatting to Elekes. There was a ring at the door. Anna brought his belongings. She put them down.

'Thank you, Anna,' said the young master and pressed a hundred kroner note into her hand. He escorted her to the door and told her to wait for a second. He reached into his pocket, took something from it and gave it to her. 'This is for you too.'

Anna stopped in the street to see what it was. In the paper bag were some roast chestnuts, rather small, burnt and blackened, but still warm Hungarian chestnuts.

Now she saw that the young master was no longer angry with her.

15

Winter

The Romanians too started packing in November. The advance guard of the national army reached the Danube at eight in the morning on Friday, 14 November 1919. Pest was still officially administered by the military police when the ceremonial eagle-plumed shakos of Horthy's cavalry swayed down Attila utca and the combat helmets of regular troops shone resplendent in the Budapest sunlight.

Everybody gathered to look out of the windows, waving handkerchiefs at the stubby lowland boys marching strictly in step. On the other side of the river people hurried to their balconies clutching telescopes, hoping to catch a glimpse of the first soldiers.

For days the wagons of this battle-kitted army continued rattling down the main orbital roads. Old bugle calls sounded once again; at nine at night they blew tap at the Ferdinand Barracks to call the poor troopers home tra-la. On the eighteenth – it was a nasty foggy morning, and the flat red disk of the sun hovered low in a polar sky – accompanied by bells and serried ranks of bishops, the supreme commander himself rode in along Fehérvári út. Kornél Vizy was there too, top-hatted, among a delegation of civil servants. Mrs Vizy was part of the ladies' parliamentary delegation, giving out flowers and tricolour ribands draped in scraps of funereal veil.

Anna was working alone. The house was empty and

silent. There was not a sound to be heard. She leaned over the balcony and shook out her dustcloth, went inside as if looking for something then came out again. As she aired the flat, pleasant bathroom smells continued hovering on the breeze: they had eaten their way into the very furniture.

'Can you hear her?' said Mrs Vizy to her husband as they relaxed in the sitting room after their return. 'She's singing.'

Anna was humming some merry little song: *On Friday night, on Saturday night, I'm off to meet my darling in the pale moonlight . . .*

'That's unusual,' she commented. 'She has never been one for singing before.'

'So what? She's in a good mood. Would you prefer her to be in tears?'

One morning she was stripping some meat on the table. There was a sharp intake of breath.

'What happened?' gasped Mrs Vizy who was sitting nearby.

'I've cut myself.'

Blood covered her hand. The knife, a big kitchen knife, had slipped and cut her thumb clean through to the bone almost severing her knuckle. It was an ugly gaping wound.

'Why aren't you more careful?'

'Please leave it. It'll be all right.'

She washed her thumb in the sink, applied plenty of table salt and bound it in a scrap of cloth. The cloth was soon soaked through with blood.

They sent her up to the doctor. He smeared some stinging ointment over it, gave it a proper dressing, stroked her cheek, and told her it would all be healed by the time she got married. The doctor was a very kind and sensitive man.

A severe winter followed. There was terrible frost and such a thick fog you couldn't see two steps in front of you. The sky was full of rooks. Then came the snow, burying the streets; trams ground to a halt and even the bus service across Lánchíd, the Chain Bridge, was suspended. It snowed incessantly. The fat policeman woke the local caretakers at crack of dawn and ordered them to sweep the pavements, threatening to report them if they didn't. At five o'clock while everyone was still sleeping Anna was out in her gingham frock, the only thing she wore nowadays, gazing round at the falling lilac-coloured snow. A deep silence lay about her. Sparrows hopped from twig to twig. She broke the ice with an axe, took a spade to the snow and swept the way clear.

There was no one on the streets at that time. By eight though clerks were ambling towards their workplaces in the Vár, cigars in their mouths. Moviszter too ambled downstairs. He wore a winter cap with ear-flaps tied close round his sensitive ears. Sometimes he would stop at the gate and ask her how she was, take her aching thumb in his hand, examine the dirty dressing and declare it needed changing.

Working as she did that winter the wound kept opening up, her hand ached, froze and grew pockmarked, and coal dust settled in the cracks of her skin. All women lose part of their beauty in the winter, but servants grow so ugly that one is hard put to recognize them in their rags after having seen them in kinder weather. Anna too was becoming plain. Her hair was falling out. Every time she combed her hair more tangles remained between the teeth. She didn't want people to see her.

For the first time she began to feel tired, a kind of drunken exhaustion so acute that once she had finished at night she couldn't bear to lie down straightaway but walked about swinging her arms and slapping her shoulders, wandering up and down the corridor and in and out of various rooms. Once Mrs Vizy asked what she was doing in the dark. Anna shuddered. She didn't know what she was doing there or even what the matter was with her.

The young master no longer ate with them, though he was often invited to come whenever he wanted, and particularly on Sundays and other official holidays. He came but once. Some time later Anna spotted him in the window of a coffee house: with a long stick in his hand he was leaning over a green table. That was the last she saw of him.

As the days passed something in her grew numb and

indifferent. She forgot everything that had happened. Yet she continued suffering. For though she had forgotten everything she felt its loss. She was like an animal that lives in the eternal present, an unfed dog who doesn't quite know what ails it and yet keeps wandering back to its empty bowl, sniffs at the rim, and, seeing it is empty, retreats dejected to its kennel, casting the occasional look back.

One evening she was wandering about empty-handed and in a daze before the entrance to the attic.

'Pop in for a second,' said Stefi. 'I want to show you something.'

She brought out a pink dress, a beautiful pink dress that she had made for herself. Blushing with excitement she blurted out the secret: there would be a ball soon, a fête at which some hundred couples would perform the Hungarian Circle Dance for the assembled gentry. The girls would all be well bred, the daughters of solicitors and doctors, and she was included among them, so now she had to attend dancing classes with a very severe instructor. This piece of good luck came her way because she was being courted by a guardsman, a tall ramrod-straight youth of the kind respected by the whole community, and he had put her down as his partner.

Anna listened to her, and Stefi was pleased to have an audience at last. After this she often invited her up. She suggested they should go together to the cinema, it would be all right, Stefi would pay for both of them. Anna hemmed and hawed, said she had nothing to wear, but in the end succumbed to the temptation. It was the first time she had seen a film. Cars sped across the screen, somebody fell into a pond, a count and a countess kissed each other in the garden. Stefi talked about her guardsman. He followed her about constantly but she kept him at arm's length. 'Let him suffer. It doesn't do men any harm, the beasts.' In the meantime she explained the film. She was particularly taken with a thin actor; whenever he appeared she touched Anna's arm. 'See, that's my type. Tall and pale. What's yours?'

143

Anna didn't know what to answer, she didn't even know what she meant. In any case, the moving images and the people in the auditorium confused her. She thanked Stefi for the treat but didn't go again. She had no time anyway.

She spent practically the whole day stoking the stoves. They had a lot of trouble with the heating. The stoves in the flat were deteriorating from day to day. She began on them as soon as she had finished sweeping the snow away. She lit a candle and stumbled down to the cellar. The cellar was deep; the damp ran down the walls and she was over-powered by its stale warmth. She filled two scuttles with coal and didn't dare look round. There were rats here that had tunnelled their way in from the street, they squealed behind the wood-piles and frightened her. The dining room was supposed to be warm for breakfast. She heaped coals on the stove, blew on it, flapped at it with her apron but the fire merely flickered and filled the flat with suffocating smoke. It was like this every blessed day in every room.

Mrs Vizy would often get cross. 'Why don't you call the chimney sweep?'

'He was here yesterday.'

'Mr Báthory?'

'Yes.'

'Then it must be your fault. You're not be using enough kindling.'

Mr Báthory – Árpád Báthory, a stout yeoman with three forenames – lived opposite and did the sweeping in the Krisztina district. He was a regular visitor to the flat, clearing blockages and burning the chimney flues clear. Next day the status quo would be reestablished: lots of smoke and no fire.

On one occasion when her mistress was out she took the initiative herself and called him out. He came at once.

'What's the problem now, Annie girl?'

'I can't get it to light.'

'Well, we'll soon fix that.'

He leaned his ladder against the wall, kicked off his slippers and examined the offending stove barefoot.

'I spend ages on it,' complained Anna.

'Too bad,' the chimneysweep wagged his head, 'Too bad.' He sympathized with her as one workman with another. But he paid no more attention to her: he concentrated entirely on the stove. He shook the grating, tapped the lining and in his curiosity practically stuck his head right in.

'The draught keeps blowing it back,' said Anna.

'Hang on a minute,' he suddenly exclaimed. 'Where's the attic key?'

In the twinkling of an eye Mr Báthory was out on the snow-covered roof and skilfully and powerfully making his way up to the ridge. He was like a cat. He stood beside the chimney stack with his broom, black against white, a black tom cat. He was fussing with the ventilation flap. Anna was watching him from the courtyard. Soon he came down the attic steps.

'Were you not afraid up there?' she asked him.

'What is there to be afraid of?'

They went back together into the flat. She wanted to light the fire again.

'Leave it,' the sweep advised her. He reached into the still hot stove with his vast hands, emptied it out and lit it himself with a sheet of newspaper.

They squatted and watched the flames licking the walls of the stove and the shower of sparks crackling and rising.

'It'll burn all right,' said Mr Báthory and stood up. They waited for the kindling to heat through before he piled some coal on as well. He knew just how much to put on without stifling it. After a couple of minutes they could hear the coal snapping and yielding to the flames. They warmed their hands at it. Warm air billowed from the stove. The iron door began to glow.

'Well,' laughed Mr Báthory, his teeth bright against his dark face. 'What did I say?'

'Thank you.'

'My pleasure, Miss Annie. Any time. Call whenever you need me.'

145

All three chimneys in the Vizys' flat were merrily pouring their smoke into the sulphur-yellow sky. Every so often Mr Báthory would enquire if everything was all right.

'Does it burn?'

'It burns.'

'Just as well. So it should.'

On Wednesday a heavy rain swept across the town, the wind bellowed and the house shook. The Vérmező field outside was as storm tossed as the Balaton in winter when one couldn't see the shore.

Mrs Vizy went to the spiritualist. Anna warmed herself by the fire and listened to the storm. Golden embers breathed and collapsed in showers of diamonds. The stove's iron door stared at her with its five red eyes.

Somebody quietly knocked at the outside door. When Anna opened it she found the chimney sweep waiting.

'You frightened me!' she whispered.

'Me?'

'Yes.'

'Why?'

'You're so black.'

The sweep stood in the corridor in his black trousers and belt, the black spade on his shoulder, the black rope in his hand.

'How can you get so black?' exclaimed Anna, half frightened, half smiling. 'You look like the devil.'

'Come now,' Mr Báthory joked, 'we're not so wicked.'

He came in. His chain clanked in the half-light.

'Is nobody at home?' he asked. He moved towards the light of the kitchen. He had big blue eyes, quite improbably large eyes, like an actor in make-up.

'What are you doing?'

'I was going to bake some rolls. And you?'

'I thought I'd drop in.' But he remained standing at the kitchen door.

Anna took a tray and put in leaven, butter, sugar and salt. She poured warm milk over it and sprinkled flour on. She

146

started mixing it. The sweep watched her working. He stood for a long time watching her then said, 'I'll have to be going.'

'You're in a hurry?'

'I have to get home and see if my daughter's there. She tends to stray everywhere.'

'When did your wife die?'

'Two years ago. In the autumn.'

'What did she die of?'

'She was consumptive.'

Anna put down the wooden spoon and fell to musing, like someone reading a good book, full of life.

'The girl needs someone to look after her,' said the sweep. 'I can't manage it. It needs a woman.'

'You'll find one. How old are you?'

'Thirty-five.'

'You're young yet. And you make a good living.'

'I've had offers. There's one now. A widow in the Erzsébet district. She has a small house.'

'There you are then.'

'But somehow I don't fancy her. Now if it were you . . .'

'Stop messing about,' she cut him off sharply, without a trace of coquetry. She didn't feel like being praised because she knew she didn't look pretty.

Something in her attracted the sweep: it might have been her unhappiness and this sudden pain, since a man will always sniff out the degraded, exploited quality in a woman and often find it more alluring than beauty itself. He leaned against the doorpost. He waited for Anna to finish moulding the pastry in the baking tray.

'I must be going now,' he repeated.

'You really had better be going, Mr Báthory. They'll be home any minute.'

Báthory didn't stay to argue the toss. Once he met her in the street, by chance, and mentioned again in a general way, that really he needed a woman round the place, yes a woman. Then, as was proper, he sent a message, by Mrs Ficsor, that he would gladly take Anna for his wife if she were willing.

147

The caretaker's wife positively put herself out to accede to his request. She spoke to the girl, told her how lucky she was and that not for the world should she allow such an opportunity to slip by, she praised the sweep as a sober hard-working man who had been very good to his first wife. Anna didn't say no but asked for time to think. Báthory for his part asked her to come over and take a look at his home.

On her day off he met her at the Vérmező and escorted her to his flat on the fourth floor, ushering her into a room overlooking the courtyard. A cold wintery moonlight trembled on the frosted window, and gave their bodies a metallic, rather deathly appearance as they stepped into the dark room. They stood some distance from each other. Anna went straight over to the window and looked out. She could see the Vizys' house and recognized a tree, then her own window and marvelled at how small it seemed from up here. The sweep lit the spirit-lamp and hung it on the wall beside the window.

The room was full of things. Two large cupboards, two beds together with bedding, all the necessaries, a settee, a kitchen cabinet, a table. Mr Báthory opened the cupboards. He showed her the white linen, washed and apparently untouched – six blouses, three underskirts, three nightgowns – one bright-red Himalayan scarf. He spoke to her with great respect. Anna fell to thinking and a faint thrill of happiness ran through her.

Later the daughter came home, a scowling fourteen-year-old adolescent in muddy open shoes. Her father told her to say hello so she did so then sat down in a corner. Anna cooked supper, potatoes in paprika. The three of them ate it quietly.

The sweep escorted her downstairs. 'What do you think?' he asked anxiously.

'I haven't decided yet.'

Mr Báthory emphasized that it was a matter of urgency.

'Let's leave it for now. We'll talk about it after the holidays,' answered Anna. So they left it at that.

Just before the holidays, when she was at her busiest

making poppyseed and groundnut cakes, her brother, whom she had not seen for five years since the French took him prisoner, appeared. He had grown up and had even grown a moustache. He had a whip in his hand. He had driven up from the *puszta* and had a present for the masters of the house. He asked how she was, then went away again.

It was a spectacular Christmas in the house. The Drumas were the first to receive the herald with the gifts, mostly for the baby. Stefi received a gold wristwatch and Etel a bolt of canvas from the Moviszters.

The Vizys were the last to light the Christmas tree having invited the Moviszters and Drumas for the occasion. The honourable lady and his excellency kissed each other. Mrs Vizy surprised her husband with a cigar-case; he bought her twenty-four handkerchiefs, as he did every year. The mistress handed Anna her present. It was wrapped in fine tissue paper.

It was a waistcoat, a hardy brown woollen waistcoat. They gave it to her so she would not be cold sweeping the snow.

As Anna unwrapped it by candlelight, Mrs Druma nudged Mrs Moviszter. She recognized the vest. It had been Katica's present previously, and she had worn it too, but when she was dismissed she had contemptuously left it behind.

16

Matter, Spirit and Soul

At Epiphany, the Vizys were returning from tea at the Tatárs where two ministers of state had been among the guests. On arriving home the woman suddenly stopped before the kitchen door.

In the kitchen sat a stranger, a man she didn't recognize. He was seated at the table and beside him – though some distance away – was Anna. On noticing her the unknown man respectfully stood up and bid her good evening.

She could see him more clearly now that the lamp illuminated his pale face and silky blond hair. He wore a light grey suit and a long tie. Mrs Vizy stared at him in growing uncertainty, trying to place him in her memory.

'I see your ladyship doesn't recognize me,' said the man in a not unpleasant baritone voice and smiled. 'I'm the chimneysweep.'

'So it's you. I see. I didn't recognize you. I've never seen you like this, Mr Báthory. Good evening.'

The uninvited guest did not trouble them for long. He waited for the mistress of the house to go in, then, after a little hesitation, long enough not to make it seem as if he were running away, he quietly left.

Now Mrs Vizy saw what was afoot. She shook her head in disbelief. She wouldn't have credited it. She had never imagined that someone else had an interest in Anna, or could have an interest in a creature that belonged so intimately to her; that anyone at all might simply come in and sit down at her table. It was all so unpleasant and indelicate, a clear usurpation of her domain, as if she had found the chimneysweep calmly smoking his pipe, sprawled across the white couch in her bedroom. The impertinence of it stung her but she didn't say anything. She broached the subject gently.

'Tell me, Anna, does this man often call on you?'

'He looks in sometimes.'

'What do you mean "sometimes"? You mean this wasn't the first time? He has been here before?'

'Yes.'

'How often?'

'Now and then.'

'I don't like it. You know I don't. A strange man in my home. It isn't done anywhere in the world.'

'He calls. I can't chase him away.'

'Come, come, that's not the way things work.'

'As far as I'm concerned he can stay at home.'

'Then why don't you tell him so? Why not?'

'I can't, your ladyship.'

'In that case I'll tell him. You have other things to do.'

'Tell him if you like. It really doesn't matter to me.'

Mrs Vizy talked with the chimneysweep and he didn't call again, but the matter didn't end there. While Anna was cooking she would keep nagging her. 'Was he courting you?'

'He'd talk to me.'

'He has filled your head with talk. He wants to turn your head.'

'Where's the butter, your ladyship?'

'There on the windowsill. Careful, Anna, be very careful. He'll muddle up your life. What sort of things does he say?'

'Once he said . . .' But at that point she went to the sink to run some water into the jug so Mrs Vizy didn't hear the rest of the sentence.

'So, what did he say?' she persisted once Anna had put the jug on the stove.

'He said he didn't have anybody.'

151

'Nothing else?'

'And that he needed a woman round the place.'

'Interesting. And what did you say?'

'Nothing.'

'That was wise. It's ridiculous. He's not for you.'

Anna openly admitted she was right, and probably thought so in her heart of hearts, but since her mistress gave no reasons she was disturbed.

The news that Anna had an admirer did not remain a secret: the whole house got to hear about it and there were two clear opinions on the matter. Mr Báthory had taken care to secure some advocates in his absence in order to sway public opinion. First and foremost he depended on the servants. Mrs Ficsor, to whom he had promised a present if Anna could be brought round, was undoubtedly on his side. She in her turn converted Stefi to the cause and Stefi encouraged Anna to get smart and not to be so choosy or she would end up like her, unmarried and still a servant at thirty-two. The Moviszters' maid, Etel, was not absolutely convinced. She admitted that a wedding would probably be nice but laughed and asked why a servant should get married; one is much happier as a single girl. The Durmas were firmly against a marriage. Mrs Moviszter retained a benevolent disinterest and waited to see how things would turn out.

Everyone was full of advice. One urged Anna to hurry, another warned her against a hasty and fraught decision since she had plenty of time. Anna's ears rang; she was almost deafened by advice, and when she tried to gauge her own feelings she found that more than anything she wanted to be left in peace. Let them decide between then. She loathed the whole affair. She always agreed with whoever spoke to her last.

It's impossible to say which was the telling blow, who had spoken to her most recently, who had not, or which of all the conflicting pieces of advice she finally listened to; one day, however, it happened.

Anna was peeling potatoes when quite calmly and simply she told her mistress that she should look for another girl, since she was going to get married as soon as possible, as soon as a new maid could take over, preferably by the fifteenth of the month, or if that were not possible, by the first of the next. The notice was formal but not unfriendly.

Mrs Vizy said nothing to dissuade her yet, but acknowledged the notice as formally as it was given. She gave Anna a long hard stare, as if she were a stranger, then proudly marched out of the kitchen.

The blow was not unexpected, since it had been in the air for weeks, but perhaps it was all the more terrible for that.

Anna had been with her almost six months, longer than any previous maid. She had grown so used to her she couldn't begin to imagine anyone else in her place, either better, or worse. She didn't even look for anybody. After the first excitement she surrendered to a fatalistic impotence, some groundless hope which was only strengthened by her visits to the spiritualist. At a seance she asked her guardian spirit, in a rather indirect manner, what she should do; the answer came that what she feared would 'under no circumstances come to pass' and that in the meantime she should 'act in a stern manner'. This reassured her.

Shortly after this she fell ill. Her husband found her one day at noon, lying in the darkened bedroom with a cold compress on her head. A beetroot smell emanated from an open medicine bottle. Her illness, which recurred at longer or shorter intervals, always took the form of an attack. Suddenly, without warning, she was seized by a weeping fit, her head began to throb.and could not be soothed for hours at a time, not until her upset stomach forced her to vomit. This then relieved the condition and the headache slowly passed away. The doctors called this 'hysteria' but could do nothing about it.

Vizy didn't even greet her. He threw a disapproving glance in her direction then turned his back on her. His wife's illness tended to anger rather than frighten him. He took it as a personal insult that she dared to be ill.

In the afternoon the patient's condition grew worse; she

was moaning and wailing, and clapping her hands together, then, after a very long time, she began to be sick. Anna kept bringing her the bowl.

The doctor could only come once surgery was finished. He glumly hung up his coat and went into the bedroom, first adopting his more benign social expression. When he lit the small electric lamp on the beside table the patient complained that she couldn't bear the light and took one of the many handkerchiefs which lay about her to cover her eyes up tightly.

The first thing Moviszter did was to suggest that they should open the window, since the room was very stuffy. Vizy stood at the head of the bed ready for action. He addressed his wife as 'angel', the name she was given as a girl and the one he always used when there were strangers present. He solicitously asked after her health. The doctor chided his patient. He took her hands in his and held them for some time without saying anything. Having taken her pulse he also measured her temperature. He nodded: there was no fever, everything was all right.

Then, so it should look as if he were doing something, he gave her the usual examination. He uncovered her body and looked it over. He knew it well enough; as a piano tuner knows a frequently tuned piano, every key and hammer was familiar to him; but he also knew that the mechanism wasn't everything, that in order for the keys and hammers to function it needed the agency of music or life or some other force, since this tangible self-contained object was only part of a bigger scheme of things, from which it could not be isolated as easily as it might appear, since it was not a fully independent or foreign body but one whose fate was tied to everything else that lived on earth or in heaven. He sceptically went through the ritual as he had done so many times before. He pressed her stomach, poked at her liver and kidneys, asked her to sit up and breathe deeply; he listened to her lungs, tapped at her heart and politely thanked her for each effort.

Her husband practically held his breath throughout the

examination in order to facilitate the doctor's task. Vizy belonged to that rank of educated twentieth-century men whose blind trust in medicine – which was taught at university and diplomas in which were usually awarded by the same scientific body as awarded his own – equalled that of any religious zealot. He regarded doctors as superior beings who knew more than he did about himself, so he tended to perceive them in a peculiarly mystical light. He watched Moviszter's movements with due reverence. When the doctor shook the thermometer and the button on his cuff rattled, he thought it was the official medical rattle of the thermometer. The rubber tube of the stethoscope and the bell of the listening device awoke a similar awe in him. He waited in anticipation of the moment when the doctor who was bent over his wife would suddenly cry out that, there and then, he had finally arrived at the root of the problem.

On the contrary.

'I can't see anything wrong,' said Moviszter.

'It's not her stomach?'

'Nothing wrong with that.'

'Her lungs.'

'Functioning perfectly.'

'What about her heart?'

'Her heart is in excellent shape.'

'What should she eat?'

'Whatever she fancies.'

'What about a light soup?' Vizy suggested helpfully.

'That'll do.'

'Is there no prescription?'

'I could write you one,' Moviszter said in an abstracted tone. He did write one. Vizy continued solicitously. 'I'll send down for it straight away.'

'It's not so urgent.' Moviszter gave the prescription to the patient. 'If you would be so good as to take ten drops of this with a cube of sugar. You can take up to fifteen if you're unhappy, but only then. You should rest and enjoy yourself. Is your head still aching? See – it has stopped. I told you there was nothing wrong.'

He put out his hand to say goodbye.

'Her problem is that . . .' and Vizy glanced at his wife, 'Angel, would you mind if I revealed your secret? Her problem is that she is highly strung. Her maid has given notice and is getting married . . .'

'I see,' said Moviszter.

'This had been preying on her nerves for a week now. She can't sleep.'

'Do you seriously mean that?' asked the doctor.

'It's certainly not very nice,' croaked Mrs Vizy. 'I trained her up and now she is going.'

'It's often the case.'

'It's because they are ungrateful and have no conscience. I laboured six months with her, wasted all that time. Was it worth it?'

'Look here, madam. I have a patient who is seventy-six years old and who has just started to learn English. By the time she has learned it she will probably be dying. But let us suppose she doesn't die just yet, that she survives until she is a hundred – she will die having learned English. Will that have been worth it? Is it worth it for us to start on anything even at the age of twenty? Of course it is: one has to fill in the time somehow.'

'Of course she was a very good servant. But she has gone mad,' Mrs Vizy whispered, 'quite mad, doctor.'

'Of course she hasn't gone mad. She is going to get married, that's all. Let her get on with it. You'll find someone else.'

'One like her? Never.'

'All right, not like her. Let's assume you find one not quite as good.'

'She'll steal from me.'

'So she steals from you. Believe me it is not good for a servant to be too good. Let her be like the rest, both good and bad.'

'Like your Etel? Forgive me doctor but I would not tolerate someone like her in my home. I always wonder how you . . .'

'I am not exactly in love with her either. She is sometimes rude, even to my patients. Last week she told one off for not wiping his feet. But what can I do? They all have some fault. It's natural. One just has to accept it. They're not in an enviable position. They go to great trouble and wear themselves out and the nature of their work is such that they cannot even enjoy the fruits of their labour, since as soon as it is done it disappears: others eat it, or we ruin it and make it dirty, and it is we, we who do that. Then let it be a consolation to them that they can be just a little remiss. We should try to understand.'

'But I do understand,' Mrs Vizy nodded, the tears that had gathered at her lashes just beginning to brighten. 'There's just one thing I can't understand. Tell me, dear doctor, why are they such utter pigs?'

The doctor saw that he was talking into a vacuum so he didn't even bother to answer but grumbled, 'Of course, of course. As I was saying, ten to fifteen drops . . .'

Mrs Vizy cast him a furious glance as he was leaving. She decided never again to call down that old ass.

But her husband, who had escorted Moviszter out, said on his return, 'The doctor is right, quite right. There is nothing wrong with you. Why are you holding your hand to your head?'

'Does it bother you?'

'Very much. I spend the whole day in the office worrying about one thing or another and when I came home you treat me to this. It's sheer pettiness. You'll find another servant and that's the end of it.'

'But can't you get it into your head that it is her and only her I need?'

'You exaggerate. You're always exaggerating. She's a sound girl, I admit that, but you can't ultimately force anyone to do anything. You must let her go.'

'Under no circumstances will I let that girl go!'

'What do you think you can do? You can stand on your head if you like, you won't stop her. Must you do this to me now, just when I am most busy? I have had it up to here

157

with this servant business for once and for all, the devil take them. Let her go to hell.'

'Don't scream at me!'

'You stop screaming then. It's ridiculous. Do you really think that nobody else is capable of doing what she does?'

'No!' screamed the woman on her knees in her nightgown and waving her arms. 'No! No one can do what she does.'

'You are abnormal,' retorted Vizy, staring at his wife who, having frightened herself, lay down again. 'You are quite abnormal.'

'And you are as rude, as coarse, as a horse-blanket, that's how coarse and nasty you are. You've been like that to me your whole life, so coarse . . . so nasty . . .'

The woman kept wiping away her slow tears with one or other of the many handkerchiefs around her. Vizy sat down and picked his nose. He listened to her railing at him, patient and submissive as an errant husband doing penance for his unfaithfulness. But then the telephone rang and he hurried to his desk. Cupping the mouthpiece in his hand he talked quietly to somebody, answering merely yes or no, then he took his coat and went out.

Mrs Vizy was left alone in the big flat. She continued sniffling for a while then growing tired stared straight ahead of her.

Then Anna was suddenly standing by the bed.

'I've only come to see,' she trembled, 'if there's anything your ladyship would like?'

The woman didn't answer. Since Anna had given in her notice she hadn't said a word to her, she hated her so much she couldn't even bear to look at her.

Anna hesitated in the air of loathing: she felt its cold envelop her. She felt sorry for the honourable lady, because she was ill and was suffering, and because she might have been the cause.

Mrs Vizy sighed. She felt that the ugly atmosphere had lightened somewhat, and the girl was waiting because she didn't want to go. She adjusted her pillow and in a scolding but calm voice spoke to her.

158

'So, you have come to your senses?'

By way of answer the girl bowed her head. Mrs Vizy's speech was carefully broken up.

'Because I have to know . . . One scene like this is enough for me, I don't want another . . . I can't keep you . . . You are within your rights . . . you can go . . . leave me here alone in the middle of winter . . . One cannot force anybody . . . If you don't like it here it's perfectly all right for you to go . . . Though I don't understand you . . . What was wrong here . . . ? Did anyone harm you . . . ? Didn't you get enough to eat . . . ? Do you need more money . . . ? Your wages are in the savings bank . . . they're piling up . . . why don't you say anything . . . ? You can take your money out whenever you want . . . you can buy something quite expensive with that amount . . . or do you want a rise . . . ? I'm perfectly prepared to discuss that too . . . What do you want?'

Anna took a step forward. The moment had arrived, Mrs Vizy saw, for her to break down that last shred of resistance. The spirit was speaking to her, telling her to be stern, quite stern.

'You don't know what you want yourself . . . Do you believe this half-wit who has robbed you of your reason . . .? I know his type . . . They promise you everything then leave you . . . He doesn't even earn enough to keep you . . . How do they survive . . . ? Where do they live . . . ? Do you want to rot your life away in a slum . . . ? Such people only want a servant, a free servant who will wash for them . . . they don't even pay wages . . . they want a fool, not a wife . . . Perhaps if he were young, this sweep of yours . . . but he isn't even that . . . a widower . . . His daughter is as big as you are . . . I know the little bitch . . . She'll scratch your eyes out . . . You want to be a stepmother . . . ? Oh, I've seen this happen before . . . I've had servants before who got married . . . they soon came back, saying how their husbands beat them, how they came home drunk, or unemployed, and ah! bless your ladyship, if only I could come back to my old job here . . . They begged me . . . But once they leave here I won't have them back . . . So what will

159

become of you . . . ? Where will you go . . . ? Home . . . ? You can go to the Jews . . . to some Jew who will . . . What did you say?'

The girl whispered something, smiling. Mrs Vizy launched a last, milder assault.

'Don't ruin your life, don't waste your youth . . . that blessed youth . . . you will bitterly regret it . . . Listen to someone wiser . . . more experienced . . . If it were something worthwhile that would be different . . . But this . . . ? There'll be others . . . later . . . who would make you a good husband, with our blessing . . . I am not going to force you . . . Just think it over once more, for the last time . . . Tell me tomorrow . . . But think over carefully first . . .'

Anna ran her fingers over her hair. 'I have made my decision.'

'Then you're staying?'

'I'm staying.'

Exhausted by her battle Mrs Vizy slumped back on her pillow.

'Would your ladyship like some supper?'

'Nothing,' she said. 'Perhaps a little preserve. I haven't eaten a thing in two days.'

Anna skipped away to serve her, happier than ever. She brought a bottle of Spanish cherries. Mrs Vizy noticed the writing on the label. It was Katica's spiky scrawl.

'This is last year's. Katica made this,' she said. For the first time in a long time she thought about Katica. While she was spooning up the dark-red liquid and spitting the stones out into the saucer, her mind dwelt on the last maid, whose entire bodily strength seemed to have been concentrated in this stoppered jar which, being opened, exploded, expelling the trapped energy. The cherries lasted a few more days. Whenever she ate them certain images flashed across her mind but once the label had been discarded in the waste-bin they no longer troubled her.

In any case there was blessed peace. Anna went across to the sweep of her own accord, and gave her refusal in such a forthright manner that he was quite insulted, and within

160

a fortnight had married the widow from Erzsébetváros, who had a little house of her own. Anna wasn't too upset. When asked whether she had made the right decision she answered that she might well have.

There was less excitement in the house. Even Stefi was no longer minded to argue the toss. She went about in low spirits. There had been some unpleasantness in her life too. Having learned the circle dance and even bought herself some lacquered shoes for the ball where she should have danced with the daughters of gentlefolk, she received a letter from the organizing committee, 'most regretfully having to dispense' with 'her services'.

Anna's conversation value declined daily. She became so much a part of the day-to-day household that she practically disappeared: no one noticed her, no one talked about her. Like many servants she began unconsciously to imitate her mistress. She picked up precisely Mrs Vizy's manner of smoothing her hair, and when she answered the telephone even acquaintances were sometimes hard put to it to know whether it was the maid or mistress whose voice they heard.

17

Carnival

The daily post was brought to József Elekes in the currency section by one of the porters; it consisted of a single item edged in black. He opened it and was so shaken by the contents he almost dropped the announcement.

Framed in black, in heavy block letters, stood the name of the deceased, his best friend, János Pátikarius.

He hadn't heard anything of him for months. Without a word to anyone, he had simply disappeared from the bank from one day to the next; he had given no notice; his name was excised from the roll of clerks. All they were able to say at his bachelor flat was that he had gone away somewhere. The Vizys thought he was in Vienna, but he had written neither to them nor to anyone else.

The announcement read:

> Ferenc Patikárius and his wife, *née* Terézia
> Jámbor, are joined in their grief by all their
> relatives, in most sorrowfully announcing
> that their only son
> JÁNOS PATIKÁRIUS
> has, on the sixteenth day of February 1920,
> quit this life
> of all solemn pursuits and intends henceforth
> to live only to amuse himself and others,
> for which reason this gayest of corpses takes

this unoriginal opportunity to invite his friends
on the day named above
at precisely twelve o'clock midnight,
at The Club des Parisiens,
to a long and hearty rout of champagne
where they may assist him in ceremoniously
interring all their cares.
Good humour is compulsory. Down with gloom!

Ashes to ashes. RIP

Elekes leant against a safe for support in his astonishment and kept turning the card over in his hand. This joke was really too much. In his terror a faint grin flashed across his face. He read the announcement through again, this time in admiration, marvelling at the ever more daring refinements and delicacies of the text. The blighter had him properly fooled this time.

Jancsi arrived that day on the Vienna express. From the station he took a cab straight to the Danubian Restaurant overlooking the river and occupied a room on the first floor. He took a bath and went to dine in the restaurant. The estate agent he had summoned by telegram was already waiting at his table. They quickly tied up the deal. Jancsi signed some statement to the effect that his flat, together with all fittings and furnishings, should be passed over freehold, in return for which the fellow immediately showed the colour of his money and Jancsi carelessly stuffed the great wad of dollars into his wallet. It was a real fast deal, big business USA style. They pressed flesh on it.

After the brilliance and sheer size of Vienna, its poor little cousin Budapest seemed so intimate that Jancsi began to feel quite sentimental. It was a mild, dreamy afternoon, idyllic and fresh, a winter afternoon when one's appetite for life is keener than ever. The town was covered in a coat of crisp snow. Snow had settled on the manes of the lions at the entrance to the Chain Bridge: they looked as though they were wearing white headscarves. Skates jingled in

163

women's hands as they hurried to ice-rinks, sleighbells tinkled. The frost, severe yet healthy, brought a glow to people's faces. Chandeliers sparkled in the Gerbeaud *konditorei* and Váci utca and Crown Prince utca, and all the old nineteenth-century streets of the city centre were aglow with shops and window displays where everything seemed more desirable, more entrancing than ever before: the shoes, the books, the flasks of mineral water arranged on a mossy rock beside a miniature fountain, the jars of quince jelly, the little piles of hazelnuts and walnuts, and the heaps of tasty, still moist Tunisian dates, everything suggesting a distant childhood and memories of presents and Santa Claus. The whole theatrical spectacle was aided and abetted by the sky which changed momently. First it loomed apple green behind Mount Gellért, then it blushed a deep pink over the Royal Palace, then again it melted into a soft ashen grey which was quickly pierced by the tiny powerful winter stars.

In the evening the Vizys had a lady visitor. The maid led her into the sitting room where she sat and waited while Mrs Vizy quickly changed her clothes in order to receive her.

The visitor drew the otter fur tightly about her as she waited. She seemed to feel the cold. As soon as her hostess entered she began chattering in a high bird-like twitter, addressing her with the familiarity of her class. She spoke about Mr Vizy whom she knew through the ministry, and about the Patikáriuses whom she had met in Eger, generally continuing to cluck and peer at the lady of the house through her lorgnette.

Mrs Vizy regarded her with some reserve. At first it was hard to tell what she wanted. She thought she might have been a member of one of those committees so popular nowadays which were for ever recruiting and trying to raise money for vague charitable causes. She kept dropping the name of a countess. She babbled quietly in a generalizing and perfunctory manner which suggested something bogus. Her green shoes and silk stockings peeped from beneath the fur. Later she removed her feather boa, opened her coat and

164

revealed her flat, powdered chest and dinner gown, which was a conventional silk piece, richly embroidered with golden pearls.

Mrs Vizy was just answering some question and, her suspicions aroused, was on the point of asking her to provide some proof of her identity when she changed her mind. Instead she took one more glance at her, stepped over and snatched off her hat to reveal a scraggy wig of roughly the same blonde colour as her own hair.

'You scoundrel,' she said. 'What are you doing here?'

'I'm off to a fancy dress-ball, Aunt Angéla. May I kiss your hand?'

'Where have you come from?'

'Vienna. Tell me,' he asked his aunt as he paraded round the room slightly raising the fur coat to reveal his legs, 'don't you think I'd make a pretty girl?'

'Oh yes. Very ornamental. Your poor father has no idea what has happened to you. What are you doing in Vienna?'

'Business.'

'You're a dealer?'

'In coal. Do you need any? How many wagons would you like?'

'Idiot. How long are you staying in Budapest?'

'Just for the day. I'm off again tomorrow morning. How are you anyway? And Uncle Kornél?'

'Haven't you heard? He is to be an under-secretary of state.'

'Congratulations. Perhaps he could do something about the state. If Uncle Kornél comes to Vienna he must definitely look me up. I have a nice flat in Rothenturm Strasse, number one. Well, I must go, Aunt Angéla, my friends are waiting for me, Elekes, the whole gang. 'Bye for now. Allow me to kissa-da-handa.'

'You're not going out into the street like that?'

'There's a car waiting for me.'

'Look after yourself, Jancsi dear,' Mrs Vizy advised him. 'And do write to your poor father.'

He entered the Club des Parisiens through a side door.

He was surprised to see how mean these side entrances could be. Some coats and canes were hanging on the rack, the waiters were still in their shirt sleeves, combing their hair. The proprietor himself came to greet him. He knew he was expecting a Viennese coal magnate. Bowing very low he ushered him into the curtained private room where they had set ten places for him as arranged. They discussed the rest of the arrangements in German. Jancsi, having asked for bouquets to be placed on the table and for a waiter to be assigned to their sole use, examined the menu. It was all in order. His final request was that the guests should be shown into the room and that his own presence should not be revealed to anyone.

He put on his black silk mask and stepped into the dance hall. The club was in full swing. The jazz band was roaring away though only a few couples were actually dancing. The staff released thirty huge balloons which slowly drifted upward in the opalescent light then settled by the arc-lights wreathed in coloured crêpe-paper, quite close to the ceiling, whence they stared down as if in mild surprise. Slowly the other masqueraders began arriving. Pierrot with his Pierrette, a single gypsy girl, a peasant in boots carrying a steel hoe and some needle-grass, a green-haired jester and another with red hair, the usual red noses, mandarin moustaches and grey beards, fool's caps with bells and paper shakos. The greatest sensation was created by a well-known fat stockbroker who appeared in a blood-red executioner's outfit, in a blood-red hood and blood-red mask, carrying an enormous executioner's axe.

Jancsi stood in a corner, observing from behind his fan as the seething human mass grew ever thicker. He sought his pals, the nine invited guests. At first he could only discover Elekes, in a long frock-coat but without a mask, who was accompanied by a blonde pussycat. It was already becoming difficult to dance. The floor was so crowded that couples could not move vertically, leaning against each other. He was swept into their midst. A man he didn't know invited him. He lost his partner in the confusion somewhere near the band. Elekes happened to be loitering there and put his arms around him, swept him on and, holding him tightly, watching his eyes shining through the holes of the mask, took him through one or two rough tours of the floor and squeezed his hands in his own pleasantly damp lukewarm palms. The whole thing was so peculiar that after this Jancsi himself took the opportunity of picking partners, men and women alternately.

By this time he could hardly wait for supper so that he could relax among his old neglected friends. At midnight, when everyone removed masks, he looked around. Under the masks were the faces of strangers. He took off his own and his wig and, unbuttoning his dress, headed for the private room.

Those gentlemen who having waved their black-edged announcements had been admitted and seated by the waiters, greeted their host with great glee, while he in his motley costume glared at them in mock disapproval. Elekes smothered him with kisses, the others raised his skirt and fumbled at his breasts. There were four of them altogether. Apart from Elekes there was Dani Töttösi, Pista Indali to whom he was bound by a vague sense of comradeship because they had attended so many parties together, and Gallovich who held an enormous ox-head in his hands and who was a rather distant acquaintance he didn't even mean to invite. Those on whom he most counted, the people from the bank, had not turned up at all. This depressed him. He quickly changed and played the proper host and rang his five missing friends but was told in every case that the gentlemen were not at home.

They waited for them a long time but eventually they had to make a start on the supper. There was plenty of eating and drinking: clear soup in a cup, pike-perch (from the Balaton) suprême, roast turkey with Californian plums, and top quality Badacsony and Rajna wines. The *maître d'hôtel* brought in buckets of icy French champagne, lightly sprinkled over with snow.

Jancsi sat at the head of the table; to his left – and closest to his heart – sat Elekes with his beautifully parted hair, his monocle and his creole complexion, to whom he confided his latest adventures, his head practically resting on his chest. Having not spoken his mother tongue for some time he was particularly talkative. All those things he had for months been wanting to say tumbled out of him for the benefit of his audience. He was wallowing in money, not only the dollars he had earned as a result of selling his flat, but two hundred more dollars on top of that, as well as Austrian bills and bonds and devalued Hungarian thousand-kroner notes. He told them how he lived in a five-room flat with his lover, a Polish dancer called Daisy, who helped him conduct his business affairs. From his wallet he pulled a signed and dedicated photo of the showgirl in question and several letters from her in German, just as proof. These were passed from hand to hand. It was certainly convincing.

Gallovich, the repulsive Gallovich, kept annoying him though.

'You keep her, eh Jancsi? How? Like you keep fleas?'

Jancsi bore this for a while then with a withering look he growled at him, 'I like a flea, especially the twittering kind,' and turned his head away.

The supper wasn't going as he had imagined. Hardly had they eaten the carnival doughnuts when strangers started appearing. Gallovich introduced one of his friends who sat down with them and started drinking. When it came to the *parfait* two women gatecrashed the party and threw confetti at Jancsi. He had a sawdust taste in his mouth after that.

When the tables had been cleared and once the headwaiter had passed round the cigars and cigarettes, lighting them with a flickering candle, Elekes drew Jancsi aside. Jancsi was happy to let him have fifty dollars. Töttösi and Indali were also given something and they went off to dance. The blonde pussycat, a little *demi-mondaine* with freckles showing through her yellow make-up, put her head round the door looking for Elekes. Gallovich filled the girls' glasses with champagne, and amused them by occasionally donning the big ox-head.

Round about dawn the bounder had the glasses taken over to another table where he continued drinking with his female entourage, leaving Jancsi on his own. The place was full of unfamiliar faces, which was not surprising since the clientele of the bar changed from week to week.

Elekes, his collar soaked through, returned from the dance floor. Jancsi grabbed his hand and wouldn't let go.

'In vain,' he sighed, 'in vain . . .'

'The rain in Spain falls mainly in the plain . . .' Elekes continued.

Jancsi shut up. He didn't know what else to say. He had said everything there was to say about his successes, his dollars, his five-room flat, Daisy and all. He felt a kind of dissatisfaction. You can't say anything to take the wind out of these fellows' sails.

He rubbed his forehead with his dry hands.

'Here, Elekes,' he said suddenly. 'I did have another friend here. Someone you knew nothing about. When I first arrived in Pest.'

'The actress?'

'No. Right time, wrong girl. Do you know who she was? A servant.'

'Tut-tut.'

'Here, Elekes; a servant, a common servant,' and he stood up, shouting at the top of his voice in order to be heard above the saxophone. 'What a peach though! Lovely skin. A virgin.'

'Really?'

'Here, old man; she was a housemaid, her heels were cracked. She was dirty and ugly. But she was hot stuff, by God, she was.'

Elekes leaned on the divan fiddling with his silver cigarette case. He was bored with his friend and was pleased when the blonde pussycat reappeared from behind the curtain and asked him to dance.

'Elekes!' roared Jancsi, as loudly as he could. 'Elekes!' and he held out his arms in supplication.

But his voice was lost. The drums in the jazzband were

beating wildly: it might have been a military court-martial preparing for execution at dawn.

He remained standing for a while, his arms stretched out, then collapsed into his chair. He was quite alone, the room was empty, he had nothing left. The thought of the gang filled him with loathing. He groped his way to the toilets and let the water run on his head. On his way back down the corridor he asked the headwaiter for the bill. The waiter did his sums with lightning speed. The total was so vast that it quite sobered him up. Jancsi warned the headwaiter that he was not drunk. They got into an argument about the amount of champagne that had been consumed. The owner gathered up all the empty bottles and explained that the gentlemen had entertained ladies at other tables too. There was also disagreement about the dollar's rate of exchange, at which point they produced last night's edition of the *Pester Lloyd* as evidence. Jancsi threw them the money.

It was a quarter past five by the time he arrived back at the hotel. After he had paid this bill too he had practically no money left. He told the porter to send his luggage over to the station, for the eight o'clock to Vienna.

He didn't go to bed but decided to get a breath of fresh air on the embankment. He walked down the length of the deserted Rákoczi út. There wasn't a soul about. How dark Pest was compared to Vienna! He was growing bored again and started looking for a coffee house, but there weren't any open. He struck out for the Jozsefváros district, ambling down those crooked parallel streets he had always liked exploring. This was dead too: no traffic, no music. They were sweeping up in a few corner bars where the streetgirls who had weathered the frosty night sipped their little milky coffees. Only the most desperate or the most hard-working whore still cruised the streets.

Jancsi wandered down one of these narrow streets which seemed to lead him on and on, his face turned up to the sky, whistling into the air. The sky, which in the afternoon had been filled with miraculous colours, was now almost black with snow-clouds. Rime was slowly gathering on the fur collar of his overcoat. Somewhere, about halfway down the street, opposite a vacant lot that had been empty for years, a woman was still standing in front of a slum tenement; not a young woman but a woman past forty, leaning against the gatepost with an expression of subhuman boredom on her broad and heavy face. Her hands, which had once pickled gherkins for a living, were hanging at her sides. The surprising thing about her was that she was wearing an apron and a patterned peasant headscarf. Her folksy appearance suggested domestic bliss and was calculated to awaken someone's unsatisfied desire for neat little housewives. It was an idyll intended to appeal to the patient imaginations of uprooted countrymen making their way to city factories, or to the apprentices rolling home on Saturday night. She wouldn't normally have dared to solicit an elegant young man so different from her usual customers.

'God,' thought Jancsi as he passed her, 'how strange it would be. But,' he thought again, 'God, how disgusting.'

He neither slowed nor quickened his pace, but the woman loitering by the door guessed his thought and quite boldly sneaked up behind him and whispered in an indescribable voice, 'Come in. You won't regret it.'

There was something so awful about this – about the flirtatious and repulsive confidence of her tone – that the boy stopped. He still had his back to her and didn't even glance round but heard her passing through the door of the tenement which was now open. Jancsi followed her.

She lived right at the back of a yard beside a lean-to or woodshed. Her door, which opened on to the yard, creaked with frost. A single lamp glowed at the centre of the table on a maroon velvet cloth. When the woman turned the light up Jancsi saw a couch, a towel and a pillow and on the wall a portrait of Kaiser Wilhelm wearing his full set of medals.

Later as it grew lighter and the grey February morning pressed its melancholy face against the window, he paced up and down, lit an Austrian *dritte Sort* and threw a cigarette to the woman too. She bent down to pick it up off the floor, wiped it with her blouse and stored it away. She never smoked.

Jancsi felt curious and took stock of her belongings. On the table he discovered a book bound in worn green velvet, its corners tipped in copper, which shed a few pages as he opened it. It was her commonplace book. He let his eyes run over it. It was mostly messages of best wishes, and little nuggets of wisdom gleaned from the classics, particularly those which conjured up broadly symbolic images, such as the dawn of life, the anchor of hope and so forth.

He more or less read it through. Somehow he had to kill the time before his departure.

'Who wrote this?' he asked, pointing at one leaf.

'A friend of mine.'

'When?'

'A long time ago.'

'And this?'

'An acquaintance from Gyöngyös. Sometimes guests write things too. Why don't you write something?'

'What?'

'Make something up.'

She brought him ink in a bottle and a rather rusty pen. Jancsi pushed these aside and produced his new Waterman. He racked his brains for something to write. 'What's your name?'

'Mrs Piskeli,' the woman answered as at a police station.

'Are you a widow?'

'No,' she replied and repeated. 'Mrs Piskeli, Mrs Józsi Piskeli.'

'Is your husband still alive?'

'He's an upholsterer. In Transylvania. He won't give me a divorce.'

'It's not important. That's not what I asked. 'What's your Christian name?'

'Ilona.'

Jancsi frowned deeply and continued in thought, his gold pen raised in his hand. Then he began to write in a round

172

and ornate hand as carefully as if it were a copybook. He wrote.

> I picked a violet in the wood,
> The violet before me stood,
> And whispered low so I could hear:
> Best wishes to you, Illy dear!

And he signed it with his full name and, for some reason he couldn't even explain to himself, added an exclamation mark like this:

János Patikárius!

He dried the ink by the heat of the lamp and passed the commonplace book to the woman who thanked him.

'What lovely handwriting,' she said. 'You must be a clerk or a solicitor.'

Jancsi just made his train.

18

The Terror

There was ever more talk of Kornél Vizy's pending elevation to under-secretary. The candidate enjoyed the complete confidence of the government. Many times it seemed the appointment would be made the next day but there was always some little hitch which resulted in postponement. Then people would agitate on his behalf and the whole thing would begin again. His chief advocates were Gábor Tatár and his friends. The message from parliament and from party ranks was that everything was in place.

In the meantime spring arrived. The white blossom flared on the chestnut trees in Krisztina, the oval Biedermeier entrance to the Alagút underpass shone in its frame of green boughs through the golden dust of April and cobblers in old-fashioned leather aprons took up their usual positions before their workshops.

On the Saturday before Easter Sunday, Mrs Vizy joined an afternoon procession to mark the Resurrection. From where they gathered in Attila út she could see the ancient church where Count Széchenyi had sworn eternal faithfulness to Crescentia Seilern. The banners above the crowd had begun to sway as if of themselves when Gábor Tatár approached her to offer his congratulations: she was now the wife of the new under-secretary.

The following day the news was in the press. Vizy's most spectacular dream was fulfilled: he was an under-secretary of state – only an assistant under secretary that's true – but with such a wide field of responsibility that it quite satisfied his ambition.

They had a continuous stream of visitors anxious to pay their compliments throughout the Easter holiday. These were received in a fitting manner. The Vizys had used the long period of suspense to smarten up the flat. A crystal chandelier hung from the ceiling and new bracket lamps with red silk shades cast a theatrical glow on the new wallpaper. Flasks of cognac and boxes of cigars and cigarettes took up permanent residence on the table. Vizy was already being driven about in a government car.

The party could not be postponed much longer. They had to invite all the friends to whom they felt an obligation. This was to be the biggest party they had thrown since the war. When they prepared a list of absolutely indispensible guests they found there were about thirty of them. Vizy, in his best parliamentary manner, emphasized that the evening should be appropriate to the occasion.

She for her part considered engaging a second maid, but for the time being there was no servant's room available and the kitchen was too small to lodge two.

The party was finally held on a mild and sunny day at the end of May. By now the whole house had been transformed into a restaurant-cum-*konditorei*. Etel volunteered to bake the pies, Stefi the cakes. The first whirlwind of activity lasted for days and blew itself out by the afternoon, only to be succeeded by the second. They solved the problem of seating the guests by practically emptying the study, the dining room and the living room and arranging tables in all three. The Drumas and the Moviszters loaned their chairs and silverware. The whole house sparkled.

When Ficsor, in his ceremonial uniform, opened the gates to the guests that evening the illuminated stairwell gave the house the air of an enchanted castle. A red staircarpet ran up to the first floor, where, on the highest stair, stood the host in his dinner jacket, genially waving greetings to the guests as they arrived; he looked years younger and

175

handsomer in the knowledge that he had arrived at the peak of his career.

There were friends from the ministry, business acquaintances, some army officers and a few priests, the Tatárs with their two daughters and Jancsi in a frock coat. He brought a great basket of flowers for Aunt Angéla. At precisely nine, the minister, his deputy, and his wife sailed up the stairs. Vizy hastened to greet them two steps down, kissed the hand of the right honourable excellent lady, made some comment to the minister at which they both laughed, then escorted them in. The remaining guests were left to be greeted by Druma who acted as his representative.

Etel and Stefi served the guests dressed like the maids of the aristocracy, in white aprons and neat caps. Anna remained in the kitchen. She was preparing the fried chicken, and sprinkling fat on the tender young goslings. The other two, who came and went with their trays, brought her occasional news of the progress of the party. Her ladyship was sitting next to the minister, wearing her purple velvet dress and her big golden earrings, while his excellency was chatting up the minister's wife and Jancsi, if you please, was flirting with the doctor's wife. First the minister made a speech, then his excellency Mr Tatár, then Druma, and finally Vizy himself.

There was repeated clapping and cheering.

When Etel brought in the May wine and returned with the tray she informed Stefi that their excellencies had retired to the sitting room.

'What are they doing?'

'Talking.'

'What about?'

'What about? About the servants.'

'That's all they ever talk about anyway,' pouted Stefi.

'Let's eat,' suggested Etel.

She took a dish of the goose roast, put it on her lap, picked up the parson's nose and began chewing it. Stefi ate in a more refined manner, with knife and fork.

'Why don't you eat something,' Etel asked Anna.

'Later.'

'Why save it for them?' Etel urged her. 'You don't need to feel sorry for them.'

'There's plenty in the house now,' added Stefi.

'That's right,' Etel nodded. 'They'll be having a clear-out here. The rag and bone men will have a real time of it. Soon they'll want a cook and valet.'

'Yes, and a butler,' added Stefi with a mocking smile, 'like we had at the count's.'

Etel turned the food over and over in her mouth. Stefi stared into the fire.

'Where I worked the butler even had to warm the newspapers.'

'Why?'

'Because they were brought in from the cold. The old count once sent the butler away to warm them up and it became a custom after that. And Etel, do you know what the cook used in the war when a really fierce fire was needed? Lard. He threw great ladles of lard on the fire. Just like that.'

'Didn't do you any harm, did it?' Etel asked her, her mouth full.

She chewed the chicken necks and broke their skulls open to suck out the brains. She dipped lumps of bread into the sauce.

'They were right to do it,' she said, 'while they could. At least you got some benefit from it. The main thing is that there should be enough to eat. All you ever really have is what you eat.'

Etel had still not finished eating. She gnawed and sucked at a few left-over bones. She wasn't fussy about hygiene in such high company. She poured the remnants of the wine out of the various glasses and drank it down.

Inside someone had struck up on the piano. Etel opened the kitchen door so they could hear it properly. She nodded her head in time to the music, her white cap bobbing up and down. She looked like an old fat angel.

The dancing had begun. Ethel and Stefi pulled the tables

177

out of the way but there still wasn't enough room and some couples spilled out into the hall. Jancsi steered Mrs Moviszter out. As a joke he danced her right round the flat, through the bedroom and back. As they passed through the bathroom on one of their circuits the young master squeezed her tight and kissed her neck. The pretty doctor's wife burst into deep-toned laughter.

Anna, who was moping in the hall, heard them. Her ears were red from the fire in the stove. She cast a glance in their direction. She wanted to run back into the kitchen but bumped into the wall. The lamps flared up as though they were squinting at her.

The jollities lasted for some time. Moviszter made his usual solitary escape after supper but everyone else remained. Even the minister stayed put. He felt just fine. Everyone else felt just fine too. Perhaps because the minister felt just fine.

There was a gay light-hearted universal din. No one argued, they simply melted and sprawled in the triumphal atmosphere. Minor pieces of gossip circulated: who was divorced, who was dead, who had put on weight, who had lost weight. People who had mistaken one vague acquaintance for another were relieved to find, once they had realized their mistake, that the person they had been told was divorced had in fact remarried, the one that was alive was dead, and the one that was thin was in fact fat and vice versa.

The gaiety of her guests made Mrs Vizy progressively more nervous as the evening wore on. She kept suppressing anxious little yawns. She had been exhausted by her duties as hostess, and most of all by the empty congratulations to which she had to respond with equally meaningless words. She watched her husband through the smoke, far away from her in the third room, as he fluttered round the minister and bowed to the ladies with that endless reserve of false bonhomie that tends to increase rather than decrease with the spending.

Somewhere in the window recess she came upon a pretty

blonde Austrian girl she had not yet engaged in conversation. She was the wife of some big businessman. As she spoke no Hungarian she could take no part in the general conversation and therefore felt as isolated as she did. Mrs Vizy sat down beside her. She told her the story of her daughter's death in great detail. But she had told it so often that she was aware only of a stream of empty words, without even the consolation of accompanying grief. She watched the grandfather clock and could hardly wait for everyone to go.

At three the minister rose. The air was thick with smoke. Blue wreaths of it blocked out the light of the chandelier, its glimmer as dim as a streetlamp in a November fog. Vizy was drowsing at the table, his head drooping. He heard the minister's car revving up, and the distant dying babble of guests departing. Everything had gone well, he thought. It had been very nice and now it was over and done with. But he had started belching. He took some bicarbonate of soda and went to bed.

His wife remained at the table. She surveyed the havoc round her. A smear of yellow apricot jam stared capriciously at her from a glass plate, part of some futurist daub which included the handle of a knife, a piece of cabbage strudel, a mound of cheese, a toothpick, some mayonnaise, a patch of damp tobacco, a stain of May wine and a sprig of rank woodruff. She would have liked to tidy up, or to sweep everything off the table with her hands. She was so tired she began to ask herself why it was necessary to eat at all.

The three servants came in and she had them air the place. She sent Stefi and Etel upstairs. Anna continued to fuss with the table right next to her. She picked up a jug then put it down again.

'Leave it,' wailed Mrs Vizy, covering her face her hands. 'I'm so sick of the sight of you, why don't you just go away. For heaven's sake, stop rattling about. Close the windows and go to sleep. You can tidy up in the morning. I want to have a good sleep.'

Her husband was already snoring though the light was

179

on. She unhooked her dress, threw it down anyhow and almost fell into bed.

Hardly five minutes had passed – perhaps less – when the door of the dining room opened and Anna stepped in. Without lighting the lamp she went back to fussing at the table. Maybe she was determined to clear up after all so that she'd have less to do in the morning. After all the screaming and shouting it was quiet again. The snores of her master in the other room only emphasized the silence.

Suddenly there was a great clatter which echoed through the untidied rooms. It was as if someone had set off a gun. Anna wasn't acquainted with the strange furniture and had upset an oak chair, one of the Moviszters'; it had toppled over and was lying full length along the floor. She waited to see what would happen. Her employers were in the first cycle of deep sleep and heard nothing.

A dog nearby was howling at the full moon. It was Swan, the big white dog she had often seen in Tábor utca. Anna was walking around. She ran back into the kitchen, gobbled down something in the dark, whatever lay close to hand. A chicken's leg, a lot of pies.

Then she leaned against the hall door as if wanting to go out. But she thought better of it and ran quite loudly into the bathroom and from there through the yellow-papered door into the bedroom.

Mrs Vizy woke to find someone sitting on the bed. She rose a little from the pillow and stared at the figure. In the ambiguous moonlight it looked like a ghost, with a surrounding halo of silver mist. Whoever it was was unafraid. It put out its left hand and took hold of hers. Their wide-open eyes met and stared at each other.

'What do you want? Mrs Vizy whispered. 'Is that you Anna? Go to sleep.'

The visitor did not reply but carried on sitting there, holding her hand and not letting go. She was moving very slowly, and this was the frightening thing about her, the peculiar slowness of her movements. One longed to see what she would do.

Mrs Vizy put out her free arm to grasp the girl's neck and push her away, but she did it so clumsily that the girl merely tightened her grip. She was in fact embracing her.

'Kornél!' she suddenly shrieked out. 'Kornél! Who is this? Help! Kornél! Help, help!' Then she felt a blow on her chest, an enormous blow like she'd never felt before. 'She's mad,' she said faintly and sank back on her pillow.

Vizy, whose head was heavy with wine and sleep, mumbled something, then leapt out of bed and stood in the middle of the room in his long nightgown which hung below his knees.

'What's going on,' he roared. 'Who is that? Help! Murderer, murderer!'

He saw the flash of the blade, the blade of the enormous kitchen knife. The girl was waving it around. But who stood there, what she had done, whether it was a man or woman in her way she had no idea. She only saw that someone was flitting towards the door, trying to escape. Then they joined in battle. Anna was terrified that he wanted to hurt her and was as frightened as her master. Her arm, which had been strengthened by hard labour, got hold of his waist. She tried to throw him down. For a while they wrestled. At the white divan Vizy lost his balance and fell, first on to the divan then to the ground. The girl in a wild fury knelt on his chest and stabbed him wherever she could, his chest, his stomach, his throat. Then she flung the knife away into a corner and staggered through into the sitting room.

She washed her hands with soap at the tap then returned to the sitting room. Something was dripping in the other room, drip drip like a tap that hasn't been properly turned off. The blood ran down. The man was gurgling and moving, but the gurgling was ever fainter. Anna lay down on the settee and fell asleep . . .

At six in the morning the dustman rang at the gate. Anna rose intending to take down the bin and give it to him so that she could clear up. It was a bright dawn. She rubbed her eyes and surveyed the mess left by the party, a chaos of colour, still unaware of where she was and how she had got

here. Then she stopped, stood still. The doors of the bedroom were closed, only the merest slit remaining between
them. It seemed she must have closed them behind her as
she tottered out. She didn't dare look inside. She listened.
She heard nothing but the deep deep silence.

Then, clapping her hands over her face, she felt a surge
of self-disgust. She was so afraid her heart turned to ice. She
rushed hither and thither gathering up her rags and tying
up her travelling pack. She must get out and escape, she
must get out. The house was still sleeping after last night's
revels. She could have run up to the attic or down to the
cellar or hidden behind the mangle. But she was afraid that
someone would be waiting for her in the stairwell. She
threw her belongings down.

She opened all the windows to Attila utca in order to feel
less lonely. Thrushes were already busily singing to greet
the beautiful summer morning. Trams tinkled their bells,
Swabian women were carrying milk into the house next
door.

Until eleven no one disturbed her. She sat hunched on
the couch, her elbows on her knees. After eleven someone
rang at the outside door, and kept ringing and wouldn't go
away.

'They're asleep,' Ficsor shouted at him from below. 'Stop
ringing that bell. Give it to me, I'll make sure they get it.'

It was the apprentice boy from Viatorisz's grocery. This
was the time he used to deliver the herbs.

'There was a big party here last night,' added the caretaker.

Mrs Moviszter sat down at the piano as was her custom
and began to play and sing above. The telephone rang. Anna
picked up the receiver then put it down again. The telephone kept ringing after that.

About two in the afternoon somebody beat at the door.

'Open up. Can't you hear? Open up for heaven's sake.
They can't still be sleeping, can they? It's impossible. Let's
see if we can see anything from the street.'

They did indeed go and look up from the street.

'Hey, is anyone there? Who is there? There is somebody. I'm sure there is. Look, they've opened the windows.'

There were more and more voices to be heard, here, there and everywhere.

'But I tell you, excellency, they haven't gone away. We would have seen it if they had. Anna! Anna! Are you asleep. We must wake her. Go on, beat louder. Break the window! Smash the door down, yes the door. Prise it open.'

'You mustn't do that,' she heard Druma's voice. 'Go straight for the police.'

The constable arrived. He had heard about the big do last night. He too tried ringing the bell then tapped the doorhandle with his key, but he felt suspicious so he sent for a locksmith. He arrived and broke the lock open. The constable asked for two witnesses and having obtained his excellency Mr Druma and the locksmith, he entered accompanied by them and by Ficsor.

'I told you there was someone here,' boasted the caretaker when he caught sight of Anna standing by the settee. 'So you're here? Why don't you open the door? Are you deaf?'

The constable paid no attention to her but hastened with giant strides towards the bedroom. He pushed open the doubledoors and was confronted by a scene straight out of the fairground chamber of horrors. Even he was taken aback. It was the first time he had come upon a murder like this.

He practically ran to the girl, grabbed her by the shoulder and shook her violently and uncontrollably.

'Did you do this?'

Anna closed her eyes as if in confession.

'Why did you do it?' screamed the constable, his large mouth gaping under his walrus moustache, his eyes bulging from their sockets. 'Thee'll be hanged!' he screamed, still out of control, passing sentence as if he were the first court of appeal.

Anna knew it. And yet her heart, which had remained in a state of frozen animation throughout the deathly tensions of the night, suddenly felt a kind of warmth rushing through it, a warm summer breeze that responded to his intimate form of address. The policeman was a peasant like her, like the lads in the village. He naturally addressed her as thee; in him she saw not the paraphernalia of office but the person who fulfils it, who was of her blood and who might have been her brother.

The hall was full of people, a mixture of strangers and fellow lodgers. They were peeking into the dining room. The constable roared at them to stay out.

'Break it up now,' he said. 'It's murder. Everyone leave the flat. In the name of the law. Are you the caretaker's wife? Lock the gate. No one may leave this house. I'm making you responsible.'

It was old Antal, Antal Szücs the local bobby, who was taking charge. Anna knew him well. Everyone looked at him and felt reassured. It was good to see, in the midst of this awful and incomprehensible nightmare when the blood rushed intoxicatingly to one's head, such cool level-headedness in a representative of law and order, to see him striding about and gesturing with such self-assurance. He was an enormous and healthy slice of life with his big broad shoulders and fat belly, a policeman who rose above this vale of sickness and pain and was a real pillar of society.

'Where's the telephone?' he asked Anna. She indicated where it was with a nod of her head.

'Hello,' said the policeman. 'District one headquarters ...? Hello ... hello ... Antal Szücs, officer number 1327 respectfully reporting to the desk officer, sir ... There has been a murder ... a double murder ... 238 Attila utca, first floor ... Vizy ... What's his first name ...? Gornél ... yes, sir ... Kornél ... Both are dead ... I have apprehended the criminal ... I have taken charge of the premises ... Yes, sir,' he noted the desk officer's instructions, 'yes ... yes ... yes ... yes ... yes ... yes ... yes ...'

He led the girl over to the sitting-room fireplace and told her to face the wall so she shouldn't try to escape. From that time he kept one eye on her and one on the door. He took off his cap, wiped his brow. He was breathing hard because of all the excitement. Ficsor stared crestfallen at the floor. Druma and the locksmith were whispering to each other.

Within a few minutes the police sirens sounded down Attila utca. Two cars had been sent. In the first sat the officer in charge accompanied by a commissioner from central HQ, the magistrate and the police doctor. The second was packed with detectives.

'I beg to report to his excellency the commissioner,' Antal Szücs saluted him, snapping to attention. 'As the officer on this beat at two o'clock this afternoon . . .'

'Is this the murderer?' asked the commissioner, cutting across him.

'Yes, sir.' The policeman pointed her out. 'The maid.'

They looked astonished. Never in their long experience had it happened that the murderer had made no attempt to flee the scene of the crime. It was most peculiar. They quickly surrounded her as if afraid that she might try to escape now. They looked as if they were about to murder *her*.

'Good,' said the commissioner and signalled to the magistrate that they could now examine the premises.

The fingerprint expert discovered two useful and clear prints. The quilt and the pillowslip were hurried away for further examination. The photographers got on with taking pictures. Druma introduced himself to the commissioner who allowed both him and the other witness to go.

The police doctor, accompanied by the commissioner, the magistrate and the desk officer passed through into the bedroom.

Mrs Vizy lay on her back in the bed without a drop of blood on her. She looked as if she were merely sleeping. The knife had pierced her straight in the heart and she had only one large wound. She must have died immediately and painlessly as a result of internal haemorrhage.

Vizy lay by the divan in a black pool of congealed blood. He had nine wounds. A fingernail had scratched his throat, and there was a longer scratch under his eye. It was obvious he had struggled to his last breath. He died hard and – as the doctor declared – much later than his wife. His death throes had lasted a long time. His jaws were clamped together, his aquiline nose rose, stern and angry, from his drained white face, his fists were clenched. He looked almost noble in his posthumous strength; there was something fine and old fashioned about him, something that was and is no more.

The victims already bore the marks of decomposition.

Though they had seen many horrific scenes in their time the officers shrank from this bestial and merciless assault. Each time one of them crossed into the living room he wore the look of horror. Every face bore the same look since they couldn't understand what had happened and were striving to understand it. Anna's face alone remained clear. She didn't understand, any more than they did, why she had done it, but she knew she had and, since she had, she knew deep down that there must have been some urgent compelling reason for it. The view is necessarily clearer from the inside than the outside.

They found the knife in the corner and put it away as evidence. They made an inventory of the furniture, measured out the room to the centimetre, made a sketch plan and indicated on it the positions of the two bodies. The doctor dictated the report.

Then the commissioner emerged and instructed the detectives to search all the rooms.

They had been waiting for this. Like a pack at a huntsman's whistle they set off in pursuit, wreaking havoc in every room of the flat, searching everything and slamming all the doors. One tore the cover from the couch and stuck his head under as if he were looking for somebody. They raised the lid of the piano and even examined the left-over food, poking the iced cakes and fishing in the cream with a long spoon. They must have been looking for the stolen money and the valuables. They didn't find anything.

They took Anna's campbed to pieces in the kitchen. They found her belongings tied up in a handkerchief on one of the chairs. In it they discovered everything she had brought with her to the house: a pair of ragged handkerchiefs, a few headscarves, the hand-mirror, the iron comb, the toy trumpet and a paper bag full of burned chestnuts; only the two dresses and the pair of laced man's shoes were missing. She had long worn these out.

'Her bed was not even made,' reported one of the detectives to the commissioner.

'That's important,' said the commissioner. 'Make a note of it. She had no intention of going to bed. She must have planned it in advance.'

He had Anna brought to him from her place beside the fire, and made her stand before the window facing the powerful summer light.

'Did you do this?' he asked her.

'I . . .'

'Why did you do it?'

'I . . . I . . .'

'What's all this "I" business?' growled the commissioner. 'You're repeating itself. I asked you why you did it? Why?'

'I . . .'

'Did you have a grudge against them? You wanted revenge? Did they harm you? There must be a reason.'

Anna wrinkled her young but prematurely wrinkled brow. She kept wringing her hands and sighing. 'Oh dear,' she said, 'oh dear,' and twice ran her hands over her hair in the absent, mannered way she had learned from her mistress.

The police doctor said something to the commissioner.

The doctor made her stand close to the window. He held his palm before the girl's eyes and snatched it away once, twice, three times as though it were a game. He felt behind her ears and pressed hard against the area behind her earlobes. He asked her this and that. He sat her down on a chair and tapped her knee. It was then he noticed that there were two bloodstains like little poppies on her frock.

'It's her time of the month,' the doctor explained. The crowd of men glanced shyly at Anna then quickly looked away.

'Otherwise there are hardly any traces of blood on her,'

187

said the commissioner while the doctor continued his examination, lifting her arms and letting them fall again.

'Only here. And here. See? Have you washed yourself?' he asked her. 'Where did you wash? They'll give her a strip-search at the station anyway,' he told the others.

The gentlemen were once again talking among themselves. Talking and writing. They were always talking and writing.

'What did you do during the time of the commune?' the commissioner harried her. 'Where did you work then? For who? What was their occupation? You didn't have a Communist lover? Some terrorist who might have left some documents with you? Revolutionary documents?'

They were forced to go back to the robbery motive, though that was hardly likely either since the cash and valuables had remained untouched.

'What did you take away?' the commissioner continued his interrogation. 'Be a good girl and tell us. Where have you hidden it? It would be better for you, dear, if you told us. We'll find out in the end anyway.'

He ordered her to be searched.

'Raise your hands,' barked the policeman. Anna clumsily raised her two arms, her elbows slightly bent.

'Straighten them out,' said the policeman.

So she held them straighter and for a second the young murderess reminded them of some ancient, awkward religious statue, holding up the sky.

The detectives carried out the body-search. They were looking for knives and guns. They ran their fingers over her breasts, over her skirt. Front and back.

'Nothing,' they said. 'Nothing.'

By now they had finished searching the premises. The van could come and take the bodies away. The police doctor and the commissioner were signing forms at the table. The commissioner turned to the detectives and instructed them to take her in.

Anna was still holding her arms up. There was no point

in it since they had forgotten about her. The detectives waved at her to lower them.

'Let's go.'

She didn't move. So one of them took hold of her arm but she casually pushed him away. The commissioner who had been walking up and down, stopped.

'Handcuff her,' he told the detective. The man put one wrist above the other, encircled them with the metal, then quietly closed the lock. Anna allowed him. She stared curiously at her handcuffed hands.

It was a brand-new pair of handcuffs, still bright; the chain was cheap and thin but strong. It was impossible to break the links. She had imagined them to be thicker, rustier, with a clumsy ball at the end. And yet it seemed she recognized them from somewhere, from some dim past, perhaps from folk legends, some story where the royal palace always backs on to the prison. She no longer found them strange. She stared at them indifferently and stood there as if she had grown used to them, had always worn them.

The detective put on his black bowler and led her away. People were whispering on the corridor: '. . . the murderer . . . look it's the murderer . . .' Stefi and Etel were leaning over the second-floor gallery; pale, they clapped their hands in astonishment. The whole house was shaking.

Later two black coffins were carried up the same stairs. They lifted the bodies in and took them away to the mortuary for dissection, then cold storage.

But one surprise gave way to another. Half an hour later the detectives returned and took away the Ficsors under suspicion as accomplices to the crime. In the course of the enquiry there was some suggestion that they might have been in league with the killer, and that their relatives might also have been involved.

Back in the shattered house Etel took over the caretaker's duties and Druma assumed overall command. He sent Stefi to the post office with two telegrams: one for the late Mrs Vizy's brother in Eger, the other for Jancsi who had already returned to Vienna. He was in constant touch with the police. It was he who attended to the reporters who began arriving in droves once the news was out. They wanted to interview him, and the servants too, anyone who might be able to provide some colourful copy.

Otherwise everything went to pieces. Moviszter made only the faintest attempt to keep up his surgery then went over to see Druma. The lodgers, all hungover from yesterday's party, huddled together sleepy and shivering. Mrs Druma offered milky coffee and rolls to the visitors, who were all naturally preoccupied by the horrific events.

'I don't understand,' wailed Mrs Moviszter. 'However I try, I don't understand, I just can't get it into my head. A girl like that, such a decent creature . . .'

'I've had my suspicions of her for some time,' said Mrs Druma. 'There was a wicked look in her eye. She had a sly face.'

'But she had been with them almost a year. And we all knew her. She looked so reliable.'

'Wait!' Mrs Druma clapped her hand to her brow. 'I've just remembered. I used to have a pair of little nail-scissors. I was very fond of them. They disappeared after Christmas. Stefi and I looked for them for weeks. Remember I told you I couldn't find them? We had no idea who might have stolen them. After all no one comes here. Stefi doesn't steal, neither does your Etel. There you are then: she took them.'

'You think so?'

'I do, my dear. I am convinced of it. A person who is capable of murder is capable of anything. It's not just idle talk – you know us, we're not like that, thank heaven. But I'd stake my life on it: she took those scissors.'

'Incredible,' mumbled Mrs Moviszter. 'It's quite terrifying for a person to realize one really doesn't know the people one's living with. It gives me the shivers.'

There was a solemn, nervous atmosphere in the room. Mrs Druma sat her little boy on her lap, kissed him and shuddered as she looked round the smart dining room with all its middle-class comforts. Her husband stood up. He still couldn't forget his experience of the afternoon, what he had seen with his own eyes. He began to orate.

'They have poisoned the soul of the whole Hungarian nation. The swines and scoundrels. It would have been unimaginable before. Such a monstrous deed. But this is the result of all that Communist propaganda, those schools of agitation. It's the last fling of Bolshevism.'

'And the war,' Moviszter added.

'I believe,' started Mrs Moviszter, 'that she must have been mad. A sane person doesn't act like this. Ultimately she had no motive. It is inexplicable.'

'Inexplicable?' Druma retorted. 'I beg your pardon, excellent lady. It's easy to say that. And what about two human lives? They should string her up. And you Miklós? Do you regard it as inexplicable?'

'At the moment she committed it, certainly. But in any case . . .'

'You hear that? Even her husband thinks so, though he is a doctor. Fine, let's all go and get ourselves murdered! No, string her up. Even if she is ill. We have to cut her out like a poisonous growth. They were all in it together: Ficsor, that Bolshevik scoundrel, his wife, the whole gang. You can't cure this with a piece of medical mumbo-jumbo by claiming that she is pregnant, or highly strung; you need proper legal insight. Think what would happen to society. I insist, we must burn out this nest of serpents, we must wipe them out, all of them. If someone disturbs the social order they must pay for it. There must be no mercy. Hang her, I say. Hang her . . .'

The Drumas' little boy began snuffling in his mother's arms. She snatched him up and walked him to and fro to settle him down. Druma too was jumpy. Where was Stefi all this time? After all she only had to run to the post office in the high street.

Now a girl stole into the house and up the dark stairwell. She drifted silent as a shadow to the first floor. She stayed close to the wall. No one saw her. She stopped before the

Vizys' door, which now bore a large police seal, and rang the bell repeatedly.

She waited for minutes and when no one came she sat down in front of the door and burst into bitter tears. Etel ran to the Drumas.

'Please come down,' she gasped, out of breath. 'Katica is here.'

'Katica?' they repeated, startled, since on this ill-fated day everything seemed to be a harbinger of disaster. 'Who is Katica?'

'The girl who used to be the Vizys' servant.'

'What does she want here?' Druma spluttered nervously. 'Why wasn't the gate locked? Who let her in?'

They all piled out into the corridor. There they were deeply moved to see the servant, the previous servant, in a white skirt, pink blouse and lacquered shoes, sitting before her dead employer's door like a living statue of faithfulness, a loudly lamenting revenant.

'She's mourning for them,' whispered Etel, and she too wiped a tear from the corner of the eye. Indeed the sight was so affecting, so beautiful and unusual it might have been the last chapter of a cheap paperback novel. Even the miscellaneous crowd of strangers who had made their way into the stairwell found it fascinating.

Druma instructed Etel to go down and send the intruders away, to lock the gate and bring the girl up. Katica was inconsolable. The hot tears kept coursing down her cheeks. Etel slapped her back. She had needed considerable physical support to get up the stairs and into the Drumas' kitchen. Here they sat her down. But no sooner had she opened her mouth to speak than she started blubbering again. Eventually, with some difficulty, she managed to explain how she got here.

She told them she had just read the news in the evening paper, got dressed immediately and ran as quickly as she could to catch a last sight of his and her excellency. Finer people never lived.

'I knew it would happen,' she gasped for air. 'I felt it, and dreamt it.'

'What did you dream, Katica love?' asked Etel.

'I dreamt she was a bride,' she sobbed.

'The honourable lady?'

'Such a beautiful pale bride, she was. With a white veil. A wreath on her head.'

'That's a bad sign. Weddings always mean bad news.'

'And we were busily cooking and baking, we slaughtered so much poultry the fat was fairly dripping.'

'Receptions are even worse.'

'I actually wanted to come over and warn her. Oh if only I had come! Oh if only I had never gone away! The best place in the whole of Budapest.'

Katica squeezed her nose. Her handkerchief was as drenched as a washing-up cloth.

To distract her from her grief, Mrs Druma asked, 'And where are you working now, Katica?'

'Nearby. He's an engineer at the gasworks.' She burst into tears again.

'Come along now, come along. No more tears. Look, here's Stefi.'

She poured some milky coffee into a cup, topped it with thick, rich cream and offered it to her.

'Drink it, Katica love. There's a couple of nice fresh rolls there too. Stefi dear, have some coffee yourself, you haven't even had tea yet. Bring some fruit, you'll find it in the sideboard. What about you, Etel. Wouldn't you like a cup of coffee? Go on, all of you, have something to drink. What can we do? Sadly, what's done is done.'

They left the servants to themselves. The three maids sat red eyed and silent. Katica was drunk with grief. The thick rice-powder on her face had soaked through and was beginning to curdle. But when the other two servants started to describe the murder in mouth-watering detail her interest was aroused. Even with her limited imagination she could follow events, and she was intimately acquainted with the scene of the crime. She kept asking for ever more detail, her curiosity was insatiable. And later, when the girls had run out of things to say, she herself repeated the whole story, entering into the spirit of it to the extent that she experienced it all quite graphically, and felt the horror as clearly as if she had been there. She was only sorry that the poor things had been taken away before she arrived. She would have liked to see them once more, or at least the honourable lady, frozen in her blood, in the bed that she herself had so often made for her.

'You see,' said Druma, 'this shows what kind of people they were. If even their ex-servant is so grief-stricken, they can't have been such bad sorts. What sort of a girl was Katica, anyway?'

'A well-meaning girl,' his wife answered.' Hard working and, as far as I know, morally reliable. She was their best servant. I don't understand why they let her go in the first place. If she had stayed the whole thing would certainly not have happened. Don't you think so, doctor?'

'Possibly,' replied Moviszter, in deep thought, 'possibly.'

19

Why

Such sensations are quickly forgotten. For a couple of days while the news is hot everyone talks about it, then it evaporates in its own heat.

It was the same in this case. At first it was feverishly debated throughout the district, without any clear conclusions as to its causes. Viatorisz's greengrocer shop became a haven of gossip. Day after day ladies and servants discussed it among the tubs of caustic soda and the sacks of beans. The question everybody was asking themselves and others was 'why'? But no one had a satisfactory answer, not for themselves nor for anyone else.

Society showed its solidarity by attending the funeral in great numbers, at the end of which ceremony the victims were laid to rest beside their only daughter, Piroska. Because of the crowds the police were brought in to keep order. Street urchins ran after the coffins hoping to snatch a flower from the various wreaths, bowling each other over in the process. The speeches at the graveside took on a certain political tone. A number of celebrities were observed in the cortège, to say nothing of the guests who had attended the party, the relations of the deceased and Mr and Mrs Patikárius from Eger. Only Jancsi was missing. Apparently he had failed to get the telegram. On the other hand Etelka Vizy, Kornél's estranged sister, who used to sell fake Egyptian cigarettes, was there sobbing behind her veil, loudly lamenting her brother, her successful and powerful brother.

Anna Édes made her confession at the police station and was arrested. They took her fingerprints, made her sit for three photographs, then escorted her across to the public prosecutor's office at the prison in Markó utca. As soon as she stepped in she felt the walls collapsing on her.

She saw a towering iron edifice glimmering in the grey light of dawn. It was full of iron doors and stairs that rang and rumbled constantly like an enormous mill that is forever grinding. Her warders took her up to the third floor and locked her in a cell. It contained a bed, a chair, a table and a closet, but it was relatively clean, and lighter and more spacious than her kitchen. She could hardly believe that this was prison. She thought prison was a place where the inmates slept on sacking, while snakes and toads glared at them in the dark. She sat down in the chair. She didn't cry but spent a long time in thought. In the evening she knelt by her bed and prayed.

Even after minutely studying the police reports, the examining magistrate had no clearer idea of the whys and wherefores of the case than those whose information consisted of nothing more than casual gossip. The prosecutor's office thought it important to get to the bottom of this complex affair, which might have far-reaching political consequences, especially now, so soon after the collapse of Bolshevism, when order had not yet been conclusively restored. The examining magistrate fell to his task with great gusto. But the more he knew the less he understood. It was one cul-de-sac after another.

The first concern was to understand the role of the caretakers. The police took them in 'on remand'. The Ficsors swore blind that they were innocent; so fervent were their protestations that by the next day they had run out of things to say. Their defence consisted of blackening Anna's name: she was a sly, secretive girl, capable of anything. In any case there was no material proof against them. Viatorisz's delivery boy testified that Ficsor had sent him away angrily, telling him not to ring the bell because they were still asleep. After the night of a big party Ficsor's reaction did not necessarily indicate bad faith. After two days the magistrate released the pair of them.

But he examined the accused every day.

When they first came for her Anna crossed herself and prepared to yield her soul to heaven in the belief that they were taking her straight to the scaffold. They brought her instead to a thin balding man with a pin in his elasticated tie and a big gold ring on his hairy finger. Anna had thought that this overworked and modestly paid representative of justice would be a very great, very rich man. Later she saw he wasn't a bad fellow. He spoke to her kindly and gently and she grew used to him, indeed rather tired of him, since he kept nagging away with his questions. She had to repeat time and again what she had been doing at this time and that time. He encouraged her to recall other things which were very difficult and would often help her out because he remembered everything so much better. By now they had built up a picture of the sequence of events in those last days, from hour to hour and minute to minute.

Anna looked him straight in the eye; she seemed neither broken nor confused. She didn't deny anything, on the contrary, sometimes it seemed she was accusing herself. The magistrate completed his report of the investigation, paying particular attention to her potential accomplices, though it no longer seemed likely that she had any. The facts agreed, the accused had not altered her confession since she had been taken into custody. The only question she couldn't answer was why she had done it.

They questioned the inhabitants of the house in turn.

Druma's statement seemed to be the most important. He had seen the girl on the night of the murder, searching through the sideboard and the drawer from which – according to his evidence – she took the knife, and he saw her lurking in the bathroom while the guests were leaving.

Etel gave a verbose and muddled statement in which there was one eye-catching detail. One Sunday afternoon in spring she had gone out with Anna to visit the citadel on Mount Gellért. Anna lay down on the grass and fell asleep. After a few minutes she woke, startled, and started running down, waving her arms and shrieking like a lunatic. No one knew what was the matter with her and she only stopped when Etel shouted at her, and even then she continued trembling for a long time.

Stefi, for her part, had met her a fortnight before the murder, in Márvány utca, lurking along before the house where Master Jancsi used to live. Anna noticed her and ran into the stairwell and when Stefi asked her later what she had been doing there she couldn't give a coherent answer. Even now Anna was incapable of explaining the incident. The magistrate summoned János Patikárius but he wasn't at his Vienna flat, having, according to the Vienna police, 'left no forwarding address'. He had been living with a Polish dancer, but she had left the five-room dwelling and returned to Warsaw. None of this seemed particularly important since János Patikárius had not lived in Budapest for over six months.

They summoned the accused's parents too. István Édes arrived on the train at dawn, with a pack and a pair of chickens. He was followed by a neat peasant woman, much younger than himself, in red leather slippers. She wasn't carrying anything. As it was early and they didn't know their way round the town, they enquired at the Vérmező where the Vizy's house was, and settled themselves in at the bottom of the stairs, waiting for the Drumas to wake. They presented the honourable lawyer with the two chickens, a pot of cream and some fresh curd, saying it was good to stow something away in case of slack business in the legal profession. Druma explained to them where they should take the official document.

The magistrate examined them too. Anna's father was a slightly bent and skinny day labourer, long past fifty but not yet grey. His blonde hair had merely faded, grown slightly ashen with time, like broken straw. He twisted his hat in his hand as he answered the magistrate's questions but kept on glancing over at his spouse with one unhealthy eye whose expression seemed to alternate between humility and cunning. Being a peasant nothing surprised him. The great dramas of life, such as a murder, he accepted as naturally as he did all birth and death. But the old fox attempted to cover this up. He spoke too piteously, his voice creaking and wheedling as if he were intoning the last rites at a funeral. He told how he had married his second wife four years ago and how his daughter, that bad, that wicked girl, was ever like this, headstrong and disobedient, and had been the cause of much trouble at home too, which was why they had sent her away to Pest to be a servant. The stepmother – a clean, hard-working and pretty little thing – kept nodding. She had something to add to his evidence. She leant confidently towards the magistrate and described in horror how Anna had almost hit her once with the sickle, and might have killed her too if her father had not intervened. She chattered on tirelessly, with apparently infinite energy. But then she began to contradict herself. The examining magistrate took stock of the situation and sent them both home.

He examined the mental condition of the accused. The official medical consultant had Anna brought to his surgery and prepared a certificate which stated that the accused was anaemic but perfectly responsible. Having clapped this document into his file along with the others the examining magistrate completed his investigation, and passed the file on to the prosecutor who prepared the charges. Anna Édes was to be tried for two premeditated murders.

They appointed someone to defend her, a small-time, recently qualified barrister whose only experience so far had been with legacies and a property suit and who now threw himself into the case determined to establish his career as a criminal lawyer. He paid frequent visits to his client in prison. He comforted her by saying she shouldn't despair, he would take care of the matter. Anna spoke to him as she had done to the police officer and the magistrate. Later she was visited by the blue-veiled sisters from the mission who urged her to repent and submit to her fate, and left behind some religious booklets in which she might discover the consolations of faith.

The trial was held in the middle of November, and because of the interest in the case they used the great central hall of justice.

It was a dark cold winter's day. The gas fires were turned up high and flickered green in the great hall. Clerks bellowed the witnesses' name. There were eleven of them: six for the prosecution, five for the defence.

The raked public seats of the hall were filled to overflowing with the victims' friends and acquaintances to the right. Gábor Tatár sat with his wife just behind the journalists' row, and greeted the witnesses as they passed him to take their places at the front. There were all the inhabitants of 238 Attila utca – masters, servants and all.

At precisely nine the bench entered: the presiding judge (or president of court) and his two assistant judges. The president rang his bell. 'I declare this hearing open. We will hear the case of Anna Édes who is accused of murder. Where is the accused? Lead her in,' he commanded one of the guards.

Anna had been brought down to the basement at eight o'clock and was patiently waiting in her cell. The doors opened and there she stood in her calico dress which had grown quite ragged. Two guards with fixed bayonets escorted her in. She didn't so much walk as stumble dizzily to the accused's bench before the judges. The guards who were right on her heels made sure she was sitting properly then snapped to attention.

Anna took in the crowd, the pictures and the lights and felt very warm. The six months of imprisonment had had no ill effect on her. Her face had rounded out a little as many prisoner's do, and her skin looked like marble with its subterranean pallor. She conveyed an air of great calm.

'What is your name?' asked the president, his eyes already moving past her to one of his fellows on the bench. 'Are these your papers?' And he quickly read out the details

200

himself. 'Twenty years old, spinster, childless, no criminal record. Sit down,' he ordered without looking at her.

The accused sat down, and the two guards sat either side of her, the butts of the rifles between their feet.

The charge was read from a scarlet piece of paper. It began: 'Anna Édes, Roman Catholic, unpropertied, Hungarian . . .' It was a long list whose reading took half an hour. In the meantime the public inspected the judges who sat on their raised bench without wigs or gowns, in ordinary suits and ties with hard-collars, but with a certain impersonal authority. If they seemed ageless it was because it was their miraculous earthly vocation to see the truth clearer than others; this had been their study and their livelihood and when they died their tombstones would bear the word: judge.

The president was searching through a book; his elder colleague, the *rapporteur*, a long-nosed, moustached man wearing a lorgnette, was gathering documents, while the short, thick-set younger man – the so-called voting judge – propped his elbows on the table and rested his heavy head on his right hand. Somewhat to the left of the president a little man was being conspicuously busy. It was the defending counsel. He greeted his father, his mother and other relatives who had come in great numbers to witness his first major performance. The prosecution was lost in his own thoughts.

Once the charges had been read the president asked Anna to stand up. 'Anna Édes! Do you understand the charges?' He spoke to her in a loud clear voice as one might speak to a deaf man or to someone not quite of one's own intellectual capacity. 'The prosecution charges you with the murder of your employers. Do you plead guilty?'

'I plead guilty,' Anna answered. There was whispering in the auditorium. The *rapporteur* stared at her, the voting judge propped his head on his left hand instead.

'In that case,' continued the president in a more anecdotal manner, 'tell us nicely what happened. In detail please. Before you start, let me remind you that if you confess to

201

all the charges that will count in your favour, on the other hand if you deny any one of them,' and again he raised his voice, 'then you can only harm your case, because we have enough evidence to convict you of them all. So, you may begin.'

The lawyer indicated for his client to begin. But she stood there wordlessly, incapable of speech. The president hastened to help her.

'I believe you were the servant, and had worked some ten months at the Vizys'. Perhaps we could begin with the evening of the party on the twenty-eighth of May, the big "do",' he tried to affect a popular manner. 'You spent the evening working.'

'I was cooking.'

'Correct,' nodded the president in approval. 'You were going about your domestic chores. The guests arrived but you did not serve them. Now, they have long since finished their supper. It's about two o'clock in the morning. Where are you then?'

'In the kitchen.'

'That's right, that is where you are. You are already searching the cupboard and pulling out the drawers, looking for the knife.'

'I don't remember that,' Anna's voice shook as she glanced at her counsel, who nodded back at her, satisfied.

'It will be testified against her. Then what did you do?'

'Then I went into the bedroom.'

'Let's not get confused. You didn't go into the bedroom yet. That came later. First the guests left. At that time you were lurking in the bathroom, lying in wait, preparing for the deed. Do you not remember that Mr Druma looked in and saw you there?'

'No.'

'No matter, that too will be established later. We have the witness. Let us continue. Let us return to the point at which you have aired the rooms and your mistress tells you to go to bed. But then, instead of going to bed, you waited for them to go to sleep.'

'And then I went into the bedroom.'

'No, no. You still did not go into the bedroom!' cried the president striking the table.

Anna shifted from one foot to the other, her mind running to and fro in an attempt to recall the past. She began to feel a little faint because of all her travelling.

She was stuck. Her lawyer rose.

'Your honour, honourable bench! With due respect I request the court to summon an eminent psychiatrist so that here and now he may establish the mental condition of the accused. Her confession is so disconnected, so incoherent, so pathological that in my honest opinion she cannot be held at all responsible for her actions.'

The president quietly conferred with his fellow judges and expressed their view.

'The bench rejects the request. As the honourable counsel himself knows the accused has been examined several times by specialists and has been proclaimed by them to be responsible. In any case, I instruct the court to make a record of all counsels' requests.'

'I humbly withdraw the request,' said the lawyer.

The president returned to the topic in hand, and proceeded carefully through her testimony, helping the accused, leading her towards the truth, until he himself was lost in the dark and had to wait for her to lead him towards some source of light in the hope that one of these might illuminate the whole case. They went along together like two closely bound blind men, first one then the other leading, neither seeing anything.

'So,' he began, 'just try to recall. Why did you pick up the knife? What did you feel as you did so?'

Anna was silent. The president tried to interpret her silence, to describe her indescribable feelings and render them plain in plain grammar.

'You felt angry with them, the blood suddenly rushed to your head, you were no longer in control of your actions. You might have remembered how the woman had told you off, and you wanted revenge. But why?'

203

Again he was forced to continue.

'And did not your conscience rise in revolt, did your soul not raise its voice in protest, did you not consider what you were doing or the consequences of your actions, that you would have to answer for your deeds to man and God? After all, the deed was out of character for you.'

The president felt there might be some hidden secret here, a secret no one knew, perhaps not even the accused herself. But he went on. He knew that an action could not be explained by any one cause, nor even by a combination of causes, and that behind every action stood the whole person with his whole life, which a court of law was incapable of examining. Even so, while he knew full well that people were incapable of fully knowing each other, he had his duty to perform.

'Speak,' he urged the accused. 'When you entered the bedroom your employers were already asleep. What did you do then?'

'Then I . . .'

'Go on. Say it,' said the president, very sternly. 'Then you went over to the woman's bed, and while she was still sleeping you stabbed her through the heart with a knife. With this knife here.'

He lifted the giant knife from among the exhibits, and swung it in the air so the court let out a gasp of horror, then he held it out towards the defendant, and, still turning it over and over in his hand, he asked her, 'Was this the knife?'

'Yes,' answered Anna and started back because she felt the knife was being twisted in her heart.

Finally she stuttered out how it happened. Not so much in her own words as in the words used by the police and by the examining magistrate. She was quite coherent by the end of her account.

'You killed your mistress,' repeated the president. 'You killed the woman who fed you, who never harmed you. Let us proceed. What did you do then?'

'I ran through into the sitting room.'

'No, you did not run out yet. Let's not be too hasty. Let us remain in the bedroom for now. You stabbed your master too, like some common assassin, stabbed him nine times with the knife. Is that correct?'

'Yes. But I didn't want to harm his excellency. He scared me.'

'What scared you was your crime, and your conscience, and so you committed another murder. What happened then?'

'Then they came for me.'

'No, of course they didn't. No, you lay down on the big couch and there . . .'

'I fell asleep.'

'And could you sleep after such an abominable deed? Were you not, even then, aware of what you had done? Of your guilt? You didn't say anything to anyone but remained hiding there until the door was broken down. Are you at least sorry for what you have done? Pardon? Would you do it again?'

'No!' cried Anna, startled. 'No.'

'You may sit down,' said the president.

The prosecution's chief witness was Szilárd Druma, the red-faced solicitor. When he rose and approached the bench he visibly grew with pride.

'You have no quarrel with the accused?' the judge rattled out the formalities. 'You are not a relative of hers?'

The witness never even answered but smiled in a superior fashion at the amusing suggestion that he might have any kinship to a creature like her.

Methodically, he summed up the objective facts that settled any doubts about premeditation. He answered the prosecution's questions briefly using appropriate technical terms. He described how the girl's nervous demeanour had already aroused his suspicions, and that he had kept a careful eye on her thenceforth, that at two in the morning the accused could only have been seeking a knife in the kitchen drawer, one which she must have hidden somewhere, and then how he saw her for the last time when she was lurking in the bathroom, and even offered her a tip but she had leapt back startled and disappeared into the bedroom.

When faced by this evidence, Anna broke down and admitted it was so.

But Druma wasn't finished.

'I would like permission,' he said, 'to throw some light on the political background of the accused, and in passing to refer,' and he pointed to Ficsor and his wife sitting among the other witnesses, 'to the role of the caretakers. These people, your honour, behaved in such an extreme Bolshevik manner at the time of the commune that the whole house lived in terror of them. For my part I can see every reason to suspect that it was they who were the prime movers and intellectual . . .'

'Excuse me,' the president broke in, 'there has already been an enquiry in this direction too but the results were negative. The prosecution did not see fit to pursue it.' And he glanced at the prosecutor who shook his head. 'This is irrelevant.'

Druma stood with his half-finished sentence hanging in the air.

There was a short debate between the defending and prosecuting counsels. The prosecution asked that the witness should take the oath, the defence objected. Druma was released from his oath. Again the defence requested that it be wiped from the records.

Antal Szücs, the local constable, described certain significant incidents before the official inspection of the scene of the crime, and made mention of the accused's indifferent reactions.

Mrs Druma said the girl was secretive, and brought up – in passing – the question of her missing nail scissors. She expressed a high opinion of the Vizys, particularly the husband.

Mrs Moviszter appeared in a slit skirt and premièred her latest make-up, which would have done honour to a theatrical matinée. She talked in a relaxed manner and flirted with the prosecution. According to her the girl was not secretive but rather open and good humoured, and she was amazed that she could do this kind of thing since her mistress was a veritable angel, and what's more, was fond of her. She would happily have chattered on but, alas, her cross-examination was soon over.

The president advised Ficsor that since he was related to the accused he could, if he wished, decline to give evidence, but Ficsor wanted to be examined.

'I must warn you,' the president said, 'that you are bound to tell the truth, because I may ask you to take the oath, and the law deals severely with perjurers, with imprisonment for up to five years.'

The caretaker, who was already reeling from Druma's previous speech, was further frightened by the mention of five years imprisonment and was more determined than ever to save his skin. He repeated everything he had said to the examining magistrate that summer, and when the little lawyer tried to provoke him by questioning the validity of his evidence he lost all sense of proportion.

'That's not the only thing she said, if you please, there were many more incidents. Once, when the honourable lady told her off for breaking a mirror, she came down to us and said that she was going to leave, but before she did she'd do something she would herself regret – she would burn the house down.'

'When did she say this?'

'Shortly after she took up the post.'

'You are certain you remember this?'

'Quite certain.'

'Think it over. Would you repeat it under oath?'

'I would,' answered Ficsor, with real resolve.

So he took the oath and bowed to the bench, such a deep bow that it would have been humanly impossible to bow lower.

Then Mrs Ficsor rose to give evidence. The fat woman was quivering like jelly. She was already feeling sorry for Anna and would have like to say something in her defence, but was afraid of contradicting her earlier statement.

'What about you now, Mrs Ficsor?' the president asked her. 'What sort of a girl did you think she was?'

'She was always sort of suspicious, if you please.'

'What do you mean suspicious?'

'She was sort of shifty.'

'You mean with you.'

'With everyone else, too.'

'What made you think so?'

'She was always thinking of something.'

'Do you mean she was contemplating evil thoughts?'

'No.'

'Then what?'

'I mean, she was always mournful.'

'But in your statement to the examining magistrate you said something different. Look. Read it. You stated that on one occasion she had already wanted to murder someone.'

'Yes, when she struck her mother with the scythe.'

'Did you see this yourself?'

'No I didn't. I only heard about it.'

'From whom?'

'From her mother.'

'You mean her stepmother. I think we've heard enough about this,' said the president with a gesture of boredom. 'Let's leave it.'

'I've nothing to say against her otherwise. She used to be a good girl, but . . .'

'Yes?'

'But later she was bad.'

'The court is already aware of that,' remarked the president, to universal hilarity.

'Your honour your excellency.' objected Mrs Ficsor with a certain stubbornness, plainly wounded, 'I can only tell you what I know,' and when the public burst into laughter once again, she carried on fuming, 'I, if you please, can only tell you what I know.'

'Thank you, that will do. Please return to your place.' The president waved her away.

The statements were full of such useless details and quickly declined into mere gossip.

The president called the next witness. 'Miklós Moviszter, doctor of medicine. Where is he? Did he receive the subpoena? He didn't appeal against it. Where is he?'

Where indeed are you, old doctor, you who are supposed to be dying, incurable, with your eight per cent sugar? Have you in fact died, or are you lying helpless, languishing in the trance that precedes death in cases such as yours? Are you too lost? Is there nobody left on this earth? If you are still alive, if you have but a spark of life in you, then this is where you should be, then it is your duty to attend.

He had attended. He was sitting right at the back, lost among the other witnesses, lost in his fur coat this November day, growing ever cooler as death drew near. It took him a little time to come forward, leaning on his stick, his body bent and shrunk to such an extent that some members of the public had to stand up to see him.

'Present,' he said, bowing to the bench.

The president, seeing his condition, said he might sit down to give his evidence. He ordered one of the guards to fetch a chair for him. He wouldn't accept it, rather he seemed to stand a little straighter, or at least as straight as he could.

'Now doctor,' the president asked him, 'are you too prepared to stand by your previous statement?'

'Yes,' said Moviszter, almost inaudibly, so the judge had to cup his ear to hear him.

'Kindly explain to the court the views you there expressed.'

Moviszter looked as if he were preparing a speech. He was urging himself on. What are you waiting for? Do your duty. You're only one man. But what is greater than one man? Not two, not a thousand add up to more. Now step forward, just one step – so – and just one more step. It's your turn. Raise your head, Moviszter, *sursum corda*, and be strong, only be strong.

'I didn't hear you,' said the judge, 'a little louder please.'

Why a little louder? Not a little louder, but much louder. Shout it out – his heart was beating fast – shout it out as the ancient Christian priests and martyrs did, when they spoke against the pagans, in the cemeteries, in their very graves, appealing to heaven, disputing with God himself on high, that just but terribly stern God, demanding grace for sinful humanity. Have you not repeated quietly to yourself, every day, the prayer before death. Do you remember what it says? *Ne tradas bestiis animas confidentes tibi.* Cast not those that trust in you to the ravening beasts. *Et animas pauperum tuorum ne obliviscaris in finem.* And abandon not the souls of thy poor. Try now yourself to cry out in the arena, outroar even the lions, brave catechumen.

His voice grew firmer. 'I fully stand by my previous statement. I can say nothing but what I said there.'

'Yes,' said the president, leafing through a sheaf of notes. 'We have here what you said. But we want some facts. Did they beat her? Or starve her? Or overwork her? Did they not pay her? I see from this,' he quickly said, 'that at Christmas they even gave her a present, though it wasn't of much significance. A waistcoat. What have you to say?'

'They behaved coldly towards her,' stated Moviszter, his voice again firmer. 'I always felt so. They gave her no affection. They were heartless.'

'And how did this heartlessness show itself?'

'It is hard to say precisely. But it was distinctly my impression.'

'Then these are only feelings, doctor, mere suspicions, such delicate shades of behaviour that this bench, faced by such a brutal and terrible crime, can hardly take them into account. Because on one side we have facts: bloody facts. And we too require facts. Besides, the other witnesses all disagree with you. They directly contradict you. According to them the couple loved and respected her. The accused herself has made no complaint, neither to the police nor to the examining magistrate. Stand up, girl,' he told Anna. 'Did they hurt you?'

'No.'

210

'You may sit down. It was highly unlikely in any case.'

Look at the girl, Moviszter, how numbly she sinks down again between the guards. It's not a pretty sight, but look at her, and look at the judge too, as he adjusts the cheap lorgnette at his wrinkled blue eyes and starts scratching his ear so you shouldn't guess his thoughts or his emotions. He is merely the representative of earthly justice. But he does try to see the truth impartially, to take a wide view as far as it is humanly possible. Don't you feel – he encouraged himself – that he is on the way to administering heaven's justice too and is already on your side? Let him fret away with his arguments a while, after all it is his duty, then speak again yourself, don't be afraid of him or of anybody, for God is with you.

'And even if she had been ill-treated,' reasoned the president, 'then it was her right under law to register a complaint against her employers at any time; she could have given in her notice and left within fifteen days.'

'They forced her to stay.'

'How did they force her? You can't tie someone down with ropes.'

'She was such a simple helpless creature.'

'That's no reason for her to commit this dreadful crime,' the president meditated, then added more sternly, 'It is no excuse.'

'Then why did she do it?' asked Moviszter, forgetting himself. 'My impression,' he stubbornly repeated, 'my impression is that they did not deal with her as with a human being. To them she was not a human being but a machine. They turned her into a machine,' he raised his voice almost to a shout. 'They treated her without humanity. They were beastly to her.'

'I must reprimand you for this outburst.'

The public shifted uneasily and murmured furious approval of the president's action.

'Quiet please,' said the president, and carelessly tinkled his bell. For whom did this brief bell toll?

'You have nothing else to add?' asked the *rapporteur*.

211

'Nothing else.'

The public felt that the doctor was at death's door, verging on senility, or in any case severely handicapped. Indeed Moviszter was handicapped. He had one chief handicap, without which his stature would have shrunk to nothing or been lost in the vast empty spaces of the soul.

The quicksilver little lawyer sprang from his seat and asked the court's grace to register the witness's testimony by swearing him in. The prosecution objected on the grounds that Moviszter's evidence consisted of insignificant generalities.

The president made a quick decision.

'The bench overrules the objection. Swear the witness in.'

The public in the auditorium immediately rose noisily and excitedly, as if at the theatre. Even the president stood up as he addressed the witness, who was waiting, his right hand on his heart, three fingers of his left hand raised.

'Repeat after me.' And he dictated the formal oath.

'I . . . solemnly swear . . . before the living God who sees and knows all . . . that I have told the truth . . . and nothing but the truth . . . neither neglecting . . . nor altering any part of it . . . so help me God.'

Moviszter repeated it loudly and clearly. He shuffled back to his seat among the other witnesses, who moved away from him as he settled down. Moviszter didn't care. He was never one of them anyway. Not them nor anyone else, having never been a Communist nor a bourgeois, nor a member of any party but that of humankind generally, those who had lived or were living, the quick and the dead.

He soon left in any case and went about his business, not bothering to hear the rest.

There were a few more helpful witnesses to come. Etel, dressed in her cook's outfit and Stefi wearing a hat, as befits a maid who once worked for aristocracy. When they read out her personal details Stefánia Kulhanek added a reference to herself as 'household staff' and blushed. They both took the oath to swear the truth and nothing but the truth, as did the others, who were always sincerely telling the truth, from their own point of view. They praised Anna, but they praised the poor honourable lady and his excellency, her husband, equally.

Anna, who had been sitting indifferently on the accused bench, suddenly became alert. She had spotted Mrs Wild, the warehouse owner's wife who had given her her first job as children's nurse, when she first arrived in Budapest at the age of sixteen. She grew very agitated.

And there before the president Mrs Cifka, Bandi's great aunt, was already giving evidence, and Bandi must be quite big now, possibly going to school. Now she was really nervous. She thought of a thousand things at once.

The hearing ran on and on. The judge tried to speed things up: as soon as the prosecution had finished, and the defence had lodged his twenty-seventh objection, he declared this part of the procedure finished and ordered an adjournment.

At two o' clock it was time for the counsels to make their final speeches. The prosecution did not take long. He claimed that the charges had all been proved and that this was increasingly clear from the proceedings, and quoting particular paragraphs and clauses asked for an exemplary sentence.

The little novice lawyer had prepared himself to the last detail and his speech was full of fine phrases and literary references. He made a superhuman effort to clear his client and to loosen the noose that witnesses and accused alike had contrived to slip round her neck. His over-enthusiasm was comical. He found arguments to show that the accused was not responsible for her actions at the time of the crime, and that she had killed her master out of self-defence. He recounted her childhood and previously unblemished life in details that would have made a novelist envious. He urged that a hundred guilty should go free rather than one innocent suffer.

Every time they thought he had finished he would begin again.

'And now,' he said, drinking a glass of water, 'I ask the honourable bench to consider the psychological causes. Yes, let us examine her psychology; the facts, your honours, of her psychological state. Consider, if you please, this village maiden, this simple child of the people, and before bringing judgement, let us be honest with each other. Is the woman sitting on the accused bench truly the criminal type that Lombroso calls *uomo delinquente*?'

No one was listening by now. The door kept opening and closing. The public, exhausted by the long procedure and by the unbearable heat, was taking to its heels; soon only the journalists remained to laugh, and the lawyer's relatives who were obliged by their sense of family duty.

Druma was out in the dark corridor, enveloped in a wreath of cigarette smoke, talking to some people and weighing up the motives for the crime. He was in no doubt that it would be hanging for her.

When they drifted back into the court the defence was still speaking. He was quoting long extracts of a psychological study by Pierre Janet. The presiding judge consulted his watch, the *rapporteur* was already drafting the text of the verdict on a piece of paper.

Finally the orator began to wind up his speech, and produced his most affecting sentences, enunciating them with such lyrical force that those who had run out of patience grew positively angry, and those who had some understanding of these matters began to regard him with sincere contempt. He was quoting from Madách's masterpiece, *The Tragedy of Man*. Then he finished.

The bench retired to consider their verdict.

In the meantime sleet began to fall. Those who had come out without an umbrella worried about how they would get home.

Three quarters of an hour later the three judges returned and practically ran up to the dais. The accused hadn't yet arrived.

'Bring her in,' ordered the president and looked up at the ceiling, the sentence in his hand. Guns clinked. Anna Édes was quickly ushered in. They stood her in her place. She looked deathly pale now. She was very frightened at the thought of death and of the rope. She kept swallowing: her throat was constantly moving.

'I now announce the verdict of the court. In the name of the Hungarian state . . .'

The benches grew loud again. One could only hear the odd word of the sentence.

'. . . guilty by her own admission . . . and for this reason the court . . . fifteen years in prison . . . loss of political rights . . .'

'Fifteen . . .' people echoed in surprise, 'fifteen . . .' and most of them felt moved by it, since they felt the sentence was just. A few women began to weep.

The little lawyer cast a triumphant glance in the direction of his relatives. He was convinced that his speech and those quotations from Pierre Janet must have had something to do with it.

The verdict went on to say that the bench considered the merciless quality of the crime an aggravating factor but it took into account the extenuating circumstances of the accused's previously unblemished life, her obvious sense of guilt and the fact of her simplicity and low intelligence.

'Do you understand the verdict?' the president asked Anna in his previous loud voice. 'The bench has sentenced you to fifteen years' imprisonment. It is your right to appeal.'

The defence and prosecution fell over each other to lodge appeals, but by this time the public had gone and Anna was left practically alone with her judges.

'Take her away,' the president said quietly to the guards.

Two days later she was taken to the local prison, and here she awaited the result of two appeals, one to the Royal Panel and one to the Curia. The first was to come in spring, the second a year after the trial, about Christmas time. Both allowed the verdict of the bench to stand. The newspapers said nothing about this, public interest in the affair having exhausted itself.

One cold day in January Anna Édes was escorted by two guards on to a train for Mária-Nosztra. The prison gates slammed behind her. Her name was registered, her hair was shorn, she was given a bath, a number, and a coarse uniform; she began her proper sentence.

Now and then her name might be mentioned in the Krisztina district, but these occasions grew rarer.

Once a woman stopped before the house in Attila utca and said to her husband, 'This is where she lived. Don't you remember her? Such a tall girl, strong, with dark eyes and big hands.'

'She was plain,' said the man.

'No, she was quite pretty,' replied the woman, 'decidedly pretty. When the Romanian army was still here she had a Romanian soldier for her lover.'

And so all memory of her faded. By now nobody knew who she was or anything about her. She was quite forgotten. She simply disappeared, and it made no difference to anyone whether she was in the prison at Mária Nosztra or resting under the acacias of the graveyard beyond the Danube, in the village of Balaton-Főkajár.

20

Dialogue before a Green Fence

Autumn has come round again. They are selling grape juice in the pubs, children are playing with ripe and glossy wild chestnuts. Leaves are falling.

But the unit of currency, the korona, is also falling. Its value: 0.22. People are in despair. How to eat, or dress, or heat the flat at this price. They wait in trepidation for the coming winter. At noon the stock market is in uproar. It's inflation, people are winning and losing fortunes. What remains of Hungary after Trianon is accepted into the League of Nations. Another year passes. It is now 1922.

What has happened since? Every Sunday a military band plays on the promenades of the Vár and pedestrians instinctively fall into step with the blaring brass.

The Tatárs are out for a walk, without their younger daughter who has got married in the meantime. A clerk at the ministry is courting Ilonka. He once heard that Jancsi was in Poland and is a gigolo.

What used to be Kornél Vizy's house looks much the same, except that it has a new caretaker, the other having moved out to one of the occupied territories.

Mrs Moviszter continues to play the piano and recite the verses of Ady. She makes dates with ever younger men. She paints her hair canary yellow and is running to fat. Her husband is still alive. He shouldn't be, but despite being prematurely consigned to the grave by official science, the consultants, his colleagues, acquaintances and admirers – and by the late Kornél Vizy – he continues mysteriously to confound every objective evaluation of his condition as well as the forecasts of his friends. No one knows why. Obviously something must be keeping him alive. He is the most trifling detail in anybody's life; he patiently bears Etel's increasing moodiness, as well as the humiliations heaped on him by his wife. Everyone smiles at him pityingly.

Szilárd Druma has legal charge of the house which was given over to his care by Ferenc Patikárius, who had inherited it under the unfortunate circumstances. Druma has persuaded the agents to let him move into the Vizys' old flat because of the needs of his large practice. He has even repapered it and lives there with his family. A lovely little girl has been born followed by a boy. A German girl looks after the three children who are growing up happily. Stefi still works there but wears glasses as her eyes are weakening. There is also a little wet-nurse with wide mongoloid cheekbones and a coal-black pigtail like a Chinese. Druma's office takes up the second floor, where his old, more modest flat used to be. Two secretaries tap away at typewriters and visitors have to fill in a form to declare their business with the learned solicitor. He is playing an ever more important role in public affairs too. Soon he intends to stand as a candidate in the local elections, in a ward where no one will oppose him.

One afternoon, as the street lamps were being lit but the autumn sky was still pleasantly bright, Szilárd Druma was returning from the Vár, descending the Zerge Steps, with two friends of his. They ambled slowly homeward down the gentle slope of Tábor utca.

Near the bottom they were passing by a green fence when they glanced through the wrought-iron gate. They saw a glazed verandah in the garden, with a table set for tea. The small illuminated glass cage with its air of cloistered silence awoke their curiosity. All three stopped. Disguising their curiosity but with genuine envy they gazed at it, thinking, as all outsiders do when they look in, that all happiness and contentment must live within those walls.

A small blond boy in a school uniform sat at the table. It was after tea and he was busily setting up his lead soldiers on the cloth covered with crumbs. He had begun to hum a military march, beating the table with his hand. His mother sat sewing beside him, her serious and intelligent face bent over her work. A shadow lay over her absorbed features and her head was topped with a knot of thick hair. From time to time she would say something to the boy. He kept asking for advice, how the Hungarian troops encamped around the milkpan and teacups could beat the larger force of Frenchmen with their tanks and poison gas.

A tall, untidy man in a working jacket stepped out of the flat into the verandah. He was smoking. He poured black coffee into a glass. As he raised it to his mouth his gaze met those of the three men, who, embarrassed by their eavesdropping, set off along the fence.

'That's Kosztolányi,' Druma said, after a while. 'Dezső Kosztolányi.'

'The journalist?' asked one of his friends.

'Him.'

'I remember something he wrote,' said the second friend. 'Some poem or other about the death of a sick child. Or was it an orphan? I don't know. My daughter mentioned it.'

'He was a big Communist,' said Druma.

'Him?' marvelled the first friend. 'He is a devout Christian now.'

'Yes,' enlarged the second friend. 'I read it in a Viennese paper that he supports the White Terror.'

'He was a fervent Bolshevik,' repeated Druma. 'He worked with the Committee for Paganism. There's a photograph of them all together on the Vérmező.'

'And what was he doing with them,' enquired the first friend.

'Observing them,' answered Druma, conspiratorially.

219

'Then I don't understand?' the first friend shook his head. 'What does he want in any case. Which side is he on?'

'That's simple,' Druma resolved the debate. 'He's for everybody and nobody. He minds which way the wind blows. First he was in the pay of the Jews and took their side, and now he is hired by the Christians. He's a wise man,' he winked. 'He knows which side his bread is buttered.'

The three friends concurred in this. They stopped again at the end of the fence. It was obvious they still didn't fully understand. One could see that they were indeed used to thinking one thing at a time; one could see that two thoughts were beyond them.

They shrugged shoulders and proceeded down the slope. Druma made one more comment at which they laughed light-heartedly. Unfortunately it was impossible to hear the comment.

Swan, the white sheepdog, heard their voices and, aware of his responsibilities as keeper of the domestic peace, ran to the corner of the garden and set up a fierce din, so that their words were entirely lost in the sound of barking.

H. E. Bates

A Month by the Lake & Other Stories. Intro. by Anthony Burgess. Seventeen stories by the English master (1905–1974): the "so gifted . . . contemporary and worthy colleague of Evelyn Waugh and Graham Greene."—N.Y. Times Book Review. Cloth & NDPaperbook 645. A Party for the Girls. Six long stories by "the Renoir of the typewriter."—Punch. Cloth & NDP653. Elephant's Nest in a Rhubarb Tree. More stories. Cloth & NDP669.

Kay Boyle

Death of a Man. Novel set in fascist Austria: "all the elegance . . . No sentimentality—a painful dose of the early poisons that tasted so sweet."—Grace Paley. NDP670. Life Being the Best and Other Stories. Intro. by Sandra Whipple Spanier. Thirteen early stories. Cloth & NDP654. Three Short Novels [The Crazy Hunter, The Bridegroom's Body, Decision]: "showcases Boyle's morally probing, emotionally charged writing" (Publishers Weekly). NDP703.

Mikhail Bulgakov

The Life of Monsieur de Molière. Trans. by Mirra Ginsberg. A vivid portrait of the great French 17th-century satirist by one of the great Russian satirists of our own century. Cloth & NDP601.

Joyce Cary

"Second Trilogy": Prisoner of Grace. Except the Lord. Not Honour More. "Even better than Cary's 'First Trilogy,' this is one of the great political novels of this century."—San Francisco Examiner. NDP606, 607, & 608. A House of Children. Reprint of the delightful autobiographical novel. NDP631. Mister Johnson. "A wonderful book, one of the best novels about Africa . . ."—John Updike, N.Y. Times Book Review. NDP657.

Maurice Collis

The Land of the Great Image. "A vivid and illuminating study . . . make[s] the exotic past live and breathe for us."—Eudora Welty. NDP612. She Was a Queen. Marvelous real-life rags-to-riches saga of 13th-c. Burmese queen: "pure enchantment . . . the darkest possible deeds in the brightest possible sunlight."—Daily Express. NDP716.

Shusaku Endo
Stained Glass Elegies. Stories by the great Japanese author of Silence and The Samurai: "sombre, delicate, startlingly emphatic"—John Updike, The New Yorker. NDP699.

Ronald Firbank
Three More Novels. "An inexhaustible source of pleasure."—The Village Voice Literary Supplement. NDP614.

Romain Gary
The Life Before Us (Madame Rosa). Trans. by Ralph Manheim. "You won't forget Momo and Madame Rosa when you close the book."—St. Louis Post-Dispatch. NDP604. Promise at Dawn. A memoir "bursting with life . . . Gary's art has been to combine the comic and the tragic."—The New Yorker. NDP635.

William Gerhardie
Futility. A fabulously amusing and absurdly touching novel of love and the Russian Revolution. "I have talent, but he has genius."—Evelyn Waugh. NDP722.

Henry Green
Back. "A rich, touching story, flecked all over by Mr. Green's intuition of the concealed originality of ordinary human beings."—V. S. Pritchett. NDP517.

Madame de Lafayette
The Princess of Cleves. A great work of French literature and perhaps the first of all "modern" novels. "Nancy Mitford, a delicately devastating observer of the aristocracy herself, is an ideal selection as the translator.—Virginia Kirkus. NDP660.

Siegfried Lenz
The German Lesson. Trans. by Ernst Kaiser and Eithne Wilkins. "A book of rare depth and brilliance . . ."—The New York Times. NDP618.

Henri Michaux
A Barbarian in Asia. Trans. by Sylvia Beach. "It is superb in its swift illuminations and its wit . . ."—Alfred Kazin, The New Yorker. NDP622.

Henry Miller
Aller Retour New York. Miller's long unavailable second published book: an account of his 1935 visit to New York and return to Europe. Vintage Henry Miller from his most creative period. Cloth.

Vladimir Nabokov
Laughter in the Dark. Novel of folly and disastrous love: "a cruel little masterpiece" (Times Literary Supplement). "A far more daring, or, if you prefer, a far more wicked book than *Lolita*."—John Simon. NDP729.

Raymond Queneau
The Blue Flowers. Trans. by Barbara Wright. Novel. A medieval knight duke and a 1960s Parisian barge dweller romp through history: "inventive, word-mad, and funny . . ."—The Washington Post. NDP595.

Kenneth Rexroth
An Autobiographical Novel. Revised and expanded edition ed. by Linda Hamalian. "Illuminates the texture of an era and portrays the joy of being utterly true to oneself."—The N.Y. Times. NDP725. Classics Revisited. Sixty brief, radiant essays on the books Rexroth called the "basic documents in the history of the imagination." NDP621. More Classics Revisited. "Anyone who wants to be globally literate . . . could ask for no better guide than this."—Booklist. Cloth & NDP668.

William Saroyan
The Man with the Heart in the Highlands & Other Early Stories. "Probably since O. Henry nobody has done more to endear and stabilize the short story."—Elizabeth Bowen. Cloth.

Stendhal
Three Italian Chronicles. Novellas of life-and-death romance and sensational crime. "Adored by Proust, admired by Valery, envied by Gide, Stendhal was far too prepossessing a *writer* . . . to satisfy anyone as merely a *novelist*."—Richard Howard. NDP704.

Niccolò Tucci
The Rain Came Last. Intro. by Mary McCarthy. Stories which brilliantly succeed by "simultaneously breaking our hearts," as Brendan Gill noted, "and making us happy." NDP688.

Robert Penn Warren
At Heaven's Gate. A novel of power and corruption in the deep South of the 1920s. "Great poetic intensity."—The Sewanee Review. NDP588.

NEW ADDITIONS TO THE REVIVED MODERN CLASSICS

Sherwood Anderson
Poor White. "No novel of the American small town in the Middle West evokes in the minds of its readers so much of the cultural heritage of its milieu as does *Poor White*."—Horace Gregory. NDP763.

Dezső Kosztolányi
Anna Édes. A classic work of twentieth-century Hungarian fiction. Anna is the hard-working and long-suffering heroine, the unhappy maid destroyed by her pitiless employers. "...a powerful novel." (Times Literary Supplement) NDP772.

Muriel Spark
The Public Image. Set in Rome, Spark's novel is about movie star Annabel Christopher, who has made the fatal mistake in believing in her public image: "orchestrated by the harsh polyphony, the technical adventurousness and formal elegance [of] . . . Muriel Spark." (The New York Times Book Review) NDP767.